Night Flight

Anne DaVigo

Published by Quill Driver Press, 2500 9th Avenue, Sacramento, CA 95818

ISBN 978-0-9745722-3-9

Printed in USA

Cover and text design by Karen Phillips
Author Photo by Beth Baughman

Night Flight

Anne DaVigo

1

Outside in the driveway, a car horn blasted, like the timely arrival of the cavalry in a western movie. The lake had frozen early this year, the ice was perfect, her friends were waiting. Hannah took a last look in the mirror. The birthmark on her cheek, usually red as fresh blood, didn't look quite so bad tonight.

She swept down the hall, hoping she was quick enough to avoid a confrontation with her loathsome stepmother. Shooting a glance into the bathroom, she caught sight of Nancy crouched on the floor beside the tub, bathing the twins.

"Hannah!"

Too late. Nancy's eyes fastened on Hannah, examining the heavy sweater, laced figure skates, and saucy red skating skirt. "What day is it?" her stepmother asked, as if she really wanted to know.

Hannah rolled her eyes. "Friday."

The horn blared again.

"And what is it you promised me you'd do for me tonight?" Nancy asked.

"I don't remember." *Bitch*, Hannah thought.

"You said you'd babysit so I could get out of this shithole and see a movie."

"I'm not your servant, and those aren't my kids. Call an agency."

"Nobody's available on Friday night."

"Right. The week's over, and everyone's got plans, including me."

In the background, her half-brother Marcus splashed a fan of soapy foam into his brother's eyes. Screaming, Jasper pushed his twin under water.

"Boys, boys, stop that!" Nancy grabbed for a towel and leaned over, only to be soaked by another infantile foray. Her shirt and jeans were dripping. "Beau will hear about this," she yelled over her shoulder at Hannah.

In seconds, Hannah was out the front door. Actually, she owed the little brats. The distraction had allowed her to make a getaway.

The flagstone walk in the front of the house was slippery. She'd arisen while it was still dark, pulled on coveralls and shoveled before school, but another cold front had moved across the Rockies after lunch, dumping an additional three inches of snow. The unfairness gnawed at her. Why should *she* be responsible for babysitting, house-cleaning, digging them out after a storm?

Winter should be like it was before, when her older brothers shoveled the snow and did chores, but those worthless shits had skipped when their mother died and her father, Beau, took up with Nancy. Clyde was at the University of Chicago now, and Boomer'd enlisted in the Army.

And Beau, after spawning another family, took a job with the Western Trucking Association, off to Seattle on Tuesday, gone until the weekend, and shuffling everything off on Hannah.

A light tap from the pickup's horn roused Hannah into motion. She tossed her skates and bag in the truck bed alongside a stack of bricks and lumber. Inside the cab, she squeezed into the shotgun seat beside Rosemarie, who was sandwiched in middle. Paulette's hand was cocked on the wheel, a cigarette between two fingers.

"Your new skate skirt is fabulous," Rosemarie said.

Hannah thought it was Rosemarie who looked fabulous. Her trim figure barely needed a panty girdle, an item invented by the same person who designed the straitjacket. And Rosemarie's dark, glossy ponytail looked like the one featured—along with the fashionable poodle cut—on last year's *Life* magazine cover.

Not that her good looks had helped Rosemarie navigate high school's social landscape. Her father, Aaron Stein, was the rabbi at the only Jewish synagogue in suburban Denver, and Rosemarie was one of two Jewish students at Woodlake High School.

"The skirt's not pretty—it's hot." Paulette tossed her cigarette out the wind-wing. "I'm insanely jealous." She shifted into reverse, narrowly missing the elm tree growing alongside the driveway.

"Enough to shock the Pops?" Hannah fingered the hem of her red felt skirt.

"Their jaws will fall open," Paulette said.

The Pops was the trio's name for the high school elite: girls selected for every honor from home coming queen to science club secretary. Nothing made Hannah's day like showing the Pops how little she cared about their snobbishness. Some of them, she hoped, would be at Sloan's Lake tonight.

The pickup skidded down the icy street, but Paulette didn't slow down. She had lots of driving experience, sneaking the pickup out of the garage since she was thirteen, late at night while her mother was passed out on the couch after a day of drinking.

They traveled east on Twentieth Avenue. The street wasn't particularly steep, but the few miles from home toward the center of Denver were a ladder in the hierarchy of teen life in Colorado's capital. Their school, Woodlake High, had the best reputation in the middle class suburbs; Edgewater High, halfway down the hill, was lower by a few rungs; Manual and North were at the bottom of the hill and the social scale. Boomer said Manual High was where Negroes went to learn a trade, and North High was where the Dagos went to drop out.

Woodlake High didn't have any Negroes and only a few Mexican and Italian students. Boomer called it Wonder Bread High, and maybe that was true, but every time he said it, Hannah got a tight feeling in her chest at the unfairness of it.

"There's the Hoggs' house," she said. They were passing a two-story brick mansion on the lake shore. Her father'd told her the story of the Hogg family years ago as they drove past on the way to his law office.

Paulette laughed. "Hog as in hog pen?"

"H-O-G-G," she said. "The mansion was owned by the Hogg family for decades. They were a legend back in the Twenties, throwing fabulous parties, but when Grandfather Hogg died, he willed all his money to his two sons—on the condition they didn't change their last name."

"And did they?" Rosemarie asked.

"Of course," Hannah said. "But they spent the money first."

The story made her sad. Not because of Hogg's lying sons but a longing for the lost closeness with her own father. In those years, Beau'd taken her with him while he worked on Saturdays, assigning her small chores while he labored at his desk. She'd felt important, as if she were part of the firm, and someday they'd be partners. His current job, counsel for the trucking association, was one of a myriad of things that had changed when her mother died.

The world seemed strange tonight, the crunch of crusted snow under the pickup's tires, the needle-sharp points of the new moon. Hannah wished she'd brought her camera to take a black-and-white photo. As they approached the lake shore, she spotted the bundled figures of Kenny Nilsson and his father, Olof, pushing snow shovels to clear the ice of the afternoon's snowfall.

"I love that boy," Paulette said. "If only he'd look my way."

Kenny was in their senior class, probably headed for DU on a hockey scholarship next year. He and Olof often volunteered to prepare the ice if the city crew had already left for the day. Olof had been a hockey player in Sweden when he was young, before he married and emigrated to the United States.

As Hannah climbed out of the pickup, the air's icy clarity filled her lungs. It was thin and intoxicating, enticing her to shrug off family problems and suffocating expectations of the school elite.

Twenty or thirty skaters circled the ice to the strains of a Strauss waltz being broadcast over the loudspeaker. The three friends brushed snow off a bench and sat down to pull on heavy wool socks and lace their skates.

"Look, the king and queen are here." Paulette's breath rose in a cloud, obscuring her long, thin nose. "Aren't they so, so perfect?"

On the ice were six or eight members of Pops royalty, including Woodlake High's homecoming queen, Odessa Stamos. She and her boyfriend, Henry Killan, skated with gloved hands clasped. Their shoulders touched and lips hovered close.

"She's wearing his class ring on a chain around her neck," Rosemarie said. "I saw it Wednesday in French class."

Hannah wiggled her toes to check that the skates were laced tightly. With her red cap pulled snugly around her ears, she glided onto the ice. It was still early, before the traffic of too many skate blades had carved ruts in the surface. Her skating skirt swished saucily against her tights. It was her first visit to the lake this year, but it took only a few moments for her to gain a firm balance on the blades.

She did a quick forward circuit around the rink, the steel hissing as it cut the surface. On the second round she reversed and skated backward, glancing over her shoulder to avoid a collision with other skaters.

Kenny leaned on his shovel and called out, "Coming later to Tiger's Lair?"

Hannah waved, but didn't answer. Her earlier restlessness returned. She and Kenny, along with a group of kids from surrounding neighborhoods, had attended school together since they were young, and now were finishing high school along with students from many other feeder schools. She'd remained close to Paulette and Rosemarie, but had lost track of Kenny a bit.

He was blond, athletic, and genuinely nice, but because Olof was a janitor at the school, the informal student hierarchy left Kenny out of its constrictive elite.

Tonight she yearned to free herself of those boundaries, including the predictable Friday night dance, Tiger's Lair.

Rosemarie slid alongside Hannah, ponytail swishing across her back. "Paulette's having trouble, poor thing." Only Rosemarie would call prickly Paulette a poor thing, but it was clear their friend was unaccustomed to ice skating. Paulette wavered, her ankles sinking inward and her butt sticking out. Hannah skated over to her.

"Hold onto me." Skating backward, she clasped Paulette's forearms and guided her slowly around the circle. Face to face, the residual scent of Kools hovering between them, Hannah was aware of how rarely Paulette dropped her steely exterior or displayed a moment of weakness.

"Can't believe I'm making a fool of myself in front of everyone. I'll hear about it on Monday for sure," Paulette said.

Hannah raised her eyebrows. "But you can drive forty on slick streets. Nobody else has bragging rights on that."

"When I drive, I'm in perfect control. Not in this devil's playground."

The music changed to Elvis. Hannah wiggled her hips as she skated, and Paulette loosened up, laughing and managing a complete circuit without support.

"Hannah, come on." Rosemarie beckoned her to the center, where the two of them cut figure eights and practiced spins. A cluster of Pops had gathered near the concession stand. The group darted glances in their direction and whispered to each other.

"Let's get something hot to drink," Rosemarie said.

"Not now." Hannah didn't want to beam a fake smile at them. On Monday, they'd still be gossiping about her skirt and her birthmark.

When the Pops returned to the ice, Hannah and her friends slipped rubber guards onto their blades and clomped to the concession. The apple-cheeked concession attendant was selling doughnuts, brownies, and packaged Lorna Doones in addition to hot chocolate and cider. Because Hannah'd skipped dinner, the sweets tempted her, but she didn't want sticky hands inside her gloves. She ordered cider instead. The first sip, fragrant with cinnamon, seemed to dissolve some of her bitterness.

As she took a second swallow, two cars—a Caddy and a Buick Special—pulled into parking spaces just behind the concession shack. The surly rumble of engines stopped, and two men emerged from the Caddy. Car doors slammed, and on the ice, conversation ebbed.

"Holy Christ, they're goombas," Paulette whispered.

The men from the Caddy did look like North Denver men. Dark haired and olive skinned, they wore thick alpaca overcoats. Snap-brim hats shaded their faces from the parking lot's lights. Were they members of the Smalldone family? Sensational stories in the *Post* and the *Rocky Mountain News* about the trial of Checkers and Flip Flop Smalldone had created an expectation of hulking gangsters, but compared to Hannah's father and brothers, these men were short.

No matter that they were five-six, the Smalldones controlled the state's gambling, loan sharking, and drug trafficking. The driver of the Buick Special, however, was different. He stood about six feet tall, bareheaded, and his crewcut announced that he wasn't a member of the crime family.

He gave the girls a long stare from under his dark, thick eyebrows.

Rosemarie tugged Hannah's arm. "Let's go down by the ice and drink our cider."

Hannah squeezed her cup, splashing hot cider on her wrist. "Why should we let these old guys scare us off? What are they going to do, shoot us?"

"Who knows?" Paulette said. "They wiped out the mob in Pueblo and probably shot Joe Roma in North Denver. Smalldones are kings of the Rockies."

"Nobody was ever arrested for Roma's murder," Hannah said. "The *Rocky* said so in a big story on the Smalldones a few weeks ago."

Huddled together, the girls threw covert glances at the trio. The men talked briefly, then crossed to the Caddy, with the Buick driver slipping into the back seat. After the doors slammed shut, the passenger windows opened a few inches, and smoke drifted out.

"The short one with the mustache, that was Young Eugene, Checkers' son." Kenny's deep voice at her elbow made Hannah jump. "He must be out on bail."

"What did he do?"

"Something to do with slot machines, I think."

He gazed at her, maybe looking for some sign she favored him over other boys. Hannah liked Kenny—the solid set of his shoulders, his easy good nature—but tonight she felt too edgy to encourage him. He dug the toe of his hockey skate into the ice. "See you later, I guess."

Hannah gathered their cups and dumped them into the trash bin behind the concession shack. The Caddy was parked just beyond a mound of plowed snow. As she pulled on her gloves, the tall man opened the car's rear door and stepped out. The Caddy churned snow from its back tires as it pulled out, then sped away. The remaining man strode toward his Buick.

Glancing up, he stared at her. "Are you spying on me?" He edged closer. "I know you. You're the girl with the birthmark who goes to Woodlake Methodist."

"What a mean a mean thing to say." Tonight, confident on her skates, she'd almost forgotten about the irregular red patch in the middle of her left cheek. "Don't you have any manners?"

"It's just the truth." He didn't seem embarrassed.

The wind rose, and the force of cold air against her face was oddly cleansing. Most people didn't acknowledge the disfigurement—only her grandmother, who used to call it Hannah's Rose. To the rest of her family, the birthmark was the great unnamed, like farts or bad breath, but inescapable. People had two reactions: either gluing their eyes on it in fascination or looking past her, as if she were a tree or a rock.

Up close, the man appeared to be younger than she first thought: in his mid-twenties. He fidgeted with nervous energy like a boy, his eyes darting toward her, then veering away, hands rubbing together, weight shifting from foot to foot.

His frankness emboldened her. "Are you friends with those guys?" she asked.

"They're business associates," he said. "Legitimate business. I own the Comet Drive-In on Federal Boulevard. They want to partner with me on the Comet and other ventures. Have you ever been to the Comet?"

Hannah shook her head. "Federal Boulevard's outside our neighborhood. We go to Berry's on Colfax."

Hannah's pushback seemed to animate him, his words almost colliding with each other. "I have a completely new idea, installing small lighted kiosks at each intercom that will showcase the menu and any daily specials. Nobody's done it before. It'll be a big hit."

His gaze fastened on her, eyes extraordinarily bright. The force of his desire for success seemed futile, yet there was something grand about it, she thought, as if he were unwilling to be run-of-the-mill. Ordinary.

The shock of his interest opened her senses to the scrape of blades on the ice, the scent of cinnamon drifting from the concession shack. Energy coursed through her.

"Take a ride with me," he said.

She raised her eyebrows in mock excitement. "Like where? California? The Gulf Coast?"

"Just around." He stuffed his hands in his coat pockets.

"Stay right there." She backed up, not wanting to lose sight of him. "I'll just be a minute."

It seemed as though she couldn't untie the laces on her skates fast enough.

2

Jack watched the girl arguing with her friends, who tossed disapproving looks at him over their shoulders, trying to talk her out of leaving with someone she didn't know. Finally, with a shrug, she stuffed the skates into her bag and pulled on a pair of loafers. As she came close, he could almost feel her warmth, as if the disagreement with the other girls had ignited a wave of body heat.

"I'm Hannah," she said.

"And I'm Jack Graham." Interesting, she didn't tell him her last name. He'd used his real name—he'd already told her too much about himself for a convenient lie.

They walked around to the passenger side of his car, her shoulder brushing his arm. The Buick's chrome gleamed under the overhead lights. It was his mother's car, but he'd borrowed it for tonight. The Smalldones drove flashy cars and wore expensive suits. If he was going to do business with them, he had to look the part. What was the price tag on one of the alpaca coats they were wearing? Maybe he'd buy one himself when the deal was signed and sealed.

He opened the passenger door with a flourish before remembering he'd left a mess on the passenger seat: envelopes, boxes of papers, a bag of cookies.

"Just let me . . ." Leaning in, he bumped his head on the doorframe in his hurry to transfer the clutter to the back. *Stupid, stupid,* he scolded himself.

When Hannah was inside, Jack circled the car and settled behind the wheel. Although she was across the seat leaning against her door, he could smell cinnamon on her breath and the faint odor of the warm flesh beneath her clothes.

"Sorry about the clutter," he said. "I'm moving my business operations from the Comet to a rented space on Sixth Avenue. I have some exciting plans for the future that'll require a real office." The lie slipped from his brain to his mouth as smooth as cream.

"How long have you owned the Comet?" She leaned over and flipped shut the metal cover on the ashtray, filled with cigarette butts.

"I bought the property and began construction two years ago. The grand opening was in March." His mother'd bought the place, but Jack always told people he did the deal.

The car was stubborn, and it took a couple of attempts before the engine caught. Between the meeting with Chauncey and Young Eugene—who'd been higher than a kite—and now encountering this odd girl, his nerves were jangling. As he pulled out of the parking lot, he stole several quick glances at Hannah. She was small, with dark hair in a pixie cut like Audrey Hepburn's. Her red skirt showed off slim, strong legs. She'd be pretty if it weren't for the birthmark.

He had to hand it to her—she didn't try to disguise it with pancake makeup. Instead, the bright red discoloration, the size of a quarter, seemed to say, "Here I am. Take it or leave it."

If only *he* could do that—ignore what people thought of him. Recalling the meeting with Young Eugene and his uncle made Jack burn with fury. They had been condescending about his new idea, a car dealership, as though he were a punk kid proposing a paper route.

He drove south on Sheridan. "I need to stop by the Comet to check on how things are going," he said. "We're having a big reopening weekend after being closed two weeks for repairs."

Hannah seemed uninterested, instead staring out the side window at two passing cars full of teenagers waving and shouting at each other through open windows. Jack inhaled a couple of deep breaths. It was time for one of his favorite tricks for evoking admiration—his ability to recall things, almost like his brain snapped a photo and pasted it in an album.

"I remember one time at church," he said, "your family was sitting about six rows in front of us, your father, you, a brother, and your mother. She was wearing a black coat with a leopard collar."

He glanced over to see if she were impressed.

Hannah's wide blue eyes stared at him as they passed under the streetlights. "She's my step-mother, not my mother, and she wears that coat every Sunday." She gave him a teasing glance, looking up at him from under her bangs. "I remember your wife at church. She and my older brother were in high school together. He's in the Army now."

Shot down on that one. His foot pressed harder on the accelerator to show the power of the Buick's V-8. "Too bad he didn't go to college. I got my degree in management from DU. I've always wanted to own a business."

He'd actually attended DU for one semester. The place had driven him crazy. Professors droned on and on. The snobbish students harbored illusions they were going to be the next president of General Electric, but most of them were as dumb as dogs. When he'd quit, his mother had given him a terrible tongue-lashing.

As they approached the Comet, a white building with red trim, he stared through the windshield in disbelief. "What the hell?" The neon sign in front, depicting a speeding comet, was dark. The parking lot was empty, and lights had been switched off.

Tires squealed as Jack skidded around back and braked beside trash cans near the rear door. Dim light shone from a small storeroom window he used as an office. He jumped from the car and sprinted to the back entrance. It was locked, and a notice from the gas company was taped to the door.

No service until the bill was paid in full.

He tore down the notice, ripped it in half, and threw it on the ground. Blood pounded painfully over his right eye as he strode around the back lot, kicking mounds of crusted snow. Hannah watched him, her face luminescent in the darkness. What must she think of him? That he was a braggart and a liar.

Finally, he climbed back in the Buick and slammed the door. "Damn Public Service. Couple of weeks ago, a gas leak caused an explosion. We had to close to make repairs. It was the fault of the utility, no question, and they owed us compensation for the repair costs. I told them on no uncertain terms that I was holding up payment on our bill until we got reimbursed."

He stuffed his clenched fists into his coat pockets. "Nothing is easy when you're in business. Sometimes I'd like to be free of the whole thing."

"That's amazing," she said. "I was thinking the same thing just tonight. That I'd like to be free."

Some of the tension in his shoulders eased up. "Did something happen to make you say that? I assume it wasn't a gas leak."

A momentary smile lit her face. "Good guess. My family's a mess. Two years ago, my dad had a surprise: the woman he'd been dating got pregnant. Second surprise: it was twins. Before that, I was the youngest—my brothers are nineteen and twenty-three. Anyway, my dad and this woman got married, the twins were born, and they cried for five months straight, driving us crazy. The older brother in the Army prefers to be anywhere but home when he's on leave. The other one enrolled in college out of state. Even my dad has bailed out. He got a job on the road, leaving me home with *her* and *them*."

"A girl in a trap." The heater's warm air and the cushioned seat were as cozy as an animal den in winter. Anger at his mother was forgotten. He sniffed the girl's scent again, aroused by the intimate odor.

"Those brothers of yours, they're a couple of shirkers, running out on you like that."

"Those are the exact words I used when I talked to Dad, but he didn't listen. It's like, we're women, so it's our responsibility."

Thoughts of his wife, Lucy, home with the two kids, diverted his attention momentarily. She was probably nodding off by now. The baby slept in a portable crib just an arm's length from their double bed. The kid should have been moved months ago to the second bedroom with his sister. The feeling of being suffocated—by the business, his mother, and his wife—returned.

"Let's drive up to Lookout Mountain," he said. "We can see the lights of the city from there."

"Make-Out Mountain?" Her laugh sounded more amused than outraged. "I don't think so."

"No groping, I promise." He opened his eyes wide to emphasize his truthfulness.

"Oh, sure."

"Really, I won't do anything you don't want to."

She nodded slowly.

Too bad she didn't seem interested in sex. Maybe she got in the car for the hell of it, a way to defy her father and stepmother. On the other hand, Hannah could be intimidated by his maturity and confidence compared to the immature high school boys she knew. After all, he'd been in the Coast Guard by the time he was sixteen. His mother had lied about his age to get rid of him. True, it hadn't gone well; he'd drunk too much and gone AWOL, but that was eight years ago. One upside of his few months in the service was the older women who admired his uniform, despite his age. Thinking about the raunchy things he'd done returned his attention to the proximity of this girl's short skirt and skating tights, which were stoking a desire to put his face down there.

"Instead of necking, let's drink." Liquor always seemed to increase his success with women. "I've got a bottle of Black Label in the glove compartment. We'll drive up there and talk. Get to know each other."

"I don't know," she said, sounding doubtful.

"If you didn't want to have fun, why did you come?" Everything about this night seemed to be going wrong.

"I was tired of the same old things—my stupid family, the snobby kids at school, my life," Hannah said.

"Exactly," he said. "I feel the same way." Jack heard her exhale and relax against the seat, moving a little closer to him. This was going to work.

He turned west on Forty-Fourth, through the town of Golden, and then up Lookout Mountain from the north. As he navigated hairpin turns up the steep incline, the lights of Denver seemed to tumble beneath them. He pulled into a wide parking spot where they could scan the length and breadth of the city. The panorama stretched from Westminster on the north to Aurora on the east and Bear Creek on the south.

"They're so inconsequential from up here," she said, "the people in those houses and towns."

She sounded sad, as though she were feeling the abandonment of her brothers and father. No great tragedy, it seemed to him. They were users and liars, ignoring her for their own needs, just like the people in his family. He leaned across, brushing her shoulder as he retrieved the Black Label from the glove box. It was a new bottle, and the seal broke with a satisfying crackle.

"Be my guest," he said, handing it to her. Judging by the way she swallowed a big gulp, then leaned over in a coughing fit, he figured she'd never drunk liquor before.

"You don't chug it like Coke. Here." He tipped some into his mouth—enough, but not too much.

As they handed the bottle back and forth, his anxiety didn't ease, as it usually did when he drank. Her problems with her shitty family seemed like gasoline on the fire of his own resentment at his family. "There's only one person in my entire life that really mattered to me. That was my father." Words seemed to force themselves up from his gut. "He had a cabin he took refuge in when he wanted to escape my mother. I went there with him once, just the two of us, when I was very small. It was over on the Animas River, I think."

"Where's that?"

"Near Silverton. That trip, we slept in sleeping bags on the cabin floor. His training was as a geologist, but his real interest was prospecting for gold. The bed of his old truck was filled with stuff: a pick, shovel, other equipment I couldn't identify. I was too little . . ."

He tipped the bottle again. "When I think about that trip, the memory is like a razor cut. Has that ever happened to you? Such a clean wound you don't feel it for a few seconds."

"How could you remember that? You were too young."

"I don't forget the bad things that have happened to me. Every detail is stored in my brain."

Her shoulders curved, as if to ward off some painful memory of her own. "What happened to your father?" She took another drink, settled back against the seat. Wind whistled down from the mountains.

"He died of TB. I don't remember that part, only what happened after." Instead of going to Denver's tuberculosis hospital, the best in the country, the stupid ass had continued to search for minerals and died soon after, leaving Jack to be sent to an orphanage. And that was nothing compared to what his mother did.

A couple of long swallows burned all the way down. He opened the window to inhale lungfuls of frigid air. Below them, automobile lights flowed along Route 6. The dots looked as though they were crawling, but actually the cars were speeding so fast one would crush you in an instant.

What would it be like if you were hit, he wondered? Would you feel pain or die quickly? How long would it take between the time you were hit and you died? A second or a minute?

He wiped the neck of the bottle on his shirt. "Do you want another swallow?"

"I'm a little woozy." She spoke slowly, but her words weren't slurred. "Take me home, please."

"You want to get out and barf?"

"No." She pulled her skirt further down on her thighs. "I just need to rest."

He rolled up the window, then studied her. Her face was flushed from the liquor. Was he going to go through with this? His eyes lingered on her breasts, not bad for a slim girl like her. He and Lucy hadn't had sex since the baby was born, not counting hand jobs. The doctor said her infection would clear up soon, but that had been four months ago.

And this week, his mother had returned from Palm Beach and taken up residence in their basement apartment, telling them when to get up, when to go to bed, what Lucy should prepare for dinner.

He leaned over and nuzzled the girl's neck, inhaling the fragrance of her skin. A small part of his brain acknowledged the possibility of a patrolling sheriff's deputy spotting them, but he was hot to go.

"What about your wife?" she said, as if she'd read his mind. The vibration of her vocal cords felt unpleasant against his lips.

He lowered his voice to a seductive murmur. "The fact I'm married doesn't really bother you, or you wouldn't be here." The low hum of the engine was like his favorite song, and the fragrances of booze and warm skin stirred him like Chanel No. 5. He leaned across the seat, slipping his hand under her skirt. Her slim, firm legs moved restlessly against his fingers.

"It's just for tonight." He raised the hem of her sweater. "One night of freedom, where we're answerable to nobody."

He felt her shiver. The bare skin under her sweater was like silk under his fingers. He unhooked her bra straps and fondled her titties. He'd had enough of Lucy's nipples dripping almost constantly since Albert was born.

He was good to go in about two minutes, but wrestling her out of her shoes, tights, and panties almost drove him crazy. Finally, the clothes were off her legs and on the floor, and the bare, firm skin under the flare of her skirt felt good enough to be the Holy Grail. He pulled her over to him, positioning her legs to straddle his lap. The zipper tab on his pants was halfway down when a thousand-watt spotlight hit the car's interior.

Hannah scrambled off his lap and cowered in the corner of the passenger seat, wayward underwear hidden under her skirt. The patrol car rolled up, and a smirking officer propped his arm on the sill of the open window. "None of that along here, folks. Get a room."

3

When Hannah awoke in her own bed, her head ached. Her pillow-case smelled of smoke, residue from Jack's cigarettes that clung to her hair. The taste of Black Label in her mouth, which had been disgusting but exciting last night, was simply disgusting this morning.

It had been after 1 a.m. when she tiptoed into the house through the back door, past her stepmother, who was sleeping on the living room couch. Nancy's cheek was wrinkled against a throw pillow, and one slipper had fallen off, exposing her bare toes. Hannah had taken only a step or two toward the hallway to the bedroom when her stepmother stirred.

"Beau?" Nancy's voice had been fuzzy, calling out for Dad, who wasn't due back until midday. Hannah had held perfectly still until Nancy's breath evened out, then tiptoed cautiously to her bedroom.

This morning in the shower, hot water streamed over her short hair, washing away the smell. The unsettling impact of her encounter with Jack Graham dissolved as she toweled herself dry. It was as though the squat figures of the gangsters, the ride in the car with a stranger, and the other-worldly interlude atop the mountain were remnants of a fading dream.

As she stepped back into the hall, her father's laughter drifted from the kitchen. She snatched jeans and a flannel shirt from her closet and dressed quickly to the rhythm of melting ice dripping from the eaves outside her window.

In the wide, sunny kitchen, her stepmother was loading the dishwasher while the twins' unwavering gaze was fixed on their father.

Beau Brightman was singing "Clementine." "*You are lost and gone forever, dreadful sorry, Clementine.*" Her father hammered it up, spreading his arms wide, exaggerating the movement of his lips. Hannah had memorized all six verses and the chorus years ago when he'd sung it to *her*. He spotted Hannah and broadened his delivery even more, as if he were trying to woo her as well.

He wore a ratty wool sweater and a pair of castoff dress slacks; his hair was gray and thinning, but even so, he retained an unusual ability to snare people's attention, some combination of his wide blue eyes and the mobility of his face.

The twins' reaction to his performance reflected the boys' already strong differences. Marcus kicked his feet and banged a spoon aggressively on the high-chair tray. Firstborn and always more robust, he'd weighed twenty-four pounds the last time Hannah stepped on the scale with him. Jasper was smaller, quieter, and more intense. His watchful gaze focused on Beau as if he were memorizing the song for an audition.

Her father tilted his head to study her. "How's my beautiful daughter, the light of my life, the apple of my eye?"

"I'm your only daughter and not feeling all that lovely," she said, remembering Jack's comment about her birthmark. She crossed the kitchen and kissed her father on the cheek. Last night's anger at him faded, at least for awhile. "I thought you weren't coming home until noon."

"I hitched a ride from Boise with Roger Quint." He removed the bowl of Cheerios Marcus had overturned on his high-chair tray. "He's got a new twin-engine plane, bought by the association. I've definitely got to get one of those."

Forks and spoons clattered as her stepmother stuffed them into the dishwasher basket. "No private planes, Beau. United Airlines is within our budget."

He set the sticky bowl in the sink with one hand and stroked the back of Nancy's neck with the other. He was always touchy-feely when he first arrived home. It made Hannah uncomfortable, as if they were trying to be young again.

"Hannah didn't get home until after midnight last night," Nancy said.

"It was just after 10." It sounded like a lie, even in her ears. "You were already asleep."

"I was awake at 11, 11:30 and 12:15." Nancy pursed her lips. "When I was that age, my mother would've grounded me."

"She's seventeen," her father said. "Midnight's okay, as long as she's behaving herself."

Hannah shot him a startled look. Usually, he was strict about lapses in house rules.

"After midnight's too late. Nothing good is happening at that hour," Nancy said.

Beau leaned closer, until his lips were close to his wife's cheek. "Hannah's going to be home by midnight on weekends and 10 on weeknights from now on. Right?" He raised his eyebrows at Hannah, giving her a conspiratorial cue.

She nodded, his mood making her cautious. As a girl, she'd worshipped him. Their Saturday mornings at his office had been one of the few times they were close, because during the week he left for work early and arrived home late. But that camaraderie had vanished with the death of her mother, Chantal. Her brothers drifted away, Nancy, the woman he'd been dating, had gotten pregnant, and Beau's new job had sent him on the road.

"You want eggs?" he asked. "I'll make you some, poached, the way you like them."

"I've stopped liking eggs."

"Since when?" He folded his arms across his chest.

"For many years." She sipped a cup of Ovaltine. In truth, it had been nearly a year, after he'd begun traveling.

He shrugged and sat across the table from her, scanning want ads from yesterday afternoon's *Post*. He'd hardly begun when Jasper, now tired of sitting, began to whine, "Down, down," while Marcus kicked the underside of the tray.

Hannah ignored them. In June, she'd be free of this house, its anger, and noise, and baby stink. A stack of West Coast college catalogs sat on her desk. Rosemarie's father said California was controlled by Communists, but Hannah wanted to attend Santa Barbara or Berkeley. She longed for the fresh wind of new faces and startling ideas, a free-floating inquiry as to what mattered in life.

The telephone rang.

"Beau," Nancy said, "get that. It's probably for you."

"Not now, I've got errands." He turned to Hannah. "You want to come with me, Miss Lovely?"

"Paulette and I are going to the afternoon matinee at the Orpheum." Hannah knew he was trying to charm her, and a hard knot of resistance formed beneath her ribs.

The phone rang four more times and stopped. Nancy's eyes narrowed to slits. "Hannah can't go anywhere. I need her to get the boys down for naps."

"I'll help you, Nan," her father said. "As soon as I'm done here, Miss Lovely, it'll be like our old Saturdays."

Beau and Nancy wiped the boys' faces and hands with wet cloths and carried them off, Marcus crying and Jasper leaning over Nancy's arm for a solemn glance at Hannah, as if to determine the truth about last night.

It was an hour before she and her father climbed into the station wagon. He flicked on the heater, which blew noisily on her feet, slowly reducing the chill. Snow was piled in front of the house and perched like cake frosting on the roof, disguising its shabbiness. Years ago, the gray, single-story frame house had been the showplace of the street, with crisp white trim and black decorative shutters framing the paned windows. But with Beau out of town several days a week, the twins sucking up much of Nancy's time, it looked shabby. Paint was peeling, and the concrete driveway was veined with cracks.

Morning sun had melted the icy streets, allowing Beau to drive too fast for the bulky station wagon. His carefully trimmed fingernails tapped the wheel in a careless rhythm. How different from Jack Graham and his ragged, bitten nails. What was Jack doing today? Maybe taking his kids for a sled ride.

Jack was nothing like any young men she knew: her brother Clyde, the brainy scholar, Boomer, an idealistic patriot, and Kenny, as nice as a sunny day, but not exciting. Jack was smart, but erratic as lightning.

"Where are we going?" she asked.

"To see a man about a car."

"Another car? We don't need one. You're never home."

He glanced from the road to catch her eye. "A car for my girl."

A car! The prospect seemed to lift her off the seat. Freedom. She'd be able to pay back Paulette for a year of rides to school. To leave a Friday night party when she wanted, not when someone else was ready. Stop at Berry's after a football game. Pack Rosemarie and Paulette in the car on a summer night and head for a swim at the reservoir. It was perfect, the prospect of freedom.

Her father grinned at the delight on her face. "Nothing's too good for you."

They traveled southeast to Cherry Hills, passing the country club where Babe Zaharias had won the Women's Western Open. Each home in Cherry Hills was set on a lot of at least an acre, and some estates spread for ten or fifteen. Rolling hills were covered with unbroken snow and landscaped with firs and elms.

"Roger Quint says the people who founded Cherry Hills thought the Denver Country Club wasn't exclusive enough." Her father laughed. "I guess they were too snobbish to consort with the Douds, Mamie Eisenhower's family. She grew up near DCC."

Hannah felt torn between longing and anger. She wanted that life, but at the same time she despised it. Mothers in Cherry Hills didn't need their high-school-aged daughters to be unpaid babysitters; they hired foreign nannies to bathe and feed their children. Daughters attended Kent School and took tennis lessons from the country club pro.

But if she lived in Cherry Hills, the girls would use every sly, devious ploy, worse than the Pops, to shut her out. Even if her father had lots of money, there was no treatment to remove her birthmark, the consulting dermatologist had told them.

"Maybe decades from now, but not yet. Just be grateful you're smart and healthy," the dermatologist had said. As if the stupid ass had any idea what it was like, being different.

Her father turned into a long, curved driveway lined by slender trunks of a hundred trees, their graceful branches leafless now. The engine's growl seemed crass amidst the expanse of white and the perfection of the red-brick Tudor house. Leaded glass window panes reflected the winter sun.

"Roger owns this place," her father said. "He founded Medallion Trucking back in the '30s and made millions. Now he heads up the trucking association."

"But what are we doing here? It's not as though you're buying a Cadillac from your boss."

"He mentioned last night that his wife's niece had left for college and wanted to sell her car."

A branch of the driveway veered off to the south side of the house, past a pool and tennis court, and terminated in front of a three-car brick garage built in the same Tudor style. Beau parked the station wagon alongside. It seemed strange to Hannah, the huge home on wide landscaped acres without a soul to be seen.

A moment later, a white-haired Mexican man emerged from the garage's side door. He was short and barrel-chested, with deep lines in his brown face.

He approached the driver's window. "You Mr. Brightman, yes?"

"Call me Beau. This is my daughter, Hannah. She's looking for some transportation. Roger told me to stop by and look at the car."

"And I'm Manuel." He stared across the seat, eyes glued on her birthmark, before dragging his gaze away. "Mrs. Quint told me you were come. I open right away." He used a show shovel to loosen a crust of snow in front of the overhead garage door, then rolled it up.

Beside a pair of matching Lincolns—one black and one white—sat a light green Volkswagen.

Leaving her father at the wheel, Hannah scrambled out of the car, sliding a little on the wet pavement.

"I vacuum inside and wipe down just this morning." Manuel's wrinkled brown hand flicked a bit of dust off the VW's rear window. He extracted a key from his jacket pocket, started the car, and backed it into the driveway.

Its soft, sea green paint was unblemished and the shiny chrome bumpers, undented. Her fingers trailed across the surface of the roof, chilly as a lime freeze, but so delicious she could almost taste it. Only one other kid at school, Stu Hinkle, had a VW. All Hannah's friends jockeyed for seats if Stu was making a run to Berry's after classes.

"For me? Are you serious?" The smile on her face stretched muscles she'd forgotten about.

Possibilities jumped in her head like popcorn. Driving the VW to the ski slopes this winter with Kenny. Rolling down the windows and playing KIMN radio at max volume. She could almost feel the wind blow through her hair as she and her friends sped to Red Rocks amphitheater for a summer concert.

"I'd have to teach you how to drive a stick shift, of course, but it's got your name on it, Miss Lovely."

"It's not that hard. Stu Hinkle, from my class, has a VW. I've driven his a few times. It won't be much of a problem." She'd spin circles around the boys in her class who were rehabilitating 1930s Model A's. Their cars would look like ponderous buffaloes compared to her adept bug.

"Would it be mine? Not sharing with Clyde or Boomer when they're home?"

"All yours," her father said. "Just one thing."

"I promise I'll be a good driver. No drag racing or sliding around corners."

Manuel leaned on the handle of the snow shovel, watchful eyes flicking between the two of them. A blue jay screeched from a nearby conifer tree.

"The thing is, Nancy needs you at home, now that we have the twins." He crossed his arms across his chest.

"I'm already helping her because you're gone all the time."

"Well, yes. It's just that it's been hard on her, and now that the boys are about to start walking, it'll be tougher. She's worn out."

His words wove themselves into a net around her, sticky as a spider's web.

"But I'm a high school girl, not a mother. Right now, I can hardly go anywhere because I have to shop or babysit or hang diapers on the line."

"Yes, yes, that's true. Nan and I are terribly grateful for what you're doing. We're lucky to have a daughter like you."

Her fists clenched at her sides. "I'm not her daughter. I didn't want her, but I'm stuck with being the unpaid help, now that you're paid by the frigging truckers."

"That's why we want you to have the car, all yours."

His extraordinary blue eyes rested on her as if there were no one else in the world. "And in exchange, we want you to stay at home and go to DU for your first two years of college."

Cold crept through the soles of her loafers and up her legs. She stamped her feet, tears springing into her eyes at the pain. "Boomer enlisted," she said. "Clyde's gone away to college. Since I'm the girl, I'm supposed to stay home?"

"I need you, Hannah."

"Hire a nanny. That's what Quint's friends do."

"We can't afford it." He reached out to touch her shoulder, but she shrank away. "Listen, Hannah, in two years, Quint's retiring. He's promised me the position as executive director for the western US. When that happens, our money troubles will be over."

She felt the force of his ambition. After years in a law practice where his partners siphoned away the most lucrative cases, he was hungry for success. At this moment, he seemed tainted, with graying hair and a pouch of extra flesh around his waist. The whites of his remarkable eyes were hatched with tiny red veins.

Two more years at home. Her throat contracted, making it difficult to breathe. While Paulette escaped to San Francisco, Kenny to Minnesota, and Rosemarie to a Jewish girls' college, she'd be sleeping in the same bed her parents bought her when she was six.

The chrome-plated rear bumper glittered in a ray of sun.

She thought, suddenly, of the Hogg family. The patriarch had given his sons a choice—money or the freedom of a new name—but the boys refused to play his game. They'd grabbed the money, then did as they wished.

She was a lawyer's daughter. Once she had title, the car was hers.

"All right," she said. "We have a deal."

4

Jack squirmed in the pew. Reverend Kellems bowed his head and launched into the prayers. "O Creator and mighty God, you have promised us strength for the weak, rest for the laborers . . ."

While Kellems droned on, Jack scanned the congregation. Hannah's father and stepmother sat at their regular spot in the second row, but she wasn't there. Too bad. He'd been looking forward to whispering a few words in her ear after the service. In the midst of his erotic thought, his wife reached over and laced her fingers in his. He snatched his hand away. The pious hand-holding other couples did in church was nothing but a phony show of pretending to be happy.

"Give us, O Lord, steadfast hearts, which no unworthy thought can drag downward . . ." Kellems continued.

Talk about being dragged down. His mother, Daisie King, just back from two months in Florida, flanked him on the other side. She'd raged for hours yesterday over the situation at the Comet.

"Heal the sick, Lord, especially our president, Dwight Eisenhower, recovering now in a Denver hospital," Kellems continued, as if anyone with a brain cared about the Commie-loving president.

His mother adjusted her mink coat, thrown around her shoulders, the sleeve brushing the back of his hand. The brown hairs seemed to crawl with power, as if probing for a patch of his uncovered flesh. He jiggled his knee to settle his nerves.

"Stop it." Daisie's breath hissed in his ear. Her hand clamped down on his thigh.

Jack surged to his feet and stumbled to the aisle, bumping legs and stepping on toes. The president, and his mother, he couldn't stand it, not after yesterday's fight, and Ike all over the TV last night, him waving from the hospital balcony. Thoughts beat against his skull until he was dizzy. He sank down onto a bench in the vestibule and pressed his thumb against his throbbing forehead until his heartbeat slowed and his fury subsided.

As a small child, he'd tried to keep his distance from Daisie, sometimes having terrible nightmares that she was a carnivorous animal, her body covered with hair and eyeteeth weighty and pointed.

He wandered the church's halls, passing Kellems' office. Jack rattled the knob, but it was locked. In spite of his prayers for that asshole Ike, the minister wasn't a bad guy, a red-faced fatherly type. In the three years he'd been minister, he'd managed to get a new sanctuary built, three times larger than the old one.

An image associated with his own father rose in Jack's mind: a handkerchief spotted with blood. It wasn't until years later Jack learned his father had died of TB. Sometimes his anger at Daisie overflowed onto his father as well. The bastard had ignored his own health, leaving Jack without him at a tender age.

From this wing of the church, he heard children's voices from the nursery in the basement. Lucy had dropped the kids there before the service. He descended the stairs. The nursery door stood open, but an accordion gate blocked the lower half of the entrance to keep the children from wandering. He peered in.

Three cribs sat against the wall. His son, Albert, who'd kept them up most of the night crying, dozed in one of the cribs. Five or six boys sat at kid-sized tables stacking building blocks and assembling pioneer cabins with Lincoln Logs. A white-haired woman perched on a small chair, reading "Mary Had a Little Lamb" to Jack's daughter, Serena.

Glancing to his left, he was startled to see Hannah sitting on the nursery floor, her full skirt tucked under her. A little boy rolled a rubber ball to her across the asphalt tiles. From the child's strong resemblance, this must be one of Hannah's twin brothers.

She was prettier than he remembered from Friday night, her elfin haircut, full upper lip, and rose-colored blemish giving her a sweet, vulnerable aura. Surprisingly, Hannah seemed to like the kid. The way she'd described her baby brothers Friday night, he assumed she hated the greedy little bastards. Instead, she laughed and clapped encouragement as the toddler caught the rolling ball between his palms.

The boiling rage at his mother subsided. He leaned over the kiddie gate. "Good morning! I missed you at the service."

She didn't look at him. "Your wife was here earlier, dropping off your children."

He ignored her reference to Lucy. "I've been thinking about you. When I didn't see you in the pews, I was afraid you were sick."

"I'm okay." Finally, she looked up at him, a flash of triumph in her eyes. "I got a car."

"One of your brothers gave you his junker?"

"No, no! My father bought it just for me. A VW. Only a year old."

"Beautiful. So you're free to come and go as you please." He opened the gate and stepped into the nursery. "When are you going to take me for a ride?"

She rose and joined him, close enough he could see a small loop earring in the lobe of her pierced ear. "I don't think that's a good idea."

Before he could respond, Serena spotted him and ran over. Her fingers tugged his pant leg. "Daddy, Daddy, come play with me!"

Ordinarily, her interruption would have made him angry, but now he felt under control. Plans were stirring in his head. He leaned over and picked up Serena. "Did you have fun the other night?"

"It was, well, strange," Hannah said.

Jack lowered his voice. "I'm not trying to seduce you, Hannah. I just want to celebrate with you."

She glanced over at the white-haired woman, who'd begun reading *The Poky Little Puppy*. "You wanted to get in my pants on Friday, didn't you?" Hannah tilted her head to one side, as if she were judging her own attractiveness.

"The situation at the Comet had me on edge. I wanted you, but I was upset, not thinking clearly." He assumed his most contrite face, which almost always worked on Lucy and his mother. "I spent all day yesterday opening up and getting it running again."

Serena wriggled in his arms and patted his cheeks.

"Tell you what. My wife and mother are going to a baby shower tonight. Why don't I buy you dinner at Gaetano's, in honor of your new car?"

There were moments, he told himself, when he was extraordinarily perceptive, and now was one. Her longing hung in the air like smoke. She wanted to defy her parents and live her own secret life.

A tiny smile quivered at the corner of her mouth. "The restaurant owned by the Smalldone family?"

He felt a surge of satisfaction. It was going to be perfect. As he had this thought, strains of the organ playing the final hymn filtered down from the sanctuary. Lucy would be arriving soon to collect the kids.

"It's a family restaurant with the best veal scaloppine west of the Mississippi." His words flowed quickly. "Everyone goes there: lawyers and their clients, good girls and bad girls."

"Which am I? she asked.

"Who knows?" He smiled his most winning smile. "Pick me up at 6 at the Comet."

5

Hannah pulled into the Comet, where a banner was strung across the front: "Welcome Back! Grand Reopening!" Jack had telephoned her that afternoon, telling her to park in the rear, in one of the spaces meant for indoor customers.

"Darker back here. We're not as visible," Paulette said. "This feels like *True Confessions*."

Inviting Paulette was meant partly as a shield against any unwanted moves Jack had in mind and partly to witness to her new adventure. Hannah hadn't asked the innocent Rosemarie. Paulette's mother's alcoholism and her parents' divorce made her less likely to be judgmental about Hannah's foray with a married man. The one stable person in Paulette's life was her brother, a twenty-eight-year-old officer with the Denver Police Department.

"Get in the back," Hannah said. "Jack's legs are too long for that tiny space."

Paulette gave her a sidelong glance. "You're not letting him drive?"

"My car, I drive." The words tasted good. Her car was one of the few things she had control over. Once graduation was done, she was heading to California with Paulette regardless of her father's wishes. She switched the radio to KIMN and wiggled in the seat to "Rock Around The Clock." The song was a little junior high, but she still liked Bill Haley.

Twenty minutes passed. Business for the grand reopening was lively. Cars arrived at the drive-in stations. The carhops, warmly dressed in heavy coats and earmuffs, scurried in and out, delivering trays of food and picking up the empties. Some families went inside for Sunday burgers.

No Jack.

"Turn on the engine again. I need heat." Paulette's voice came from behind Hannah's shoulder. "Is that shithead going to stand you up?"

A clot of disappointment grew in Hannah's chest. Her first venture on the road to independence was a failure. He probably thought she was too girlish, not womanly enough. She'd stepped on the clutch to shift the VW to Reverse when the passenger door opened.

"So sorry I'm late. I . . ." With one leg in the footwell, Jack paused, peering into the back.

It was fun to see his surprise. "You remember my friend, Paulette, from Sloan's Lake?" Hannah asked.

"Sure. Good to see you again." He lowered himself into the seat and slammed the door.

Asshole. In the rearview mirror, Hannah saw Paulette mouth the word. This was beginning well.

Jack gave her directions, his fingers tapping his thighs. North on Federal, then right toward Italian town. "Here. Park in the middle of the block. There won't be any spaces farther on."

Hannah hadn't had much practice parallel parking. She backed too close to a Cadillac's rear fender, and on the next attempt ended up too far into the street. It took several tries, her hands damp on the wheel. What if she dented or scratched her new car?

The night was clear and cold. As they walked to the restaurant, Paulette nudged her. Exhaust was rising from a car parked across the street. Inside sat two men watching the comings and goings of Gaetano's customers.

"It's the police," Paulette whispered. "My brother Alonzo told me they take notes and pictures of everyone who goes in."

The exterior of Gaetano's seemed unremarkable, a red-brick building whose front entrance angled across the corner. Muted light shone from the windows. But as Jack opened the door, oh, the scents wafting out into the crisp air—tomato sauce, spicy sausage, and baking bread as warm as her grandmother's hugs.

Inside, a woman with dark hair teased into a beehive greeted them at the podium. "Jack, so good to see you. How many tonight?"

"Just the three of us, Sophia." As they followed her to a secluded booth, Paulette trailing a few steps behind, Jack's hand pressed the small of Hannah's back.

It felt strange, this touch. She'd seen men do it, as if they were driving a car or pushing a lawn mower, but now the subtle pressure was filled with sexual meaning, as if he were preparing her. The banquette's red leather was worn and soft, and the cushion rocked as Jack settled next to her. Paulette slid to a seat across the table.

Hannah had expected the restaurant to be dark and dirty, but instead it was clean and cheerful. Sunday was apparently a night for family gatherings. It was noisy, the rise and fall of voices speaking Italian, the clash of plates and silverware, the notes of Mario Lanza singing "Come Back to Sorrento" in the background.

Lining the wall were pictures of football and baseball teams the restaurant sponsored. A place of honor over the entrance was reserved for a photo of Giuseppe Garibaldi, the George Washington of Italy, with a spotlight focused on it. Through an arched doorway she glimpsed the bar, shadowy faces of its patrons reflected in the back-bar mirror.

"I don't know what all this is." Paulette held the menu close to the candle in the center of the table.

Hannah thumbed through page after page of the menu. She recognized the names of a few of the dishes, but the *zuppa verdure*, *antipasti*, and the difference between *pasta bolognese* and *Alfredo* confused her.

Jack was no help. He paid little attention to Paulette and Hannah, instead scanning the other customers, eyes flicking from one group to another.

A waiter with slicked-back hair and a 5 o'clock shadow appeared at the table. Without prompting, he set a glass of dark liquor in front of Jack, then pulled a pad from his apron pocket.

"Spaghetti and meatballs," Paulette said.

"No main course?" he asked.

"What I just said."

"And you, Miss?"

Hannah chose chicken Parmesan, a dish her mother'd prepared back when Hannah was little.

"Nothing for me—or, maybe just some caprese." Jack held a cigarette between two fingers and sipped his drink.

He seemed remote, not attentive like the other night. She wondered if she'd angered or offended him, but rejected that notion. The shift in his mood wasn't because of her. Maybe he'd invited her because he was angry at his wife or eager to show off a young woman to his friends. Hannah was sorry she'd accepted, and even sorrier that she'd involved Paulette.

While they waited for their dinners to arrive, a man approached the table. It was Young Eugene Smalldone, the one she'd seen in the Cadillac at the lake.

"Jack, *mio amico*, good to see you." His face was flushed, his pupils enlarged.

Hannah felt Jack's body stiffen. He raised his glass, but didn't return Smalldone's greeting.

"Who's these girls?" Smalldone stumbled as he slid into the booth next to Paulette, who wrinkled her nose in disgust and shrank into the corner.

"Friends of mine. Is Chauncey around?"

"I dunno. He might be in later." Young Eugene gave Hannah and Paulette the eye. "*Two* friends. Lucky guy."

"Listen, Eugene, we're celebrating a birthday. You and I can get together another time."

Eugene's lips curled back, exposing his teeth in a shark's smile.

"You don't want to introduce your friends to a Dago, that it? In *my* restaurant?"

From across the table, Hannah could feel the heat radiating off Young Eugene. She stirred, wanting to escape from his simmering anger, but Jack's wide shoulder stopped her from leaving the booth.

Jack raised a placating hand. "Italians are fine with me, and I meant no offense."

"Well, isn't that nice." Smalldone slapped the tabletop with his palm, rattling the glasses. "None taken."

"Good."

Hannah released a shaky breath.

Smalldone half-rose, then settled into the seat again. "I hear your drive-in has reopened."

"Yeah, last night."

"Too bad. I guess your plan didn't work out. No boom, boom!"

Curls of suspicion wound through her. What was Smalldone talking about?

6

After that jackass Smalldone had left, the three of them might as well have been attending a funeral, they were so quiet. Jack tapped his fingers on the tabletop and swirled the ice in his water glass. Hannah studied her fingernails as if they were the Mona Lisa.

Anxiety had robbed him of his appetite. He pushed aside the caprese without touching it. It was bad enough that Eugene'd picked up whispers about Jack's role in the Comet explosion. Was Eugene spreading it around? Did a bear shit in the woods? Of course he was.

What if Eugene started blabbing about the other thing? The Family'd refused to use their contacts to acquire the essentials for his new plan. Getting the money for the car dealership hinged on a certain essential component. It'd be difficult for him to obtain it without leaving a trail, but the Family could get it through their illegal sources, no problem.

The waiter appeared, carrying a large tray laden with food. He arranged the plates with a flourish at each place, turning them just so, but when he left, no one picked up a fork.

"You ladies lose your appetite?" Jack asked.

"My mother's pasta is better. More sauce." Paulette tossed her napkin on the tabletop.

Jack lit a cigarette. Hannah picked at her food, and the silence seemed to weigh a ton.

"How about dessert? The spumoni ice cream is great." He hated the way he sounded, as if he were pleading.

"We don't want anything, except to get out of here," Hannah said.

He signaled the waiter for the check. They retrieved their coats, but as they stood at the door, Smalldone accosted him again. "Your business doin' good?"

"Going great."

The dirty little junkie, he was giving Jack another stiletto cut about the explosion. If only things had gone right, the frigging drive-in would be in bits and he'd have twisted his mother's arm for a share of the insurance money. Public Service had been suspicious. Rumors had circulated, but investigators had eventually concluded it was an improperly installed natural gas valve. The damage had been repair-able, and no big insurance payment was in the offing.

As they crossed the street, the dark car still sat at the curb with the silhouetted figures of the plainclothes cops inside.

He tried to put his arm around Hannah, but she veered away, her face ivory-white and expressionless. Was she remembering their conversation in the Comet's darkened parking lot Friday night? He'd been stupid, telling her how much he disliked his role as manager; how he was thinking of opening a car dealership. At the time, he'd hoped his plan would impress her.

At the car, Jack plucked the VW's keys from Hannah's hand. He wasn't in the mood to sit in the passenger seat and listen to her grind the gears.

She looked angry enough to spit in his face. "It's my car. I get to drive."

He tilted his head toward the undercover surveillance. "We need to glide out, with no stalls or backfires."

"I can do that."

"Get in before they come over and ask questions." He unlocked the car, slid behind the wheel, and leaned over to unlock the passenger door. When they were in, of all the fucking luck, he killed the engine.

"Good job," Paulette said.

Hot with embarrassment and anger, he restarted and drove at twenty-five until he was out of the cops' view, then stepped on the gas. Hannah gripped the edge of the seat as he sped down Federal, dodging in and out of traffic and accelerating through the yellow lights. The small engine keened a high-pitched protest. The pavement was free of ice, or he probably would have wrecked the annoying stinkbug.

At the Comet, a lone car, loaded with mom, dad, and three squirming kids, sat at the speaker boxes. Through the wide front window, he spotted a handful of customers who'd opted for indoor/sitdown. This was normal. Business was brisk in the early hours of Sunday evening, but by eight or so, customers thinned out as they prepared for the workweek. He set the emergency brake and stepped out, his hand atop doorframe. Hannah climbed behind the wheel. Paulette resumed her spot in the front passenger seat.

Hannah's birthmark was bright red. Jack's vision seemed to blur, as it often did when he was on the verge. With a shaky hand on the VW's roof, he leaned in, close to her ear. "You won't . . . don't tell anyone what Eugene said."

She lifted her chin and threw him a chilly stare. "Just what is it I shouldn't talk about?"

"Eugene's not always rational. In fact, he spent some time at Pueblo last year."

She gunned the VW forward, forcing him to scramble out of its path.

His vision darkened. He made his way, almost by touch, into the Comet's restroom where he ducked his head under the faucet, letting frigid water run over his head until his body was shaking with cold, but his vision was clear. In the mirror, a gray, haggard face stared back at him.

When he returned to the dining area, one customer still lingered at the table, eating fries and burgers and sipping a Coke.

Ralph, the manager, intercepted him as he made for the door, but Jack swept past with a brief wave. Middle-aged and balding,

Ralph was ostensibly friendly. He'd worked here before the explosion, and Daisie'd paid his wages during the closure. With the reopening, Ralph resumed his role as manager and snitch, someone she'd hired to report Jack's failings and absences.

The new Chevy half-ton pickup his mother had bought him in June was parked in back, where he'd left it earlier while he waited for Hannah. The truck was beneath his dignity, as if his mother were forcing him into the role of handyman or construction worker. While Daisie had vacationed in Palm Beach, he cruised around in her Buick, but that perk had ended yesterday with her return to Denver.

Agitated and unwilling to go home, he bought a six-pack of Coors and drove up Lookout Mountain to the spot where he and Hannah had parked Friday night. He drank it all, thinking about Hannah, Young Eugene's big fat mouth, and the danger he might be in.

He'd been stupid to invite her to dinner. A bad mistake, but he'd been excited in the church nursery, watching her breasts move under her sweater. It had been perversely thrilling, to arrange their nasty little date while innocent kids ran around.

It hadn't been a bad strategy: bring a girl, create casual meeting with the Smalldones. Everyone knew the Dagos had girlfriends, even though they pretended to be good family men. He'd thought a stop at the restaurant and a casual encounter with Chauncey would facilitate further meetings about his auto dealership plan. Young Eugene had thrown a monkey wrench into it. Jack couldn't risk him blabbing any more about the Comet explosion. He needed to come up with another strategy.

The car clock read 1:45 when he veered into his driveway. The two-bedroom stucco place, too small for them now that Daisie was living in their basement guest suite. It should be bigger, like the places where Daisie'd lived with her rich parents and rich third husband. He imagined wheeling a Caddy into the driveway of a house with tall, white columns and fancy landscaping.

He left the truck in the driveway, one tire off the concrete into the dormant rose bushes. It was a nuisance to park it outside in the cold, but Daisie'd insisted her Buick be parked in the one-car garage.

He stumbled into the house, shoes in hand. Stealth proved to be useless—she was sitting in the living room dressed in a long velvet bathrobe. A cigarette was poised between two fingers as if she were Gloria Swanson in *Sunset Boulevard*.

"How were tonight's receipts?" Her dark eyes focused on him like a dentist's drill.

"Not bad." He attempted a cool, professional tone, but his words slurred a bit. "Steady business until closing. Pretty good, actually, considering it's the first weekend of reopening."

"Ralph called me about 10. They'd closed, but you were nowhere to be seen. He wanted to know whether you were coming to pick up the cash for the night drop at the bank, or if I wanted him to do it."

"So what if I didn't stay? I hate that place."

"You fool." She ground out her cigarette in the ashtray. "You're throwing away what I've given you. Yet again. I told you, didn't I, that if we started the business, it was a chance to redeem yourself?"

"Redeem myself? That whole mess at Hampton Automotive was your fault—your criticism and constant nagging. That's what got me off track, you interfering bitch!"

Jumping out of the chair, Daisie darted at him, her lips contorted in fury. A palm cracked against the side of his face. "What I've been through year after year—your failures, lies, schemes!" She drove him backward, reaching up to rain blows, hitting his nose and the side of his head.

He raised his arms over his head to protect himself from her long fingernails. He'd been a foot taller than her by the time he was sixteen, but he'd never gathered the courage to fight back.

"As if your thefts from the automotive store weren't bad enough." Her diamond ring scratched his eyebrow, sending blood dripping into his eye. "As if me having to bail you out of jail in Texas wasn't enough. You said you wanted to go into business, so I bought the land and built the Comet. Now you're going to throw this away, too?"

"It's the contractor's fault." He shouted, not caring whether the kids woke up. "If he'd installed the gas values right, it wouldn't have happened, I swear!"

During his years at the orphanage, his longing for her had been so deep that when he joined her again, he'd succumbed. She loved him. She hated him. She hugged him. She hit him. His mother was a wall he couldn't climb, a river he couldn't swim, a star he couldn't reach.

"Jack, what's going on?" Lucy appeared in the hallway, Albert crying in her arms.

He blinked away blood.

"After I spent hours getting Albert to sleep," Lucy said, "you woke him up." Her hair hung like string around her face. Breast milk leaked onto the front of her nightgown.

Through a bloody haze, he found his way to the kitchen. He shut the door and lowered himself into one of the chrome chairs at the table. Palms over his eyes, he blocked out the light.

He thought of Hannah, struggling to free herself from her family and her deformity.

"I can do this," he whispered to himself. "I can do it."

7

Hannah stopped the VW in Rosemarie's driveway and tapped the horn. While she waited, she opened the wind-wing to rid the car of the residual odor of Jack's aftershave. It had been a stupid decision to accept Jack's invitation. She flapped her hand to drive out any airborne reminders of their dinner at Gaetano's.

She'd lain awake last night trying to figure out why he'd invited her to join him. At first, she thought he found her attractive, but once they arrived at the restaurant, she saw he had something else in mind. He'd been using her to further some unspoken plan. Not only had she waded into trouble, but she'd involved Paulette, who was struggling with a full menu of her own problems. Paulette had stayed home today because her mother'd drunk too much, fallen on the stairs, and broken a rib.

A flurry of motion accompanied Rosemarie as she jumped in the car and tossed her books on the floorboard. "Oh, this car is the cutest thing ever! The color's perfect, and there's not a scratch or dent anywhere!"

Rosemarie's enthusiasm spread through Hannah like warm chocolate. This was exactly the response she'd hoped for. Maybe other kids at school would be impressed.

"Tell me everything," Rosemarie seemed truly delighted. "Who, where, when?"

"From my dad's boss, who sold it because his daughter's away at school." Hannah's hands cradled the wheel as if it were a lover's face.

"Is your dad's boss an angel? This car is such a trophy. I've only seen a few Volkswagens on the road."

"Stu Hinkle has one, remember?"

"But yours is a beauty queen. Stu's is a beggar man." Rosemarie slid her fingers over the dashboard. "Why did your father relent? I thought he'd laid down the law—you only get a car when you're in college."

Hannah bit her tongue, a reminder not to tell Rosemaire about her deal with Beau or her secret decision to violate it. "He really wanted to make me happy. Plus, he knew I needed it so I could run errands for Nancy."

"Not in a decade of Saturdays would the Rabbi allow me to have a car," Rosemarie said, referring to her father, as she often did, as "the Rabbi."

It was nearly 8:30, and classes would start soon. Hannah revved the engine, thrilled at the way the dual pipes made it sound like a race car. Within minutes, they were roaring into school's parking lot, where she stopped with a squeal of brakes near Stu Hinkle's dented beige '53.

Stu waved a meaty hand. "*Guten tag, frauleins*," he said a terrible German accent.

At noon, Hannah fidgeted at the lockers waiting for Rosemarie. Several boys had said admiring things about her car, but she was nervous about the Pops. Would her car impress the ruling queens of the school? After fifteen minutes, her stomach began growling, so she gave up and went to lunch on her own.

She hesitated at the cafeteria doorway. An arcane seating scheme governed lunch at Woodlake High, reminiscent of the rungs of British royalty. The athletes, for example, had an unwritten rule book decreeing that only other athletes occupied tables in the center of the room, and even there, the best were designated for football players.

Students with straight As or award-winning science fair projects knew their place, as did the class clowns, underachievers and middle-of-the-road plodders. Hannah and her two friends usually sat near the kitchen alongside the tray return area. Nearby was a table beside the trash barrel for the outcasts, like the sophomore with a deformed hand and Junie, who'd worn the same pair of ripped, run-over loafers for two years.

Then there were the Pops. Hannah knew it was shallow, her longing to be accepted at one of the two fine tables near the window where the female elite ate lunch. She didn't really like the Pops, but she wanted to be noticed. Envied. She wanted to win—at something.

Today, the benches flanking one of the Pops' tables were full. The second Pops table had only four occupants, homecoming queen Odessa Stamos and three girls-in-waiting. Their books and purses were piled on the tabletop in front of the unoccupied bench seats. Hannah gathered courage. Her VW was all the buzz in morning classes. She wanted to test whether she was on her way to being *somebody*.

Feeling guilty but compelled to attempt a change, Hannah by-passed the table where she, Rosemarie, and Paulette ate lunch every day of the school year and walked steadily over to the Pops' table. She cleared a spot for her tray and sat down.

Odessa brushed her thick, blonde hair back over her shoulder. "That spot's taken."

"It's not saved," Hannah said.

"Audrey and Carla are coming. They sit there."

Hannah slid to the end of the bench. "There's plenty of room."

"Not for you." Odessa raised a forefinger, held it in the air, and rubbed her own cheek.

Heat crept up Hannah's chest and neck. *Not now, please.*

The silent plea went unanswered. Her birthmark grew hot enough to burst into flame. She closed her fists to keep from covering it with her palm.

One after another, the other girls stared at her and rubbed their cheeks. Hannah fled, and as she passed their usual table, Rosemarie stared at her with dark, accusing eyes.

***

In the girls' restroom, Hannah locked herself in a stall. The window-less space throbbed with sounds—talk, laughter, flowing sinks, and flushing toilets. Smells of liquid soap—and worse—filled the air.

The five-minute bell rang and the noise subsided until only a few voices remained. Water splashed in a sink.

"Did you hear?" a someone said. "Brightman got her butt kicked."

"I was at the next table," said a second girl. "It was ugly. She was trying to be one of us."

"Hannah's not really that bad. She just needs to stay with her own kind."

"Over by the trash barrel." They laughed.

The door opened and closed, leaving Hannah surrounded by silence and smells.

Her loneliness seemed complete. She had ditched her friend, only to be punished for her social climbing. Maybe she should skip her yearbook class. It would be a relief to toss her skates in the car and drive somewhere, to Estes Park maybe. Her heart beat faster. Or Minnesota, or the Sierra. She thought of the snow, hundreds of miles of it, icy and clean, carved by the wind.

Stepping out of the cubicle, she was startled to see her image in the mirror, bent like an old woman. She drew closer, straightening her back and shoulders. Her eyes, the same blue as her father's, were wide and angry.

***

The yearbook was called *Tiger Tales*, an unbelievably silly name selected in the 1940s, years before Ian Lockley took over as advisor. Hannah slipped into her seat in the last row. In the high school scheme of things, a student with a last name beginning with B, like hers, normally would be assigned the second or third desk in the first column on the left. That meant she'd spent many class hours behind Sam Allen or one of the Appleton boys.

But in September, Hannah'd asked Lockley for the last chair in the last row, next to the rear door. To her surprise, he'd agreed. As the yearbook's lead photographer, she might need to duck out of class from time to time to shoot a photo.

Lockley was an elfin figure of a man, about five-three, who wore gold-rimmed glasses and long sideburns. Hannah liked him. His eyes didn't skitter away from her birthmark when he looked at her. Instead, he regarded her all at once, like swallowing a teaspoon of medicine.

"Anyone have a story?" Lockley's daily class began by soliciting students for an odd or inexplicable news item. He'd been a photographer for *Stars and Stripes*, the military's newspaper, during the Korean War and seemed fascinated by strange news events. Today, nobody came up with one, so he pulled out a clipping from the *Rocky*: a truck transporting plumbing supplies near Houston caused a huge midday tie-up when a dozen toilets slid off the rear of the trailer onto the highway

"It was a shi . . . shabby commute," Lockley said, the corner of his mouth twitching. The class burst into laughter. Hannah noticed that Lockley occasionally inserted a near-profanity into his classroom dialog. Did he do it to sound tough, perhaps to counter nasty rumors he was a fairy?

She thought she understood. Once in awhile, it felt good to do something that challenged everyone's assumptions about who you were. Not that things necessarily turned out well. If Lockley didn't watch himself, he might get fired.

What could be the negative outcome of her two encounters with Jack? Their meetings had been strange and exciting, but Sunday's dinner had put an end to it. Jack was handsome, not physically flawed like her or Lockley, but his defect was deep, lodged in his brain or his heart. And although her teacher might end up being canned, Jack might face arrest and prison.

Hannah tried to shake off the feeling she'd been infected with Jack's inner toxin.

Lockley ran a palm over his bushy sideburns and called the roll, then directed students to circle desks into clusters to work on their yearbook assignments. As they rearranged the desks, Hannah caught a couple of girls whispering and staring at her. She felt as though she and Lockley were two freaks among a crowd of onlookers.

When the desks were rearranged, Stu Hinkle and Hannah were the only two in the photography cluster; the third member of their group was out sick.

"I've got something for you," Stu said.

Hannah raised her eyebrows. She never knew what Stu would produce.

From his cardboard portfolio of pictures, he extracted a color enlargement and laid it face down on the desktop. "Take a look at this." He paused dramatically for effect, then tilted it slightly so only Hannah could see. In full color, the school's sexy typing teacher watched last Friday's pep rally, unaware her tight skirt was unzipped in back.

"After you took the shot, did you tell her?" Hannah asked.

Stu blushed, stifling a smile. "Not on your life. This'll go in my private collection."

The aberrations of human behavior, Hannah thought, seemed infinite. The Pops, despite their pretty faces and expensive clothing, were mired to their eyeballs in meanness. Her lawyer father wasn't above bribing her. And Jack, the family man who regularly attended church, had plotted to blow up his own drive-in.

"Hannah, a word, please." Lockley gestured her to his desk and handed her a hall pass. "Take the rest of the period to get photos of the cafeteria staff at work. That'll wrap up our section on support staff. Have the prints to me by the beginning of next week."

"Can't Stu do it?" After the lunch-hour debacle, she never wanted to visit the lunchroom again.

"He's unlikely to produce any prize-winning shots," he said in a low voice, "but if anyone can make something out of a sh . . . shabby assignment, you can."

Hannah understood. Freaks had to stick together. She unlocked the storage cupboard and pulled out her camera bag, containing flash gun, bulbs, and her twin-lens Rolleiflex, already loaded with film. If she strung out the assignment long enough, she wouldn't have to return to class at all.

In the cafeteria, a janitor was swabbing the floor with a large mop. The scent of today's macaroni and cheese main dish lingered in the room. Sounds of laughter and the clash of dishes emerged from the kitchen. Skirting the serving counter, she approached a trio of women scouring immense cooking pans, wiping the counters, and scraping leftover food from the trays into a garbage bin.

"What're you doing here, Missy?" The cafeteria supervisor smiled as she wiped her hands on her food-spattered white apron. "We going to be in *Glamour* magazine?" She gestured toward the camera in its leather case, dangling from Hannah's shoulder.

"Come on, Sadie." A grandmotherly woman with curly white hair rubbed a drop of sweat from her forehead. "Can't you see the girl's from *Good Housekeeping*?"

The three of them laughed uproariously.

"Much, much better than that," Hannah said. "Your picture's going to be in *Tiger Tales*. You're on your way to fame and fortune." She secured the flash attachment to the camera and inserted one of the blue bulbs.

"Make sure I look good, Honey, so I can quit this shit job and be a model," said the third woman, whose hair straggled from the confinement of a hairnet.

Hannah's sour mood lifted. These gals were different. Most of the adult women she knew were friends' mothers, churchgoers, or neighbors. Like her mother and Nancy, they'd once been nurses or teachers—but now they didn't work, seeming restricted. Not free to be playful or have oversized emotions.

"Hell, I'll retire and move to Florida. Hoooeee!" The supervisor did a little shuffle and strut step, apparently part of a routine she'd devised in the isolation of eight-burner stove, walk-in refrigerator, and oversized dishwasher.

"You ladies take a minute to make yourselves look pretty," Hannah said, "and I'll figure out the shot." While they removed their dirty aprons and combed their hair, she peered around for a good backdrop. Her eye was caught by the tall open cabinets on one wall that held dozens of large kettles and saucepans. She liked their different shapes, the way the light caught their chrome surfaces.

"Okay, here's the deal." She positioned the women around the stovetop with a large pot on a burner. Tall cabinets provided an interesting backdrop, she thought. "Sadie, hold up the large spoon as if you're asking the others to taste-test a batch of spaghetti sauce."

"Are you kidding?" The white-haired woman gave Hannah a disgusted look. "For spaghetti, we open three number-ten cans and dump it into a pot. No tasting involved."

Sadie spread her arms as if separating two boys in a fist fight. "I've got an idea." She gathered six ladles and distributed them so each held two. "Like this, the war dance of the kitchen." They raised the ladles, shaking them and laughing. As they waved the spoons, Hannah pressed the shutter half a dozen times. This could be one of Lockley's odd stories.

After the final school period, Hannah joined Rosemarie at the lockers. Rosemarie kept her back to Hannah as she finished zipping her coat and gathering her books. "Too bad things didn't work out at the Pops' table. I think I'll find another ride home," Rosemarie said.

"Listen, I'm sorry." Hannah touched her friend's shoulder, but Rosemarie shook off her hand.

"It's me that's sorry," Rosemarie said. "I guess I'm not good enough for someone with a nice car." Her voice was stiff with hurt.

For the first time that day, Hannah was ashamed. Not by the stain on her face but the flaw in her character. Even if, by some dispensation worthy of a papal decree, the Pops had opened their ranks to her, they never would've taken in Paulette and Rosemarie. Yet, at the first opportunity, Hannah'd been willing to abandon friends who'd stuck by her since elementary school.

Could she give up her dream of being *someone*? Her fantasies had focused on being elected student body president or girl of the year, but it would happen only if she were a Pop. A dark vision arose of herself sitting at the Pops' table, looking across the lunchroom at Rosemarie and Paulette, who pretended Hannah was invisible.

"Don't go," Hannah begged. "My car couldn't make it out of the lot without you."

Rosemarie slammed her locker door. "Not today; maybe not ever."

8

Jack sat at his desk and watched the second hand tick around the clock dial. This was his first week as night manager at Hertz Car Rental. It was 11. He and Eldon, the grease jockey, sat in the silent office without a single customer. Not surprising, since the location depended on arriving airline passengers at Stapleton Airfield. The last flight had landed at 10:15.

Tension made his jaws ache and blurred his vision.

He'd parted ways with Comet Drive-In. That's what he told people, but actually, his mother had fired him and promoted Ralph, the suck-up assistant.

"I think you need something that's a better fit for your skills," Daisie'd said, sweet as Christmas candy. It was the morning after the disastrous dinner at Gaetano's. The scratch on his cheek from her ring still throbbed.

Did his mother suspect he'd sabotaged the gas line? Outwardly, she supported the police version of the incident—disgruntled burglars, finding no money in the till, had disconnected the fitting. What she really believed, he couldn't tell.

How was he going to support Lucy and the kids on a salary from this place? Daisie had bought their house and given him the new truck, but he had no savings. Bills from telephone and utility companies were piling up on the kitchen table, and Lucy was already nagging him for grocery money.

He lunged awkwardly to his feet, startling Eldon, who occupied the other desk behind the counter. The service area where Eldon usually worked was cold and dark at this time of night.

"Relax. Only two hours left." Eldon licked a disgustingly greasy finger and turned a page of *Wink* magazine. He held up a two-page layout. "Man, is she something!"

The photos were a little tame for Jack's taste. Lots of cleavage, but breasts and pussy mostly covered. He went to the coat rack and took his flask from the pocket. Eldon's eyes widened with interest, but Jack ignored him.

Headlights shone in the window, and a car parked in front. A customer, at this time of night.

Slipping the flask into his suit pocket, Jack approached the counter. It was an old man, his teeth yellowed and his hair creeping untidily over his collar.

"How can I help you, Sir?"

"It's about the Plymouth I rented this morning. A pile of junk. I want my money back."

"What's the problem?" Jack flipped through the stack of paper-work from the day shift. "I assure you, we keep all our cars in tip-top shape."

"Tip-top, my ass." The old guy's cheeks flushed. "It died while I was crossing the streetcar track at Downing Street. Some high school kid helped me push it off, or your shitty car would've been smashed to smithereens."

Jack craned his neck to view the car through the front window. "An interesting story. You've managed to return it without stalling."

The customer's face turned an apoplectic red. "I had to pay Three A to come and jump it, you . . . you . . ."

Jack scooped a refund from the register and sent him off in a taxi, but closing time was still over an hour away. He gave Eldon a generous splash of Black Label in his coffee, then took several long swallows himself. He'd have to document the refund to the day manager when he came on shift tomorrow.

Leaning back in his swivel chair, he opened the *Rocky Mountain News* and slid his finger over the automobile ads. A brand-new half-ton Chevy was listed for sale at the dealership for $1,430. His was only four months old. It must be worth almost that much. Fourteen hundred was a quarter of his yearly salary.

He drummed his fingers on the desktop and took another drink. When he dialed Lucy, she greeted him coldly.

"Honey," he said, "it's going to be very late when I get home. I have some paperwork that's got to be delivered to the Englewood office before opening tomorrow."

"Oh, that's great," she said. "I twisted my arm picking up the baby's stroller, and I can hardly lift him. Your mother is in her room pouting, and Serena's wet her pants twice."

"Put an ice pack on your arm—that always helps." In the background, he could hear Serena crying and the dog barking, despite the late hour.

"When do I have time to sit down with an ice pack? You have no idea the amount of work two children demand."

As if her trivial problems were any of his concern. "Sorry, I'll be late." He hung up.

The pressure behind his eyes rose again.

He'd had a one-quarter interest in the Comet. If he'd gotten insurance money, he could've used it to kick-start his plan for the auto dealership. He couldn't fund the whole thing himself, but with money to flash, he was positive he could've convinced one of the other Smalldones, Chauncey, maybe, to be the primary investor.

What was he going to do now? Let Lucy and his mother beat him down? Their constant nagging'd caused the whole fucked-up mess at the Comet—recriminations, pushing, high-pitched voices that twisted his nerves into knots. Some days, he couldn't stand the scent of face cream, the odor of their menstruation. Women were devious. They liked to pretend they were weak, unable to lift a chair or carry a box, yet they could push you this way and that way, not stopping, yammering all day and night until your head felt bruised, like a boxer getting pounded in the ring.

He lunged to his feet, sending the chair rolling. "Eldon, I've got to get today's reports to the Englewood office. Be sure everything's locked up before you leave."

"Sure, Boss." Eldon held up his magazine and winked.

Behind the wheel of the truck, he turned on the heater. A new moon hung in the east, looking like an apple someone had taken a big bite out of. What a failure he was, working at night in a nothing job with a moron like Eldon. He was twenty-four, an age when he should be starting a brilliant career, raking in money, wearing hand-made shoes, living in a mansion in Cherry Creek. Instead, he was squatting in a stucco box with a nagging wife, two runny-nosed kids, and a mother in the basement apartment.

The road passed a truck stop with several big rigs parked in the side lot. Its coffee shop was brightly lit. Farther along, a couple of hookers stood on the sidewalk, hugging their sweaters while the wind whipped their short skirts. A carload of teenaged boys passed them, yelling out the windows, and the hookers waved.

As he took several swallows from his flask, he thought of Hannah. She could be pretty, like Audrey Hepburn, if it weren't for her face. Would she be a good lay? Maybe. She reminded him of someone he'd known but couldn't place. As soon as the deal with the Smalldones was in the bag, he'd call her. Suggest they get together.

He drove east, the land opening into fields, where only a few scraps of snow remained among brown, frozen weeds. Bridge beams squeaked under the truck's tires as the South Platte River slid beneath like a black snake.

He crossed South Santa Fe Boulevard and bounced over a set of railroad tracks. In a hundred feet or so, he wheeled the truck into a U-turn and parked on the shoulder. The engine idled. He lit a cigarette, watching the smoke drift out the open window. An owl hooted in a dead tree. His mind seemed extraordinarily clear, as if it had been polished like a gem.

A warning light at the rail crossing began to blink. A train's headlight gleamed, just a pinpoint far down the tracks. Tossing his cigarette out the window, he put the truck in gear and accelerated until it sat directly over the rails.

The train was moving fast, whistle piercing the silence. Behind him, the crossing light throbbed, turning the skin on his hands red as they gripped the wheel.

With the truck still on the track, Jack threw open the door and scrambled down the train embankment, shoes sliding in the mud.

Brakes screamed. A crash hammered his ears, but it was good. All good.

***

The intersection, deserted an hour ago, hummed with activity. A tow vehicle was hoisting the Chevy onto its bed while the engineer and a brakeman conferred with a railroad repair crew.

One police officer, a young guy about Jack's age, scrutinized the truck's damage. The other, older and with a skeptical twitch to his eyebrow, interviewed Jack.

"You say the truck stalled? It's brand-new, and the gas tank's full. What would make it stall?" The officer's pencil tapped against his notepad

The guy—about forty, Jack figured—acted like he had a stick up his ass. Jack shoved his hands in his jacket pockets to keep them from shaking. "I already told you, I was crossing the track. The damn truck stalled. I'm not a mechanic, how do I know why? I was trying to get it going when I heard the train whistle."

The officer scribbled away on his pad, but Jack could see the bulge of his tongue in his cheek.

"Listen, I jumped out and ran for my life!" He arranged his face to reflect terror and relief. "Another few seconds, I would have been crushed."

The notebook flipped shut. "Lucky for you," the officer said, "it wasn't a long-haul freight, just an engine towing a couple of boxcars to a pocket siding."

"Thank God I got away." His brain cells seemed to be tingling, calling forth skills he'd honed since he was a child to convince people of his innocence. "I was praying as I tried to get out of the truck. The door stuck, and I had to kick to get it open."

"I see you work for Hertz," the officer said. "Good company. My brother works for them. Considering that, I won't conduct a sobriety test."

"I just had one shot. Hours ago." As soon as he said it, his face flushed. The flask was on the floor of the truck under the driver's seat.

"Sure." The officer slid a citation book from the inside pocket of his heavy winter jacket. Inserting the carbon paper, he carefully wrote a ticket and handed it to Jack.

"What the hell's this for?" He resisted the urge to crumple the paper in this fist.

"A citation for careless driving, Mr. Graham."

"But it wasn't my fault. The truck stalled. No way could I get it started."

"You've been drinking." The officer's jaw jutted out. "You're driving a brand-new truck with a full gas tank. I'm letting you off easy. Don't make me toss you in jail."

***

The next night, Jack had to take the bus to work. When he arrived, he saw four of Hertz's rental cars waiting in back lot to be serviced. Inside, Eldon was not in the mechanic's shop but in the customer area with his feet on a desk.

"Evening, Boss." Eldon leaned back in the swivel chair with his boots on the desk, reading the newspaper.

"Get your feet down and go to work before I fire you." Jack didn't really have the clout to fire this little shit. He felt as though he were caught, like an animal a tar pit with no hope of escape.

It had been a terrible day. The insurance company had refused to total the truck, instead sending it to a body shop for repairs. Neither

Lucy nor Daisie were speaking to him. Instead, they'd gone out to lunch, leaving him with the kids.

Albert kept turning his head away from the bottle when Jack tried to feed him. The child wanted his mother's breast. Jack walked him for an hour, from the kitchen to the front window and back. He stroked the baby's soft hair and sang a nonsensical song, as he remembered nuns doing with babies at the orphanage, but Albert was inconsolable. Meanwhile, Serena burrowed into the cabinet under the bathroom sink and upset a bottle of bath bubbles on the floor, which he'd had to clean up on his hands and knees.

Eldon, with a defiant air, slowly lowered his feet from the desk. He shook the newspaper to straighten the pages. "There's this-here story in today's *Post*. Some guy, last name Graham, leaves his brand-new Chevy on the rail tracks in Englewood last night. When a train hits it, he says the truck stalled."

Jack's hands balled into fists. "It stalled!" Oh, how he'd like to smash the little creep's nose.

"What I want to know," Eldon said, "was why this Graham fellow didn't shift it into neutral and push it off the tracks?"

"If you saw a train about to smash your truck into a grease spot, would you stop to push it off the tracks? Get out of here before I punch you in the face."

9

Beau and Nancy were headed out for their first overnight since the twins were born—a stay at the Brown Palace Hotel after the trucking association's annual dinner dance.

The sitter from the childcare agency had cancelled at the last minute, so Beau had drafted Hannah to babysit. She was stuck at home on Friday night of the most important football game of the season when cheering fans were already watching Woodlake's JV play its archrival, Arvada. Varsity kickoff was scheduled for 7:30.

Hannah glanced at the clock. If the twins were settled in bed soon, she could tune in to the game on the radio.

"It's all right. Mommie loves you," Nancy was saying to Jasper and Marcus. She hovered at the front door, her mink stole around her shoulders, fussing over the boys. Nancy seemed torn, eager to escape the twins for a night, yet somehow oddly fearful her bond with the toddlers would be broken if she left, even for a few hours.

The boys, unconsciously sensing her ambivalence, put on a stellar performance of pathetic abandonment. Within minutes, their whimpering escalated to full-out sobs and a gush of tears.

Cold air rushed through the open door. Beau, who was warming up the car, tooted the horn.

"Go, just go!" Hannah said. She caught the boys by the seat of their pants.

But Nancy still hesitated. "Mommie will be back tomorrow, and she'll make you cookies. Won't that be nice? Cookies!"

Ignoring this transparent attempt at bribery, Jasper and Marcus broke free and toddled over to their mother. They clutched her gold satin skirt, spotting it with snot.

Nancy backed onto the front steps, but still couldn't tear herself away. "We won't be gone long, not long at all. When you wake up, we'll be right there beside your bed."

Beau rolled down the car window. "Nan, come on. We'll be late."

Hannah managed to heft a child under each arm, then kneed the door closed. As soon as the latch clicked, their tears dried up. It had been a fine performance, and she was impressed.

"Come on, you little brats." She trundled them into the kitchen, belted them into their highchairs, and sliced chunks of banana onto the trays. Marcus immediately shoved a piece into his mouth. Jasper investigated the fruit's texture by squeezing it in his fist.

Great Friday night. Stuck at home with two kids covered in goo while everyone who was anyone was having crazy fun at the game. She went to the bathroom to wash her hands. Other than the brightly lighted kitchen, the house was silent and dark. As she passed the master bedroom, she caught the scent of Nancy's perfume.

Hannah'd had a lonely week at school. Gossip about her humiliating confrontation with Odessa had percolated down to the sophomores, who whispered behind their hands and stared at her when they thought she wasn't looking. Rosemary was aloof, taking the bus to school, hurrying past her between classes and sitting with another group at lunch. She'd been unappeased by Hannah's offering of two homemade brownies wrapped in waxed paper and tucked into a gift box.

Hannah squirmed with embarrassment beneath her blanket at night when she recalled how quickly she'd been willing to abandon her friends for acceptance in the Pops' circle. Paulette, who'd been sick the day it happened, made light of the whole incident, mocking Odessa's affected lisp as they sipped Cokes at Berry's after school. The two of them hunkered down in their usual table by the tray drop-off spot during lunch. Maybe Paulette, accustomed to her mother's sporadic neglect during a liquor binge, understood better than most people what it was like to be lonely.

The telephone interrupted Hannah's thoughts. Ten, fifteen rings. She ignored it. Jack had called several times since their dinner at Gaetano's, but she'd hung up as soon as she heard his voice.

Back in the kitchen, she filled plastic cups of pineapple juice for the boys. As they talked in their private language, she was struck by how beautiful they were. Odd, to call boys beautiful, yet their wide eyes and air of wonder touched her. They deserved a happy life. She wondered if Nancy was up to the challenge of seeing them through the hard times.

She rested her forehead against the kitchen window's cold glass. The moon shone through branches of the huge elm tree in the in the backyard. Canes on the dozens of rose bushes her mother had planted were trimmed down to stubs. From next door came the muted shouts of the retired couple engaged in their customary evening argument.

What would life have been like if her own mother had lived? Better. Someone would have loved her. Hannah remembered the way her mother lavished attention on her, brushing her hair before she went to bed, slow strokes that soothed away the frustration and hurt Hannah endured because of her birthmark.

Today, when she'd walked through the parking lot after school, she passed Kenny climbing into his car. He'd gone out of his way to be friendly during the week, saying hello or falling into step with her as they walked to class.

"You going to Tiger's Lair after the game?" His question had sounded casual, but his fingers jangled the keys in his palm.

She searched for a response. Only the most hopeless high school misfits opted out of the dance at the Methodist Church hall on Friday nights, but currently she was Miss Misfit.

"You're asking me for a date?"

Embarrassment tinged his cheeks. "Yeah, I guess so. I won't be able to drive you from the game, because I'm helping coach with the equipment, but I could meet you at the dance and take you home, after."

Her eyes narrowed. Shelly from solid geometry spent ninety percent of class time twisted sidesaddle at her desk flirting with Kenny, and another girl hung around near his locker before school. Maybe he thought he could have quick sex with Hannah, the Ugly Betty.

"I don't think so," she said. "I'm less than nobody right now."

"I thought . . . I sort of asked you last week at the lake, but then you went off with the guy in the Buick."

"Him?" Hannah raised her shoulders in the pretense of a casual shrug. "He's old. We went for a ride, that's all."

A smile had lit up his face. "So, I'll see you tonight?"

She'd said yes.

***

When the boys were finished with their snack, she lifted them down, the round flesh on their arms and legs so different from the thin little limbs in their NICU incubators. She filled the bathtub, frothing it with a dash of bubble bath. Undressed and in the water, Marcus kicked his feet and splashed while Jasper investigated the soap dish and fiddled with the faucet handles.

It was sad the babies didn't see much of Beau. Because he was on airplanes all week either with Roger Quint or flights out of Stapleton Airfield, the twins spent only an hour or two with him—Saturday and Sunday—after he'd labored over house repairs, business paperwork, telephone conversations, and her brother Clyde's long-distance pleas from Chicago begging for money.

Was Nancy sorry she'd married him? Hannah remembered Nancy from before, when her mother Chantal was still alive. Nancy had owned Cut Country, the beauty shop where Chantal had a weekly appointment to have her long, dark hair washed and set. Hannah sometimes tagged along, seizing an opportunity to read movie magazines, which her parents thought were trash. Back then,

Nancy had a shiny, blonde bouffant hairdo. She seemed faded now, her hair unwashed during the week, eyes red and puffy. In the past few months, Nancy and Beau'd had several fights. Did they manage to have sex in their few private hours?

One thing Hannah knew: *she* never wanted to be a wife whose husband fed her attention like table scraps.

The telephone rang again. Jack was becoming a major annoyance. She snatched the receiver, prepared to tell him off.

"Hannah, it's Kenny." He spoke loudly over male laughter and shouting in the background. "I thought I'd spot you in the stands at the game, but you aren't here. Are you mad at me or something?"

She snaked the long phone cord from the hall table to the bathroom door to keep an eye on the twins. "I'm really sorry. At the last minute, my parents drafted me to babysit while they take an overnight. I couldn't reach you."

"You're not blowing me off for that guy?"

"Nothing like that. Can't you hear them?" She held up the handset, which caught a stream of baby talk.

"Right, sorry. I was looking forward to dancing with you."

"Is it the half? Where are you?"

"In the locker room. We're ahead, 17-13."

They didn't speak for a few seconds. On her end, the twins chattered, while on his, deep voices filled the background.

He cleared his throat. "Can I come over, afterward?"

The phone grew damp in her hand. The two of them alone. Sort of.

"I don't know. With my parents gone . . ."

"Do we need a chaperone?"

She laughed. "We've got two little brats to serve that purpose. Come on over, but park your car around the corner. We can listen to my new Fats Domino album."

An hour and a half later when she opened the door, he brought with him a wave of cold, crisp air and the scent of wet wool. They stood in the entry, giving each other quick glances that were as tasty as bites of chocolate.

His blond hair was freshly trimmed, showing a faint tint of pink scalp beneath his crew cut. In the crowded hallway, she was aware of his solidity. He wasn't tall—an inch or two less than six feet—but his body was lean and firm under his jeans and pullover sweater.

His arm slipped around her shoulders and he kissed her, his lips firm and wet. As they parted, his warm breath on her face, one of the twins gave Hannah's pants leg an insistent tug. Although she'd attempted to settle them in bed before he arrived, they were having none of it. Dressed in footed pajamas and crawling around like crabs on the beach, they stared at Kenny with wide brown eyes.

Kenny put his thumbs in his ears, wiggled his fingers, and stuck out his tongue, which set them off on a chorus of giggles.

"Don't horseplay with them," she said. "If they get wound up, they'll never go to sleep."

He held up a palm. "Promise. I'll be sober as a judge." Despite her warning, he couldn't withstand their charm. They grabbed him around the knees, like bear cubs at a tree trunk. He clomped in circles as they screamed in delight. When he pretended to chase them, they scampered away, laughing.

Hannah, who was fed up with babies, toted them to their room, which was furnished with two of everything, even matching mobiles hung above their identical white cribs. She tucked them in and clicked off the light. Standing outside the closed door, she could hear them talking in their own language.

The house was quiet. The quarreling neighbors had gone to bed. Kenny stood beside her, hands shoved in the back pockets of his jeans. She studied the dirty tips of her tennis shoes. Her clothes—food-spattered pants and flannel shirt—were no sort of date outfit. This moment should be different. She should be dressed up in something beautiful. A matching Jantzen sweater and skirt, maybe. Her birthmark felt warm, and she covered the hateful thing with her palm.

"Now what?" Kenny's voice was low and hoarse.

"Maybe you should go home." She wanted to kiss him again, feel the slick touch of his tongue, but a wave of shyness overcame her. "I've never had a boy come over. I don't know what to do."

"It's not like I'm a stranger." He slid a fingertip along her jaw line. "We've known each other since we were kids."

"I remember. It was before you moved to Minnesota and then came back."

In the third grade, he'd sat two seats behind her. Hannah was the fastest reader in the class, and Kenny could recite all the state capitals. Once, in the spring of that year, the two of them stayed in during recess. Shoulders touching, they watched the playground through the open window while girls played jacks and boys threw baseballs or swung on the parallel bars.

"We haven't danced yet," she said.

"Okay." He wiggled his shoulders, as if loosening up. "What's your Top 40 favorite?"

"The 'Ballad of Davy Crockett.'" She was teasing; the song was a twangy Western wail that appealed to grade-schoolers.

"How about 'Sixteen Tons'?" he shot back.

"Georgia Gibbs, 'Tweedle Dee.'"

Laughing, she set up her portable record player on the table in their large country kitchen where the linoleum floor was bare of rugs. They rubbed shoulders as they thumbed through her stack of singles and albums. She'd bought dozens with babysitting money— Frank Sinatra, The Chordettes, The Platters, Somethin' Smith and the Redheads.

"This one." She plucked from the stack Bill Haley & His Comets' new single, "Rock Around The Clock," and put it on the spindle.

Hannah had known Kenny would be a good dancer. Watching him skating at the lake, she saw how he moved with controlled sureness. His hand clasped hers firmly as they rocked and whirled. The kitchen grew warm. He shrugged off his sweater. Muscles under his shirt sleeves flexed and tensed as he spun her out and tugged her back against the curve of his chest.

They edged close, mimicking each other's moves, not laughing but smiling, enjoying their play. She relaxed, allowed herself to be feminine, hips swaying, shoulders wiggling. Her body moved the way it wanted, the way it needed to. This was her real self, one where the mark on her cheek hadn't disappeared exactly, but was somehow rendered insignificant.

Although Kenny seemed to like her, she wasn't sure of him. A small part of her didn't believe he could like her the way she was. Nevertheless, she loved the movement, the music, his smile, and the gleam in his eye.

The .45s dropped down the spindle one after another. When she and Kenny stopped to catch their breath, Hannah heard the kitchen phone ring.

"Hannah?" Nancy's voice was high and edgy. "I called earlier, to check on things, but you didn't answer."

"I must have been in the bathroom." She gave Kenny a side look.

"Did you have trouble getting them to bed? How long have they been asleep?" Nancy seemed unable to let go, even on a night out, with Hannah on duty to tuck them in.

"They cried a little for you." Hannah lied to make her feel better. "But they've been asleep for hours now."

"If you have any problems—anything at all—call the desk here at the Brown Palace. We're going up to our room in a few minutes."

It was 11:30. Old people's bedtime. Maybe they were going upstairs to have sex. She wrinkled her nose at the thought of her father, hair going gray and wrinkles under his chin, still wanting a hot night in the sheets.

"Don't worry. Everything's fine." She hung up feeling trapped, as if Nancy'd built a cage around all of them.

While she was on the phone, Kenny'd lined up a half dozen bottles from Beau's liquor cabinet on the kitchen counter.

"What about some of this?" He unscrewed the cap from a bottle of Johnny Walker.

The odor reminded her of last Friday night on Lookout

Mountain. "Not yet," she said quickly.

He replaced the bottles and put a record on the turntable. "This is one I imagined you and me dancing to." The Platters' Tony Williams began "Only You." His voice was sweet as warm honey as he crooned the slow, romantic ballad.

Kenny held out a hand, and she clasped it, feeling the length of his fingers and swell of his knuckles. She bent to lick his palm, tasting his skin and feeling a tickle on the sensitive tip of her tongue. The floor squeaked under their feet, the neighbors' German shepherd barked outside, the furnace whispered.

Close now, he clasped both her hands in his and curved their arms around her back, imprisoning her in his embrace. She was aware of buttons, the one on his shirt collar almost touching her lips, another on his pants rubbing against her stomach.

The song twined itself around them. His head tilted. They kissed, his lips a little fleshy, his tongue slick as it touched hers. She was flooded with sensation: the scent of her own heat that dampened her shirt, the male odor of him that made her slippery between her legs.

A fretful cry came from the boys' room. Kenny and Hannah's breaths mingled as they waited. He slid a hand down the seat of her jeans, holding her fast. Her hips rubbed against the hard pressure of his erection. In a minute, sound from the twins' room faded.

He slid his hand under the hem of her shirt. "Are we?"

"Absolutely." The was how it should be, touching this young man whom she longed for, and who liked and yearned for her. Not last Friday's shabby, secretive groping with Jack. She took Kenny's hand, led him past the windows, where the icy grass in the backyard glittered in the moonlight. Past her parents' bedroom and the twins', to hers at the end of the wing, where she'd slept in the double bed since she was four years old.

When she clicked on the bedside lamp, it seemed to signal the beginning. Low light caught the sheen on his face. Her hand trembled in his. She felt the rise and fall of his chest as he pulled her down to straddle him on the thick blanket.

Their clumsy hands fumbled with buttons, his small shirt buttons, her larger ones, then the brass buttons on his fly. She felt cold and hot, shy and eager. Clothes scattered around them.

He reached across the bed for a foil packet from his discarded jeans. "Are we going to do the real thing?"

Her lips whispered yes against the corner of his mouth and down his breastbone to the hardness between his legs.

Their lovemaking was fashioned of secret motions that would hardly ripple the air beyond her room, yet seemed momentous. Each move, curve of their fingers, tangle of tongues, touch of his lips on her nipple, slippery thrust and exquisite climax was a seismic shift, breaking apart the life she'd known and revealing undiscovered landscapes of feeling and desire. She lay back on the pillow, hand stroking his back, and gazed at the unfamiliar region of her bedroom.

Dolls from her childhood on the bookshelf. A trophy she'd won in the sixth grade Kiwanis essay contest. A complete set of Nancy Drew mysteries. A photo of their dog, Huntley, who died the same year as her mother. These objects that had once been treasures seemed to belong to another girl she'd known but moved away.

Kenny turned on his side and propped his head on his hand. A finger traced a path down her breastbone and across her stomach to the creamy slit between her legs.

"It wasn't your first time." He didn't sound disappointed, just curious.

"No, once before." Her teeth clamped against her lower lip.

"With him?" He smoothed a strand of damp hair away from her cheek.

"No, I told you I didn't. It was a boy from church camp."

"And was it better tonight?" His hand was still.

"I'm not sure."

"What?" He drew back, eyes wide and uncertain.

She laughed and pulled his head down to lick the corner of his mouth. "We need to do it again before I decide."

10

Englewood's traffic court was housed in a small room in the municipal annex. A Podunk courtroom compared to the city of Denver's, Jack thought. No dais, just a desk and five rows of wooden folding chairs. The clerk sat at a small table talking to a man with a press badge clipped to the pocket of his heavy winter coat.

Jack waited. An airplane headed for Stapleton Airfield roared overhead, shaking the building's walls. The other traffic violators stirred uneasily.

"All rise. Judge Herman Leighton presiding," the bailiff said.

The judge wore no black robe, only a rumpled brown suit, which lent a further air of insignificance to the proceedings.

Jack squirmed in the rickety chair. His feet were numb from cold. Without his truck, he'd been forced to take a succession of buses to court.

While waiting for his case to be called, he watched as a shame-faced teenager accompanied by his father pleaded guilty to driving without a license. Next, a woman with a headscarf tied under her chin told a complicated story about her ten tickets, something to do with the No Parking sign outside her apartment building being down or defaced.

Judge Leighton dismissed five of the citations. "Pay the remainder of the fines at the cashier's window," he said. "Next case."

While the woman had been nattering on, Jack caught sight of his mother slipping into one of the chairs in the back row. Her carefully cultivated look of genteel wealth was on display. She wore a fur hat and camel hair coat with a matching fur collar. He could tell she was furious. Her white skin was marred by red splotches on her cheeks and forehead as if small fires burned there. For an instant, he felt the terror that used to overtake him when he was five, and her hand was rising to hit him. Back then, he'd peed his pants.

He shifted uneasily on the chair's hard slats before the urge to urinate subsided.

"Graham? John Gilbert Graham?" The tiny bailiff was calling his name.

It wasn't the first time he'd been in court. The bad checks from the auto parts shop that led to the whole shitstorm in Texas had involved arraignment, plea, and sentencing. Daisie'd retained an expensive lawyer to replace the public defender and negotiated his release from jail.

Leighton stared at Jack over the tops of his rimless spectacles. "You're the one who wanted to contest a citation?"

"That's correct, Your Honor." He stooped a little and clasped his hands behind his back, pretending he was penitent.

The judge's eyes narrowed. "You're wasting the court's time on an infraction?"

Jack ground his back teeth. The nuns at the orphanage used to say he was stubborn as Absalom's mule. Too bad he hadn't paid attention, because right now he was in a jam. The train, which should've smashed the truck into a thousand pieces, had been moving too slowly. When the engineer braked, the train had skidded into the truck, leaving it with only a dented passenger door and a totaled right front fender. Not enough damage, the insurance adjuster claimed, for it to be totaled.

"Mr. Graham," Leighton said, "I've reviewed the officer's report. He finds no evidence of a vehicle malfunction. Your thoughtless actions created the possibility of a derailment and, worse, endangered the lives of the train's crew."

Jack felt the familiar pain behind his eyes. He took a deep breath. "Your Honor, the officer knows squat about my truck. I tried a dozen times to start it, but finally bailed out. I was facing a terrible death. Anybody in my place would have done the same thing."

"This report indicates the vehicle started right up while it was parked in the department's yard," Leighton said, flipping through the pages.

The asshole cop. He'd sneaked that into his report.

"Who knows what's wrong with the truck?" Jack asked. "It's still at the police yard. Nobody, like a mechanic, has ever diagnosed it."

The judge sighed. "You didn't pay the impound fees and get it released?"

"Well, no. I can't afford it."

Leighton tapped the desk with his gavel. "Your petition for dismissal of the infraction—leaving a vehicle on the tracks—is denied. I'm fining you $50."

Fifty bucks. Nearly a week's pay. The unfairness rushed over him; Leighton hadn't really listened to his story. The train's engineer had driven down the tracks like he was on a Sunday drive with grandma. The officer, a supercilious pig, had upset his insurance plan. And his mother'd come to court to rub it in, unable to pass up an opportunity to witness his humiliation.

"I'm innocent, and I'm not paying." It felt good to throw the decision in the judge's face.

"Mr. Graham, you're defying the court?" Rather than stern or astonished, Leighton looked amused.

The judge's subtle ridicule only strengthened his determination. "Call it whatever you like. You're not getting my fifty bucks."

"Listen to me." The judge leaned forward, forearms on the desk. "If you don't pay the fine, you'll be spending three nights in jail."

"I'm not giving you a dime."

Leighton sighed and motioned to the dwarflike bailiff. Handcuffs attached to the bailiff's belt jangled as he moved toward the audience from his post beside the rear door.

"I refuse! Put the cuffs on." Pleased with the drama he was creating, Jack offered his wrists as if he were headed for the gallows or the cross.

"Mr. Graham—" Leighton began.

"I'll pay, Your Honor." Daisie's voice from the last row cut like a diamond drill.

"And you are . . ."

"His mother." She swept to the clerk's table, coat swirling around her legs, and took charge of the paperwork. "Come with me, Jack."

From the corner of his eye, he saw the newspaper reporter scribbling in his notebook.

Jack followed her stiff-backed figure from the courtroom like a naughty boy who'd been sent to the principal's office. His fingernails dug into his palms and his vision blurred. A picture of his life rolled out in front of him. He'd be in his thirties, his forties, and she would still dog his steps, letting him know how unworthy he was, how childish, clumsy, rude, and stupid. When would he be free of her?

True, he'd done things that hadn't turned out well, but they hadn't been his fault. Three years ago, he'd really meant to pay back checks he'd written on the account of the auto store where he worked. The bookkeeper had discovered the shortage too soon, which forced him to go on the run.

The months he'd spent as a fugitive burned vividly in his mind, like a movie filmed in Technicolor compared to his black-and-white life in Denver. He'd driven all over the West—Seattle, Salt Lake, Kansas City, Saint Louis, and Lubbock—speeding across mountains and through deserts. It had been summer. Warm wind blew through open car windows. It didn't matter if the radio blasted at top volume, or he sang off key. He'd felt like a cowboy riding the range on a swift horse.

The unfortunate events that had transpired in Lubbock were the fault of local authorities, who'd created a dry county when people with any sense acknowledged prohibition was over. People were secretly drinking whiskey in Lubbock anyway. If the car hadn't crashed during the police chase, he probably would have been a millionaire bootlegger by now.

Daisie stopped at the cashier's window and fished a roll of bills from her purse. "I just love your hair," she told the clerk. "*Ladies Home Journal* says the beehive is the hairdo of the decade."

The clerk rewarded her with an unexpected smile, taking extra care to assure the receipt was legible.

While Jack waited, the sound of another plane rattled the roof.

"Come along," Daisie snapped. "I don't have all day."

They climbed into the Buick, Daisie at the wheel. As with everything else, she had to be in charge. He thought about the weeks when his mother had been in Florida, while he'd wheeled around town in the Buick. Life had been exciting: drinking booze, meeting with the Smalldones, necking on the mountain with Hannah. The danger and the threat of discovery had made him soar with excitement.

Last night, he and Lucy had sex, but he hadn't been able come, not when he was surrounded by the smell of Lucy's milk, the baby's rustlings in the bassinet, and the dark presence of Daisie sleeping in the guest apartment downstairs.

His mother guided the big car carefully into the street, chin tilted high to see over the steering wheel, and toe pointed like a ballerina to reach the gas pedal. Daisie was small, but she was deadly.

Back when he was a kid at the orphanage, the barnlike dormitory where the boys had slept was crawling with spiders. Jack had found a black widow among them. Sleep eluded him until he'd overcome his terror by carefully brushing each spider to the floor, then seizing a shoe and smashing it flat.

He tapped his sole against the floor of the Buick.

11

Saturday morning, Paulette called just after 11. "Can you meet me at the lake in half an hour?"

"There's no ice," Hannah said. "It's too warm." Colorado's capricious weather had taken a turn. During the last week, sunshine had lifted the temperatures into the forties. Snow was disappearing, even in the shade under the tall spruce in their backyard.

"We'll hike around on the path. It's only two and a half miles."

"Is something wrong?" Hannah asked. Paulette's voice sounded scratchy as a worn-out .45 record.

"I'll tell you when you get here."

Hannah pulled on a coat and a pair of boots. It had been days since she'd talked to Paulette. Kenny had absorbed her free time since last Friday night. After school, they'd sipped Cokes and hot chocolate at out-of-the-way drugstore fountains. They'd explored their bodies' secret places in the back seat of his car, but this weekend he was in Dallas for a hockey club tournament.

Kenny'd suggested attending the Junior Play together Thursday, but her answer had been no. She wanted to keep things secret. Hard-won knowledge told her the river of feeling between the two of them would be tainted once other people knew they were a couple. Kenny's friends would harbor lewd speculations as to why he was seeing the girl with the messed-up face. Rosemarie and Paulette would predict that in days, he'd dump her. And Nancy would be scrutinizing her comings and goings.

As she left the house, she heard the faint sound of Beau talking on the phone in his basement office, using the crisp tone he employed with his boss, Roger Quint. In the kitchen, Nancy, using the polished steel barber's scissors saved from her beauty shop, had spent some time giving the boys their first haircut.

Although Nancy worked quickly, fingers darting and scissors clicking, her experience as a hairdresser was not up to the challenges of the twins. The boys twisted, cried, and grabbed for the scissors. They tugged at the towels Nancy had fastened around their necks to keep the hair off. Fine, soft strands spread in a halo on the floor.

By the time Hannah'd snapped a photo of them, the twins' sticky fingers had twisted their neatly combed locks into messy clumps.

When Hannah arrived at the lake, Paulette's pickup was parked at the same spot as the night of the skating party. She deliberately blocked any thoughts of her meeting with Jack. Cars crowded the lot as families flocked to the walking trail to enjoy the milder weather. Hannah made two circuits looking for a parking spot before one opened up alongside the path.

The lake had taken on a different aspect since her last visit. Pools of water rippled where Kenny and his father'd scraped away snow for the skaters. Rather than a cluster of people on the patch of cleared ice, dozens of walkers dotted the lakeshore. An ambitious man in a canoe paddled through small waves.

Hannah pulled a cap around her ears. She strolled over to Paulette, but her friend didn't say hello. Instead, she turned away to watch the Canada geese skim the gray ponds of melted water.

"Tell me." Hannah touched her arm. Paulette's life was filled with so much drama and disappointment, the situation must be serious for her to be so reticent.

"It's about him." Paulette's lips tightened. "The asshole."

"Oh, God, it's Jack? Bothering you?"

"You could say that. Alonzo will be here in a few minutes. You'll get the picture then."

"Your brother, the policeman? What's he got to do with this?"

"Nothing good."

As they talked, a man approached them, feet crunching in the dead, brittle grass. Alonzo Merrick was tall, like Paulette, but his arms and torso were heavy.

"Good to see you again, Hannah. I hear you're becoming quite the skater." Despite the friendly greeting, his eyes probed like a physician's penlight.

Hannah backed up a few steps. "It's been awhile since I've seen you."

He nodded. "Since Boomer went in the service. How's he doing?"

"He's at Fort Ord," Hannah said impatiently. "Why are you interested in Jack Graham?"

"Let's walk," he said. They set off on the paved path encircling the lake, with Hannah sandwiched in the middle. Her legs pumped to keep up with their long strides.

She hadn't seen or heard from Jack since the dinner at Gaetano's. The unidentified caller, probably Jack, had stopped ringing and hanging up days ago. And he hadn't been in church last Sunday, although his wife and mother-in-law were sitting several rows behind Hannah's family.

"What's he done?" she asked.

"It's not what Graham's done; it's what you've done," Alonzo said.

She felt like a child accused of some unknown infraction. "What in God's name . . . I saw him twice! Nothing happened."

A gray-haired man in rubber duck-hunting shoes waved as he passed them, two Labrador retrievers trotting at his side.

"It's about the night at Gaetano's," Paulette said. "Remember the car across the street with the two men watching the place?"

"Sure. You said they were detectives keeping constant surveillance on the Smalldones, like police do on the mob in New York."

They approached a narrow spot in the trail. Alonzo moved closer. His shoulder bumped hers. "I was part of the surveillance detail, but not on duty that night. Imagine my surprise when I read the report—identifying my sister and her friend as possible associates of Denver's dominant crime family."

"Paulette and me?" Hannah's thoughts whirled in confusion. "You must have a bug in your brain. We went to dinner at a popular restaurant, the same one where the mayor, judges, and lots of other bigwigs go."

"But you were accompanied by a man who tried to blow up his business for the insurance money," Alonzo said.

"There were no charges about the explosion at the Comet!" Her pulse beat against her temples. "Jack said it was an accident."

Ahead of them, the dog owner murmured a few words, and the animals took off at a run. They plunged into the lake and scattered a group of geese into the air, which rose with a great noise and flapping of wings.

"You didn't know John Gilbert Graham had a sizeable criminal record?" Alonzo shot her a look of pseudo surprise. "He's been a forger, a bootlegger, and a fugitive from justice."

"Why would I?" Hannah tried to disguise her feeling of guilt. "He's a member of our church. His mother's a wealthy businesswoman. And even if he *has* done things, maybe he's changed."

"Haven't you read the paper? Jack's in trouble again," Paulette said.

"I've been busy." Having sex in the back seat of a boy's car. Good thing no one knew about that.

Paulette's mouth twisted. "I noticed you've been distracted." She detailed the account of the train crash and court hearing that had appeared in the *Rocky*. "It happened a few days after our dinner."

Hannah felt like a fool alongside Paulette and Alonzo, as though she amounted to nothing compared to these tough, savvy people. "Listen, I'm sorry I asked you to come that night, but I wanted a friend to back me up." She reached for Paulette's gloved hand.

Her friend snatched it back "And now, because they suspect you and *me*, Alonzo's been eighty-sixed from the organized crime detail."

Paulette's eyes filled with tears. "His boss stuck him in the property room."

Hannah's feet dragged as they crossed a pedestrian bridge. Kids, parents, dogs, and old people seemed delighted with the winter sun without giving a thought to the dead weeds and frozen fish beneath the soles of their boots.

Her thoughts picked at a knot of possibilities. "Is because of Young Eugene? He's the biggest drug dealer in the state and stopped at our table that night. But just because he said hello doesn't mean anything. His father is part owner of Gaetano's. Young Eugene says hello to a lot of people."

"We, ah, have an informant." Alonzo touched a scab on his lip. "An employee who's given us information on the inner workings of the family. That person indicated Graham and Smalldone were close associates."

Her breakfast eggs roiled in her stomach. "You think Young Eugene and Jack are plotting something."

"Graham's long Texas rap sheet, plus his two cockeyed insurance schemes, indicate that he needs money," Alonzo said. "His mother's not going to give it to him in light of his wrecking the truck and the Comet. It's reasonable to conclude he's aiming to organize a major criminal enterprise."

"That's ridiculous. Jack could no more organize a criminal enterprise than play solo violin at the philharmonic. He's a dope."

Paulette, who'd been biting her nails, tucked her hands in her armpits. "Come on, Hannah. You know he's a rotten enough to do some major crime."

"No, no. You've been watching too many episodes of *Dragnet*."

"You're smart and clever." The tone of Paulette's voice didn't sound like praise. "Whatever his scheme is, you've got to pry it out of him."

"Why are you even suggesting this? I thought you were different, that you really liked me, and we were friends."

A wave of panic rushed over her, as it had when her mother died. Beau and her brothers had been remote, wrapped in their own grief. Paulette, another lonely kid, had been the only one Hannah could talk to.

"It's like you're throwing me into the fire." Words scratched her throat. "What do I know about criminals? I'm seventeen. A senior in high school."

Any remnants of girlish beauty drained from Paulette's face, and she appeared for a few seconds as she might look at fifty. "I knew Jack was bad, but you wouldn't listen," she said. "I went to the restaurant because I was worried, and because you asked. Now Alonzo's chance at making sergeant is gone. You owe me, Hannah. You owe both of us."

"All right. I'll do it." Through a rush of tears, Hannah saw one of the retrievers emerge from the lake, black coat dripping. It held a dead goose between its jaws.

12

Daisie was making plans to fly to Alaska for a month-long visit with Gretchen. Jack's older half-sister was going through a nasty divorce and needed help managing her three bratty kids. Only someone as contrary as his mother, he thought, would choose a place colder than Colorado to spend the holidays. Not to mention, Daisie owned a house in Florida where she could drink fresh orange juice whenever she wanted. And lie in a hammock with warm breezes blowing.

His mother and Gretchen were bonded like a shark and a remora, the tiny sea creature that attached itself to the shark, feeding off scraps of prey and parasites. Jack rather liked the metaphor. Gretchen never missed an opportunity to cement her relationship with Daisie at his expense.

This morning at breakfast, his mother began penciling a list of what to pack for the trip, although her flight out of Stapleton wasn't for another week.

"I want to buy a set of X-Acto knives," she said, tapping the tabletop with the eraser.

Jack waited for Lucy or Daisie to pour him a cup of coffee, but they were ignoring him. Lucy, who'd recently stopped nursing Albert, was trying to feed the baby a bite of pablum, but he pushed the spoon away with a sticky fist.

Daisie cut her toast into four triangular pieces. "I'm going to spend the winter doing wood sculptures." Her eyes glowed with enthusiasm. "Wolves, grizzlies, vultures—those sell well in Alaska."

"You don't need money," Jack said, "and you'll probably cut yourself." He couldn't imagine Daisie spending ten minutes carving wood, but he'd already said way too much. One thing his mother hated was opposition.

"I'll need a set of artist's tools. Jack, find them for me today or tomorrow," she said. "What else do I need?"

Since the court hearing last week, she'd been in one of her periods of dynamic energy. Typically when she was like this, she started businesses, bought houses, or indulged in new hobbies.

Dread consumed him during her upward cycles, because he knew in a matter of weeks it would dissipate. Then she'd launch ferocious verbal and sometimes physical attacks against the men in her life, including him.

Jack didn't respond to her request—a command, really—about the art supplies. It was after 8. He walked to the bus stop and rode to the Hertz outlet, transferring once. The pain behind his eyes built as he thought about his mother's imperious command.

Barry, the manager, looked meaningfully at his wristwatch when Jack arrived thirty minutes late, but customers were lined up at the counter, and Barry didn't comment. Eldon, who was in the repair bay changing the oil of a Ford Fairlane, signaled Jack by tapping the pocket of his coveralls. After Barry left in the early afternoon, the two of them had fallen into the habit of drinking a bit from their flasks.

Business was steady all morning. He hated working at Hertz, especially with Barry as his boss. The *Rocky's* story about the pickup truck fiasco had nearly cost him his job, and Barry didn't let him forget it.

At 1 o'clock, Barry packed his briefcase. "We're open until 9, so no trickery. I'll be calling in to check."

Jack faked a subservient smile.

＊＊＊

"Seen the new copy of *Wink*?" Eldon sidled into the office from the repair bay a couple of hours later, flask in hand and the magazine under his arm. He sank into Barry's chair and flipped through the pages. "This one here's mighty tasty."

Jack wrinkled his nose. The mechanic smelled of motor grease and unwashed underwear. The illustration of the woman in a purple bikini untying her swimsuit top wasn't bad, but he didn't want to give Eldon the impression they were pals.

"A little tame for my taste," he said.

Customers were scarce during the afternoon. While Jack waited for the evening flights from the East to arrive at Stapleton, he sipped cautiously from his own flask. He wanted just enough liquor in his blood to calm his nerves for the night ahead.

When Eldon's shift ended at 9 p.m. and he left, Jack locked the cash drawer. From the rental car key board, he filched one for the Fairlane. It would be back in its slot before opening tomorrow. He was almost out the door when one last call rang on the office phone.

"Jack? It's Hannah." She sounded timid and a little out of breath.

"Well, this is a surprise." He tried but failed to erase the sarcasm from his tone.

"I'm sorry I kept hanging up on you."

"How many times was it, ten? Fifteen? It took me awhile, but I got the message." Giving her a bad time felt good.

"I . . . my boyfriend and I, were breaking up, that is, I was breaking up with him and didn't want to take his calls." Her words seemed to tumble out.

"That's too bad. Bad for you, but good for me, I guess." This shyer, more timid Hannah was stirring some interest below his waist.

"I was thinking we could get together tonight," she said.

Remembering Lookout Mountain and the warm, firm flesh under her skating skirt, he considered whether to deep-six his plan for tonight. How often did a gratuitous offer of pussy come his way? He felt for a second or two as if he were driving and about to run off the road. He took a deep breath and righted himself.

"Thanks, but I've got a business meeting."

"How about tomorrow?" she asked.

"I'll call you sometime." *Take that, girlie.*

***

The Fairlane turned out to be a sweet car—smooth ride and easy handling. He tested the acceleration as drove to North Denver, watching for cops in the rearview mirror. Once he left Federal Boulevard, his cruise took him on the side streets past the most popular Italian bars and restaurants, but he didn't see what he was looking for.

At 9:30, he made one last pass in front of Gaetano's. The unmarked police surveillance car was missing tonight from its usual spot across the street. He turned the corner, and spotted his quarry: the Smalldones' Cadillac, parked beneath a No Parking sign.

Clyde and Checkers were in a Leavenworth Federal Prison on tax evasion and jury tampering charges. Young Eugene probably couldn't wait to get his paws on the Caddy, symbol of his claim on the gambling and prostitution rackets.

Jack cruised another couple of blocks, left the car, and walked back to the restaurant. Inside, the air swirled with cigarette smoke and noise. Why was it Italians talked so loud?

His first time at Gaetano's, he'd worn a snap-brim hat like the ones in news photos of Mafia capos. It seemed laughable to him now, how naïve he'd been. Tonight his hair was slicked back with Brilliantine and looked just fine.

He slid onto a stool at the mahogany bar. Although his preference was for Black Label, he ordered a grappa. The bartender, a barrel-chested guy with acne scars, stared at him as liquor trickled into the shot glass. Probably wondering if he were a cop. With one elbow propped on the bar, Jack sipped his drink and surveyed the crowd. Sure enough, Smalldone was here, ensconced in a corner booth with four other men.

Jack was unsure how to proceed. He needed to talk to Eugene alone, but it would be useless and maybe dangerous to interrupt his conversation. Through the doorway to the dining room, he saw the hostess, Sophia, seating a party at one of the tables.

He rose and went to the men's room, then stopped at her podium on the way back. "I'd like to have a private conversation with Eugene when he's free," he said, leaning close enough he could smell the spray on her teased hair.

Her fingers closed around the twenty he slipped into her hand.

A few minutes later, the back-bar mirror reflected Sophia approaching Eugene in the booth. She spoke to him briefly. He nodded.

Jack had consumed another glass of grappa and a cup of espresso before the meeting broke up. Smalldone raised a finger as if he were Vito Genovese and signaled him over.

"Eugene, good to see you." Jack slid into the booth across from him, but realized his error when Smalldone frowned. He should've waited until the other man motioned him to sit.

"I hear you been in trouble," Smalldone said.

"It was nothing. Fucking cops messed up the insurance claim on my truck. I've got a good lawyer on it."

"You don't have your two girls with you tonight." Eugene rubbed a thumb across his lower lip. "Too bad."

"What I have is a business proposal for you. I think you'll be interested, now that you're the head of the family." The last part was completely untrue, but Jack needed to pour it on.

"I'm on track to open a car dealership here in Denver next year," Jack said, "and I'm in the market for a silent partner to come in on it. It'll be a top-quality operation with one of the premier automotive brands." He took a breath. The practice he'd done for the pitch was paying off.

Smalldone rolled his bloodshot eyes. "Oh, yeah? Where's a small-time guy like you getting the money to buy into something like that?"

"A big insurance payout," he said in a low voice. "Enough to pay the surety bond, lease a location, and acquire new equipment from the manufacturer."

"Sounds like a cockamamie idea to me. What's the plan?"

"I'm not saying anything yet because this is big. Very big. If it gets out too soon, the operation will be ruined. What I can tell you is that in return for your assistance, I can guarantee you a sizeable interest in the dealership."

"Yeah? How much?"

His heartbeat quickened. Smalldone was going for it. "Twenty percent."

"Forty."

"Thirty-three. That's my bottom line," Jack said.

"Done. What do you need?"

This was the moment. He could see himself shaking hands with the richest men in town as they concluded their purchase of a sleek new car at his glass and chrome showroom. "Dynamite. Twenty sticks. And the blasting caps."

"You fucking crazy bastard. I do a low-profile business where nobody gets hurt." Smalldone ground out his cigarette on a dinner plate.

"You're saying nobody gets hurt with your loan sharking or drug dealing?" Pressure was building behind Jack's eyes.

"I provide a service the big shots are too high and mighty to take on."

Jack's voice rose, and patrons at the bar turned to look at them. "How about the hits on the Pueblo mob? That wasn't you?" He struggled to keep from leaning across the table and smashing a fist into Smalldone's face.

"Get out of here," Smalldone screamed, "before I blow your fucking brains out!"

Bar patrons scattered. Jack stalked out, knowing the disgusting little worm wouldn't shoot him. A man who squeezed his victims into bankruptcy and forced women into prostitution didn't have the balls. Jack had bigger plans than Mr. Smalldone could possibly dream up.

13

Hannah felt lonely all week. How could that be, when people seemed to press around her constantly? She barely enjoyed a free moment at home. Nancy filled her mornings and evenings with meals and crises. The twins, although they were occasionally adorable, distracted her constantly with fretful demands and dirty diapers.

At school, students jammed the halls, the cafeteria rocked with noise, and restrooms had lines for the toilets. Yet she had no one to talk to. The popular girls still shunned her since the confrontation with Odessa. Paulette and Rosemarie passed her in the halls or on the stairs with barely a nod. They never telephoned. And Kenny, while he waited for her every afternoon after school, was busy with evening hockey practice at the DU rink.

Not only that, Alonzo's plan infected all her thoughts. Days passed without a return call from Jack after her failed attempt to set up a meeting.

Thursday, Kenny dropped a note in her book bag to meet at Berry's after school: *Banana splits, my treat.*

He was already at a table by the window when she arrived, his hair freshly trimmed, wearing a crewneck sweater. When he saw her, his eyes lit up.

"Hey, Hannah Montana." Warm fingers reached out to entwine with hers.

He was nice, someone she wanted want to spend hours with, talking about people, plans, dreams. More than nice. She wanted to touch, kiss, stroke, and feel him inside her. She slid into the booth next to him, close enough their legs touched. Conversation was easy at first; she was content to listen for a little while. He was in the midst of the hockey club season, and his team, the Rockets, were three and three. This weekend he would be in Laramie, but the following two games were scheduled at home.

"I can't wait," he said, tracing her lifeline with a forefinger.

A feeling of dread stole over her. What if she finally connected with Jack, and he touched her or wanted sex? Would she have to let him?

The waitress arrived with the banana splits, long glass dishes mounded with ice cream and dripping with chocolate syrup. Although Kenny attacked his with gusto, Hannah wasn't hungry. She toyed with her spoon.

"Are you mad at me?" A dot of chocolate rested in the corner of his mouth.

"It's—well, it's complicated." The situation with Jack felt like a noose around her neck.

His cheeks reddened "You're seeing another guy."

The look of hurt on his face made her want to cry. "No, no, not that! I really like you, but . . ."

"Then tell me. I'm a pretty good listener."

Her lips opened. What a relief it would be, to release the secret, which was growing like a tumor in her chest. She opened her mouth but the words wouldn't come.

"Hannah," he leaned closer, whispering, "we've done—well, you know, and we were careful. How bad could it be?"

What could she say? That she was a liar, a slut, a criminal, and a shitty friend?

"I can't see you for awhile. I'm sorry." She slid from the booth. She didn't see him pay the bill and leave Berry's, but in the VW, tears blurring her vision, she heard his car roar out of the lot. The air reeked of hot rubber on asphalt.

Saturday night, she slept poorly. The sheets tangled around her legs, and she twisted wakefully, first to one side, then the other. An hour before dawn, she climbed out of bed and slipped a coat over her pajamas and fleece-lined boots onto her bare feet.

Outside on the patio, cold air needled her face. Naked tree branches reached toward an emaciated sliver of moon. From a nearby house, the retired neighbor called his German shepherd with a shrill, demanding whistle. The backyard was bare compared to summer, when a dense canopy of leaves clustered on branches of the huge elm. Canes of the hybrid tea and floribunda roses her mother had planted were trimmed to finger-length stubs to protect them from freezing. The cushioned chairs, chaise, and picnic table had been hauled to storeroom a month ago, leaving Hannah with no place to sit.

She stood at the edge of the flagstone and lit a cigarette from a secret pack tucked in her coat pocket. The sky brightened to gray. In the cold, the cigarette's taste was particularly strong and vivid. Smoke rose from its tip like the remnant of a disturbing dream.

As she smoked, yellow light seeped around the venetian blinds on Beau and Nancy's bedroom windows. No chance to go back to bed, even though it was Sunday. Boomer, last time he'd been home from Fort Ord on leave, said getting this reconstituted family ready for church was like prepping a regiment for a big maneuver. Breakfast had to be prepared. Dishes had to be stacked, twins dressed, then contained in a playpen or bouncing chair so that they wouldn't get dirty while adults showered and donned their Sunday clothes.

The house began to stir. She heard the twins talking to each other in slow, sleepy voices. Dishes clattered in the kitchen. Still, Hannah couldn't force herself to go inside to begin another tense, lonely day. Cold crept up her pajama legs, numbing her calves. Finally, she sucked a last drag from her cigarette, stubbed it out. Her coat smelled of cigarettes, so she flapped the lapels to air it out.

"There you are, at last." The family had assembled in the kitchen. Nancy, hair flattened and the roots showing, was fastening the twins in their high chairs while Beau spread the weighty Sunday papers on the tabletop.

"Hannah, make hot cereal for the boys. Beau, leave those papers alone and start the coffee. I'll do toast."

Her father carried the *Rocky*, to the counter, where he continued to read while he spooned coffee into the percolator's basket. "Ike's still at Fitzsimons. His cardiologist says it'll be there another three weeks before he's released."

"He's sixty-five, too old to be president," Nancy said. "He should resign."

Beau smoothed back his graying hair. "Sixty-five's not so old."

"Old enough he takes a two-month vacation every year. I'd be glad to get a week," Nancy threw Beau a narrow-eyed look.

"Come on, Nan. Roger says before his heart attack, Ike worked as much as eight hours a day, even on vacation. He hardly had any free time to catch brook trout. The press calls the Brown Palace Hotel the Western White House because Ike works there eight hours a day."

"For God's sake, I read newspapers, too. Stop talking down to me. I hate that."

"I apologize." He leaned over and gave her a kiss on the neck, then plugged in the coffeemaker. "I heard from Roger that Dulles made a flying visit to Denver last week to talk to the Chief."

"I feel sorry for Mamie," Hannah said. "She came so close to losing him."

Her father flinched, as if he were reliving the pain of losing a spouse.

"Hannah, get the boys fed!" Nancy slammed a plate of toast and jar of marmalade on the table.

Here it was again, Hannah thought, Nancy, trying to erase the existence of the other family—Hannah, her parents, Boomer and Clyde. They'd lived in this house and had a history, one Nancy couldn't get rid of.

The tension was too much for Hannah. "Do it yourself." She left the oatmeal cereal cooking on the stove and locked herself in the bathroom. Would she and her father ever get over it? She was tired of sorrow, impatient to be rid of—not her mother's memory, but the constant low-level ache that flared into active pain sometimes, like this morning. Maybe loss was impossible to outlive. The idea made her angry. She had her birthmark. That was enough, the loss of any chance at beauty.

She climbed into the shower. Taking her time, she scrubbed her skin and shampooed her hair to remove any lingering smoke. By the time she emerged, the water had turned cold, and the rest of the family had left. She put on her best suit—gray wool with a belted jacket—and a small hat over her damp hair.

The choir was already processing down the aisle when she slipped into the pew beside her father. Mouthing the words of the hymn, she threw a glance over her shoulder. Was Jack here? The burden of her promise to Paulette and Paulette's policeman brother was dragging her life to a halt.

She scarcely listened to readings from the Old Testament and Psalms, delivered in a desultory monotone by the assistant minister, who'd recently been added to the church staff. Reverend Kellems took over for the New Testament reading, his booming voice filling the sanctuary to the peaked roof. The excerpt from Matthew exhorted the faithful to pluck out one's eye or cut off one's hand if it offended you.

Hannah snatched another look at the rows behind her. In the Grahams' pew, Jack's wife and mother sat side by side. Lucy's brown hair hung limply, and her skin looked yellowish under heavy pancake makeup. His mother held herself straight backed with her head held high, a fur-collared coat poised around her shoulders. Jack was nowhere to be seen.

After the benediction, Beau and Nancy paused in the center aisle to chat with friends. Hannah spotted her Latin teacher, Mrs. Adams, who fluttered her fingers in greeting.

As Hannah threaded her way through the crowd, she glanced up. Jack's wife stood a few feet away, looking directly at her.

Hannah's cheek burned. Did Lucy Graham know about her and Jack? Hannah couldn't remember if Lucy had seen them in the church nursery arranging the dinner date. Hannah dawdled, letting Jack's wife and mother move ahead. The crowd slowly filed past the stained glass windows depicting the Annunciation, Christ's Sermon on the Mount, and Judas' betrayal of Jesus.

Why did Jack want the dynamite? It was possible he had no criminal plan in mind. His mother had inherited a large ranch in the mountains near Kremmling after her third husband's death. Jack could be working to build a dam or mine on the property, Hannah rationalized. But somehow it didn't seem likely. Would Jack's mother trust him to undertake such a big project? After all, the evidence pointed to him as the one who'd opened the gas valve at the Comet.

Could he be planning to bomb the Smalldones' houses, or their front businesses, used to hide gambling and prostitution rackets?

Neither possibility seemed to fit him. Jack was smart, in a strange way; he bragged that he could hot-wire a car or repair an electrical problem, but he was impulsive, not a planner. What he couldn't seem to do was work out a long-term scheme and have it succeed.

At the church door, Reverend Kellems took her hand in his hamlike, sweaty one. "Hannah, how are you? I ran into Beau at a Rotary Club party awhile back. He said that you're in high school now."

He'd presided at Chantal's funeral, and always exhibited a fatherly interest in Hannah. "Come in and see me sometime."

"Yeah, sure." Hannah frowned, detecting Beau's manipulation at work again. He'd probably convinced Kellems to counsel her against going away to college.

As she emerged onto the steps from the tall double doors, Hannah encountered Lucy again, who scrutinized Hannah with narrowed eyes. People often stared at her birthmark. Whether in fascination or disgust, Hannah wasn't sure.

"Hello," Lucy said. "You're the girl with the darling twin brothers."

"They're darling little devils for certain." Looking more closely, she saw that one of Lucy's eyes was puffy and discolored under the heavy makeup.

Someone had hit her. A tight spiral of fear rose in Hannah's chest. It was Jack, of course.

She imagined Lucy years ago when she was the polished, confident girl Boomer'd known in high school. Why had she sacrificed a promising future to marry a loser like Jack? Perhaps she'd ignored his instability and simmering anger because she was impressed by Daisie's wealth and family connections. Indeed, Jack had bragged to Hannah his grandfather was a former county district attorney, judge, and member of the Colorado Legislature.

Daisie King also owned a large ranch in northwestern Colorado, near where Ike vacationed at a friend's vacation home where he fly-fished for trout. Ike hadn't gone fishing this year. The heart attack had hit while he played golf at Cherry Hills.

The murmur of conversations around Hannah faded, and her vision blurred for an instant. The president would be here for at least another three weeks before he boarded the presidential plane for Washington.

No, it was too farfetched. Why would Jack kill the president? But still, who knew? She remembered the newspaper photos from when she was twelve. Two guys had tried to shoot President Truman.

The twist of fear tightened until Hannah could hardly breathe. Jack's underlying violent nature, that she'd sensed early on, was getting stronger. Something bad was coming. Who would know what he planned? Not his mother, whom he obviously hated, nor Young Eugene.

Hannah summoned every ounce of her determination to smile at Lucy, who was looking at her oddly. "I saw your two children in the church nursery a couple weeks ago. They're very smart."

"I guess so. They tire me out sometimes."

"Why don't I babysit for you? I've had lots of experience, taking care of my brothers."

Lucy's good eye widened. "How about tomorrow night? My husband is out of town. It would give his mother and me a chance to go out for dinner."

Hannah's birthmark burned. What if things went wrong? Jack might become suspicious if he knew Hannah was burrowing her way into his family. She thought about Ike, about Truman. She looked at Lucy's swollen face. She had to do this.

"Okay. What time?" she asked. "And you don't need to pick me up. I've got a car."

14

Taking off for Kremmling on Sunday, Jack felt like he'd just been released from prison. It'd been a shitty few days. Daisie'd been in one of her moods. He had to practically kiss her feet in order to extract the money for this car, a beat-up sedan.

"Without a car, it takes me hours to get to work. I walk home from the bus stop in the dark," he'd told her.

"You're getting what you deserve, after the mess with the pickup." She had been working at her desk and did not look up from a stack of legal correspondence.

He used his usual tactic to pry money out of her—his wife and kids. "Lucy has no transportation to the store for groceries. And last week, Serena had a fever. Lucy had to call a cab for the trip to the doctor."

"She should have asked me. I'd have driven her."

"You were in Colorado Springs." The knot that invariably settled in his gut when he dealt with his mother seemed to harden. "Do you want your grandkids to go hungry? Suffer when they're sick? Give me two thousand. I'll pay you back."

"That would be utter foolishness. If I buy you a car, you'll wreck it—I know you." She glared up at him and took a drag from her cigarette, red lipstick leaving an imprint.

That had been Thursday. The next day, Lucy'd run out of Tide and had to wash diapers with hot water but no laundry soap. After he returned from work, the two of them had a fierce argument. Instead of blaming his mother, who'd refused to buy out his interest in the Comet, Lucy castigated *him* for the mess involving the pickup truck.

The fight had spiraled out of control, Lucy screaming at him until the pain in his forehead was unbearable. To shut her up, he'd clobbered her. The minute his hand touched her cheekbone, he'd been sorry. Getting hit wasn't new to him; Daisie'd clobbered him plenty during her violent swings.

Jack had given Lucy an awkward apology, but it hadn't mended things. She refused to look at him, turning her head when she had to ask him something. To be honest, it was Lucy who'd convinced Daisie to give him the cash—a measly thousand. After beating down the sales price at a dreary little used car lot, he'd ended up spending just five hundred for the sedan. That gave him a tidy little cushion. To make it up to Lucy, he'd driven her to King Soopers for groceries.

This morning, he was on the road.

The co-joined 6 and 40 highways out of Denver were fairly busy with skiers heading to the slopes. Jack tested the car's engine by speeding a bit when the road appeared clear of the highway cops. The car wasn't bad—a V-8 that moved well, despite one or two ominous clunks. As he drove, he hummed, flipped the radio dial to various stations, and settled on one that played Hank Thompson and Tennessee Ernie Ford.

Tapping his fingers on the wheel, he fantasized about the car dealership. Oldsmobile was holding a conference in Denver next week, showcasing its new Starfire convertible. Maybe an Olds dealership was the way to go. He could be at the conference next year, wearing a tailored suit and mingling with the Olds execs.

A small snowstorm was passing over the foothills, leaving the pavement wet. At Genesee Mountain Park, Denver's buffalo herd clustered near the fence along the highway. Snow encrusted the animals' dark, shaggy coats. When he'd been a kid, he thought they looked like prehistoric monsters ready to gore him with their impressive horns.

The road climbed up Clear Creek Canyon, past Idaho Springs, where he and a girlfriend had once soaked naked in the underground hot pools. A few miles farther, the grade steepened. The highway split, 6 veering to the south and 40 to the northwest.

His upbeat mood wavered. The sedan's gears clashed as he struggled to shift into low for the steep incline. In less than a mile, the snow-packed pavement forced him to a turnout to chain up. It took a frustrating twenty minutes to put on the cheap tire chains with missing links he found in the cargo area. When he finished, his pants and shoes were soaked. His hands, white with cold, trembled as he started the engine.

The road climbed the steep grade to Berthoud Pass in stomach-churning switchbacks. Avalanche tracks scarred the white slopes. Plows had shoved snow to the hillside shoulder, leaving two narrow lanes. He slogged uphill along the precipitous drop with only a foot to spare.

At the top of the pass, he pulled into the ski area's parking lot. He remembered this place, still marked with a wooden sign that informed travelers they were crossing the United States Continental Divide at an elevation of 11,307 feet.

He'd been nine the summer he first stopped here. Daisie, who'd just married her third husband, Earl King, arrived at the orphanage to pick him up. They were headed for Earl's ranch. She'd been at the wheel of a shiny new Packard. Excitement had raced through him, now that he was with his mother again. He couldn't sit still, squirming constantly in the seat until Daisie'd pinched his leg.

Today in his old car, warm air from the heater blew on his sodden shoes. The engine rumbled.

That long-ago trip had been six months before Pearl Harbor. Daisie was in one of her expansive moods, telling him about the barns, horses, tractor, and beautiful fishing stream at Earl's ranch.

"Let's stop for something to eat." Daisie had bounced out of the car and clasped his hand, tugging him along. The lodge was mostly closed during the summer season, the dining room dark and the ski rental area boarded up, but the gift shop was open. A few tourists speaking a foreign language browsed the postcards and Navajo jewelry.

Daisie bought him two Baby Ruth bars. The orphanage hadn't allowed the boys to have candy or any other sweets, and even now, he recalled tearing open the wrappers and immediately eating them both. The taste of peanuts, chocolate, and butterscotch had been a promise that his life was changing for the better.

Reliving that day, tears dripped down a cheek onto his shirt. He'd forgotten a handkerchief, so he wiped his eyes and nose on a coat sleeve.

***

Small drifts of snow clung to the banks of the Fraser River as Jack pulled into Kremmling. It was a small place, a few hundred people, maybe, and hadn't changed much. Highway 40 ran through the center of town, where businesses lined up like kids in the lunch line.

There it was, Brinker's Mercantile, a two-story brick building whose façade dominated the block. It sold everything.

Brinker's looked about the same as it had when Jack lived at the ranch and attended high school there for a few months when he was sixteen. The high school had kicked him out, and Daisie wrote a letter lying about his age to get him into the Coast Guard. He slowed the car, preparing to park, but his courage drained from him like piss. After letting the car idle for a moment, he drove on. Why was he getting cowardly now, just as he was putting his plan into gear?

Jack drove west on 40 for another ten miles or so. A blanket of unbroken snow covered the grasslands and pastures that had been lush and brilliant green that summer he was nine. Hope had filled his heart then, before everything had gone bad. He couldn't let his dreams be killed again. The car's tires skidded on the slick road as he made a U-turn.

Back in Kremmling, the street had plenty of empty parking spaces. He sat hunched behind the wheel, biting his nails until the tips of his fingers bled. The car dealership was almost in his grasp, if only he could pull himself together. Denver's elite would come to him for their cars, and he'd shake their hands. Call DA Bert Keating and Mayor Quigg Newton by their first names. Play golf at Cherry Hills.

The winter sun hung low when he crossed the street, dodging clods of muddy snow left by the burly trucks coasting through town. In Brinker's, a stroll down the aisles confirmed his recollections. Even though it was a small-town place, the store was crammed with electrical fixtures, well pumps, toilets, paint, sacks of feed, shovels, lumber, appliances, fence posts, a tractor, and bins filled with bolts, screws and nails.

Two people manned the long wooden counter—an overweight kid and a gray-haired guy who looked like Jack's memory of old man Brinker working on a stack of invoices. Jack had met Brinker a couple times when he was a skinny, pimply-faced sixteen-year-old. The owner probably wouldn't remember Jack, but it wouldn't hurt to be cautious, considering that he'd once purchased dynamite at this store for a construction project at Earl's ranch.

He stuffed his trembling hands in his pockets and moved to the end of the counter where the boy was reading a magazine. He wouldn't know Jack from Adam. Jack tapped his foot for awhile before the youth glanced up. "Help you?"

"Yeah, I'm doing some work at my place over near Granby. Need dynamite to blast out some rocks."

"What brand you thinkin'?" the kid asked.

"You got DuPont?" Jack liked the DuPont product. He'd used it on King's ranch and again on a construction project when he spent a few months with his half-sister in Alaska.

The older man put down the invoices. "I'll take this one, Kyle. You need dynamite?" he asked Jack. "How much?"

Jack paused as if he were considering, but he'd already worked out the exact weight, down to the ounce.

"I think, twenty, maybe twenty-five."

"Big project?" The old man studied him, tongue searching his teeth for a bit of food.

"Relocating a road. Damn rocks took the pan off my truck."

"Good luck on construction, this time of year." Brinker—if it were Brinker—scratched his palm with a long fingernail.

"Supposed to be some good weather next week. That should help," Jack said. "You got electronic caps? I need a couple."

"I can do that."

Brinker was gone for what seemed like hours. Jack fingered car keys, zipped and unzipped his military-style jacket. A couple of other customers stared at him. The axes, pointed metal fence posts, scythes, all seemed to predict injury and failure.

"Okay, here you are. You need an invoice?" The old guy hefted a wooden box to the counter He didn't look at Jack, instead staring intently at the perfectly normal scene of cars passing on the street.

"No need," Jack said. He paid, slipping a hundred into the pile of fives and tens.

15

Hannah sat huddled on the bedroom rug with the phone pressed to her ear.

"I'd like to speak to Alonzo Merrick."

The officer who answered at the police property room sounded irritated. "Officer Merrick is out ill."

"Do you know when he'll be back?" In the hours since they'd arrived home from church, her decision to babysit the Graham children seemed increasingly foolish. What did Alonzo expect her to do? Seduce Jack? Search the Grahams' home with a magnifying glass?

"Nobody's told me," the officer said. "I got called in to work his shift this morning. On my day off. Sunday, when I could've slept late."

She left a message, hung up, and called Paulette. When her friend answered, a wave of longing flooded her. The confrontation between her and Paulette at the lake had left her with an aching loss. "It's me. What's the matter with Alonzo?"

"His wife took him to the hospital last night." Paulette's voice was low and gravelly as if she hadn't slept. "He was throwing up and bending over with stomach pain. Doctors said it was a burst appendix."

"For God's sake!" Hannah's fingers twisted the phone cord. She had no sympathy for Alonzo. He'd pressured her into this situation, and now was unavailable, leaving her to fend for herself.

"I visited him first thing this morning at St. Anthony's. He was shaking like an aspen leaf. His skin was so pale he looked like the walking dead. Except he wasn't walking." In the background, Paulette's mother, Delilah, wept loudly.

"How long will it take for him to get better?"

"It could be life-threatening, but they're treating him with penicillin. Two weeks, maybe more, the doctor said."

"That'll be too late." Fear twisted her gut. She needed Alonzo in a dark sedan across the street from the Grahams' house.

"Too late? What are you talking about?" Paulette said sharply "The doctor said he should come out of it just fine."

"What I meant—what I should've said—was I need to see him sooner."

"He might be home in a week," Paulette said, "if the medicine works and he doesn't get an abscess or infection."

Her friend lapsed into silence. In the quiet, Hannah noticed the unnatural calm in the Brightman house this afternoon. After midday Sunday dinner, her father and Nancy had bundled the twins in snowsuits, then loaded them in their identical strollers for a walk around the lake at Crown Hill Cemetery.

Paulette's ragged breath fluttered in her ear. She remembered something Paulette had confided when they were in grade school— that Alonzo made scrambled eggs for her dinner every night when she was young because her mother was too drunk to cook.

The present distance between Hannah and her friend filled her with pain. She'd felt so close to Paulette after her own mother died. Hannah, her father, the older boys—each of them had eaten dinner on their own, but at least she had three people as backup. Her friend had only Alonzo, who moved out when he'd gotten married a few years ago.

"I'm sorry, Paulette. I'm sorry he's sick. He'll be better soon."

"It's just I'm so fucking scared." After a silence, she said, "Is something happening with Jack Graham? Is that why you're trying to reach Alonzo?"

"I haven't heard from Jack, but I'm babysitting for his wife tonight."

"At his house? Is it safe?" Paulette seemed to emerge from her preoccupation with Alonzo.

"He's out of town." Hannah struggled to sound calm.

"You want me to come with you?"

"No thanks. I brought you last time, and it didn't work out so hot."

"Okay. Be careful."

***

"Hannah, can you drive Beau to the airport this afternoon? I'm too busy." Once Nancy and Beau returned from their walk, Nancy had dived into repainting their bedroom. She'd spread drop cloths over the bed and dresser. The smell of the pale green paint crept through the house like fog.

"Don't you remember? I'm babysitting at 5 o'clock."

Nancy wiped a sticky palm on one of Beau's castoff shirts she wore as a coverup. "His flight's at 4:15. You can drop him off on your way."

It was miles out of Hannah's way, but when Nancy had a plan, she wouldn't be denied.

Just after 4, her father stowed his suitcase in the VW's trunk, then folded his long legs into the passenger seat. He regarded her apprehensively. "This is a first, you driving *me* someplace."

Backing out of the driveway, she intentionally steered the passenger side a hairsbreadth from the elm tree. His fingers clutched the door handle. "I'm glad I went to church this morning and confessed my sins."

"No worries." She adopted a playful tone to cover her queasiness. "This little car can squeeze through places where the big brutes dare not go."

It was fun, needling her father a bit. Years ago, he'd waved aside her brothers' minor and not so minor driving offenses, but with her, he handed out a stream of unsolicited advice and frequently circled the VW looking for dents and scratches.

She drove across town on Colfax, switching on the headlamps as the sky turned deep blue with the oncoming night. The sidewalk in front of Stapleton Airfield's passenger terminal was crowded with striking flight engineers, who paced the sidewalk with signs demanding a wage increase.

Her father kissed her cheek. "See you Saturday. And please be nice to Nancy."

"Always," Hannah said, thinking, *in your dreams*.

Her watch read a couple of minutes to 5 when she arrived at the Grahams', parking the VW on the street so as not to block Mrs. King's Buick in the driveway. In the dusk, the house had a gray, dispirited look, as if the stucco walls, as well as the residents, were sad or lonely.

From what Jack'd said about his mother's wealth, Hannah assumed he lived in a spacious brick place with a curving driveway and sculptured landscaping. Instead, the home was a boxy one-story. Lights from the ground-level window wells indicated there was a fully furnished basement apartment for his mother.

She scooped up her Latin text and a notebook from the back seat, props to give the impression she'd be studying after the children were in bed. As she rang the doorbell, a baby began crying inside.

"In a minute!" Lucy called.

While Hannah waited on the concrete step, a group of boys passed on the street, pushing each other and laughing. They reminded her of Clyde and Boomer when they were still at home.

The door opened. "Come in, come in." Lucy had reapplied a layer of heavy makeup for dinner out with her mother-in-law. "I apologize for keeping you waiting. Albert had a naughty diaper."

Lucy had tried to dress up, but a wet patch spotted the front of her wool shirtwaist dress, and a tuft of hair stood up like a thumb from the back of her head.

"Good, you're here on time." Mrs. King looked up from watching Douglas Edwards broadcast the evening news on the television, mounted in an impressive oak cabinet. "Lucy, give her the tour, and we can be off."

The house smelled like curdled milk, talcum powder, and diapers, but it didn't bother Hannah. She'd become accustomed to baby odors at home. Boomer and Clyde, however, privately held their noses when they visited.

Serena peered out from behind her mother's skirt. Hannah noticed for the first time that the two-year-old looked remarkably like Jack, with the same full lips and dark, heavy eyebrows.

"Honey, let go of me and say hello to Hannah. She's going to stay with you for just a little bit while Grammy and I go for a drive. She's going to read you a story, won't that be nice?"

Lucy led Hannah down a narrow hall past her and Jack's bedroom, where the double bed was made up with a chenille bedspread. Hannah paused for an instant, startled to see her dark form, silhouetted by the hall light, in the mirror over the dresser.

In the children's room, a Donald Duck lamp illuminated a crib and a single bed. "Albert's all fed and should fall asleep any minute." Lucy snugged the blanket around his shoulders, but the baby's eyes were wide open, following his mother's every move. "If, on the chance he should wake, there's a bottle of breast milk in the refrigerator."

"Don't worry," Hannah said. "We'll be fine." She felt sorry for Lucy, with her discolored eye. Hannah thought of Nancy, also with two young kids, but in such different circumstances: a spacious home, nice furniture, and a husband who loved and protected her.

They returned to the living room, where Mrs. King issued a litany of instructions about the restaurant, emergency numbers, fire extinguisher, and thermostat.

"Should I have Mr. Graham's number at work as well?" Hannah hoped her question sounded businesslike and unintrusive.

"No, no. He's out of town." Mrs. King settled her fur-collared coat around her shoulders.

When the throb of Mrs. King's car engine faded, Hannah turned to Serena, who crouched in front of the television clutching a doll to her chest.

"Come on. I'll read you a story. How about *Pinocchio*?"

"No." Serena shook her head, hair flying in front of her face.

"*The Poky Little Puppy?*"

"No." The little girl's dark eyelashes fluttered.

"*Cinderella?*"

"No." Serena gave Hannah a sly look.

After more back and forth, they settled on the couch with a book of nursery rhymes. Serena leaned against Hannah, who tucked an arm around her. How different girls were from boys, not bouncing and jumping and punching. She could relate to this quiet little girl with the assessing gaze.

By 6:30, Serena was settled in the bed across the small room from Albert, now fast asleep. Hannah left the door open a crack. A dark room had always frightened her. A small sliver of light should reassure Serena at the same time the nearly closed door hid Hannah's search of the house.

It took a few minutes to shed her sense of shame at snooping into a stranger's private affairs. Fortunately, it didn't take Sherlock Holmes to determine the chaotic status of the Grahams' financial affairs—a reflection of the rest of their train-wreck life. The desk in a corner of the living room was a mess. She quickly set aside yellowed newspapers, last year's Christmas cards, tax returns, photos of the kids, and an ashtray filled with cigarette butts to scan a pile of overdraft notices from Jefferson County Bank.

Flipping through them, she discovered Jack had written checks on insufficient funds for groceries, the water and gas bills, garbage pickup, and Albert's pediatrician. She didn't know much about insurance policies and liens, but fat envelopes of papers indicated they were in deep trouble.

Yet Jack was definitely obsessed with his fantasy of opening a car dealership. In contrast to their household records, the dining room table held a meticulously organized trove of clippings from automotive sections of the *Post* and the *Rocky*. A manila envelope contained carefully labeled snapshots of the interior and exterior of several local auto showrooms. From some inside source, he'd gleaned performance and mechanical specifications for various models of cars.

In a separate folder was a flyer announcing a convention scheduled next week in Denver for regional Oldsmobile dealers.

As she slipped it into her purse, she heard Albert utter a high, mewing cry. She tiptoed to the hall outside the bedroom door, but he settled back to sleep.

Passing Jack and Lucy's bedroom, she hesitated, then stepped inside. Feeling strangely excited at her daring, she sniffed the air for the odor of sex, but caught only the scent of mothballs. On Lucy's nightstand sat a packet of pads nursing women used to absorb leaking milk. Atop his was a book of matches, and in the drawer, a box of condoms. In the back of the drawer, he'd hidden a revolver.

Lucy had arranged her shoes in a straight row under the hem of the chenille bedspread. On the other side were Jack's. She leaned closer. His loafers, work boots, and oxfords had identical lumps where his little toe had stretched the leather. The heel of each left shoe was worn unevenly on the inner side. The imprint of his foot in the shoes seemed terribly personal, as if she were touching his bare foot.

Her hand had crept out to pick it up when she heard a car engine in the driveway. Her heart gave a great lurch, as if it were pounding the cage of her ribs. She stumbled to the living room and peered out the front window. A sedan was turning around to reverse its course on Mississippi Avenue.

She sank onto the couch, fighting to draw a breath. Her fist gently kneaded her aching chest. How had she ended up here, snooping like a burglar or pervert through this family's shabby belongings? Except for church, they had nothing to do with Hannah's family, her life, or her future.

Still, she owed Paulette. Hannah pushed herself to her feet, legs still shaking. Jack's mother lived in the basement apartment when she visited Denver. No search would be complete without taking a look. It didn't take long to find the sturdy brass-knobbed door that led downward from the kitchen.

The stair treads to the basement were carpeted. At the bottom, a thick pile rug signaled, without a placard or doorplate, that a different world was ahead. Mrs. King had left the polished brass lamps aglow in her sitting area. A French bombé chest sat beside a wine-colored leather armchair and hassock, and a collection of books were arranged in a bookcase. A drop-front desk was open, showing neat stacks of paperwork and monogrammed stationery. Two low filing cabinets were topped with crocheted doilies and small china figurines.

The apartment was perfumed with cinnamon potpourri that reminded Hannah of her grandmother's homemade breakfast rolls.

Above the desk, photographs of Mrs. King hung on the walls chronicling her three marriages. The first showed a handsome man in a double-breasted suit, one arm around girl about three years old, the other around a young Daisie. A cloche hat slanted low over Daisie's left eye.

Hannah drew closer to another photo, this one taken in the mountains beside a dramatic rock outcropping. Petite Daisie and the tall, thin-faced man with jutting cheekbones were as mismatched as Mutt and Jeff, yet they stood close, his arm curved around her shoulder. His heavy eyebrows clearly identified him as Jack's father.

Other photos depicted Earl King, a heavyset fellow in a cowboy hat, fine tweed sport coat, and belt with a silver buckle. By that time in her life, Daisie's butt had expanded to the extent that her expensive clothes couldn't hide it.

Three very different men, Hannah thought. How had Daisie changed herself to attract them, induce them to marry her, and mold herself to fit into their lives? In the early photos, she'd seemed young and jaunty. A little sassy. A few years had passed, and eyes of the woman who stood beside Jack's emaciated father seemed dark and frightened. By the time she'd wed King and survived his death, the lightness of her early years and the desperation of maturity had leached away. There was no softness left in the later photos of Jack's mother, only determination.

Hannah knelt and riffled through dozens of folders in the filing cabinets, but was unsure what to look for. She remembered her grandmother hiding papers in the pages of her books, but no secret documents were tucked in Daisie's. In the tiled bathroom, bottles of vitamins and sleeping pills were arranged on a tray beside the sink. A tube of lubricant lay beside toothpaste in the drawer.

She closed the door carefully, leaving it just as it had been when she entered. Behind her in the sitting room, a breath of air stirred, tinged with the odor of alcohol. She turned slowly. Jack stood at the bottom of the stairs, eyes bloodshot and face mottled with fury.

"What the hell are you doing here, you little bitch?" He lunged at her and grasped her arm, fingers digging deep into her flesh.

She cried out in pain, twisting to loosen his hold.

"Where's my wife? Where's my mother?" His free hand balled into a fist.

Hannah's mouth trembled. "They're at dinner. I'm babysitting. For the kids."

"You're lying. They'd never leave my kids with a stranger."

"Please, Jack, it's the truth. They know me." Words fell quickly from her lips, almost a babble. "Your wife and mother were at church. They were sitting behind us, the same as every other Sunday. I asked where you were, because I always see you with them, and when Lucy said you were out of town, I offered to take care of the kids to earn some extra spending money."

Her body trembled as she searched his face, desperate to detect whether he believed her.

"You don't even know my wife." His lip curled in a snarl. "You slithered your way up to her so you could spy on me."

"Why would I spy on you?" She tried to pull away, but he tightened his grip.

"Why?" His heavy brows drew together. "Fuck, it's the Small-dones. They want the dealership. Secretly, they like my idea. They've sent you to gather information. To cut me out."

He twisted her arm. The wave of pain sharpened her wits. "It doesn't have anything to do with them. It's you." She deliberately softened her trembling voice. "I waited and waited for you to call me back, but you never did. I even drove by the Hertz office after school. I missed you and wanted to see you."

He moved his jaw, as if he were chewing on this idea. "Yeah, well, I've been really busy. Business plans are coming together." His fingers loosened.

"I want to be with you," Hannah said. "Can't I help?"

His eyes focused on her suddenly, as if he was seeing her anew. "Actually, Sweetheart, you can. Meet me Tuesday at the Hertz office. We'll go from there."

She nodded, a knot of hopelessness forming in her chest.

16

"Dulles was in Denver yesterday, visiting Ike in the hospital." Daisie stirred a teaspoon of sugar into her breakfast coffee while she read the *Rocky*. "I wish I'd been a fly on the wall for that conversation."

Jack pierced the center of his egg with a fork and watched as the orange yolk ran onto his plate. "Who cares? No one in Washington even knows he's gone."

"Oh, they know all right," Daisie said. "People in power are beating a path to his bedside, Dulles, Dick Nixon, Jim Hagerty, they fly in twice a week, from what I hear."

"It's just a trick to make voters think he's well enough to run again," Jack said.

Lucy toweled a blob of strained bananas from Albert's chin. "I wonder if he's still wearing the red pajamas the Cherry Hills Country Club gave him, or if he's getting dressed now."

Jack ignored her babble. "The real ones running the country are Ivy Leaguers—like Cabot Lodge—and the Mafia. Ike's weak. The Communists are laughing behind their hands while they manufacture more nukes."

The mental image of the sickly president shuffling around Fitzsimons in his bedroom slippers made Jack's forehead throb.

"I think it's sweet that Mamie's staying in a hospital room right next to his," Lucy said. Albert had finished his food, so she laid him on a blanket on the living room floor, then lit a cigarette. She didn't inhale, instead holding it poised between two fingers two fingers as if she were Grace Kelly.

He rose and put his plate in the sink. Between smoke from her menthol cigarette and the odor of Daisie's hairspray, his appetite was gone.

"My father always said you can't dump a sitting president," Daisie said, "and my father knew what he was talking about. Jack, when are you going to get my car washed? I've asked you twice."

"Stop nagging. I'll get to it, but not today." He tightened his shoelaces and settled the knot on his tie. "I'm leaving in a few minutes. Still looking for a Christmas gift you can open while you're in Alaska."

"I got a letter from Gretchen. She says Alaska's having a very dry winter. Should make it easier to bag my deer."

That was the thing about his mother. She thought she was good at everything. He knew it was BS, but nevertheless, the stink landed on him. It made him look bad at everything.

Jack thought about Ike in the hospital wearing a bathrobe; like the fat cat he was, his robe probably featured a fur lining, and his slippers made of velvet. He imagined a sexy nurse carrying a breakfast tray to the president laden with warm cinnamon rolls, sliced ham, and a cheese omelet.

When his dealership was up and running, Jack decided, he'd hire a maid. Someone cute, like Hannah. Or even better, her friend Rosemarie. On Saturdays, he'd have breakfast in bed.

"I won't be back until late," he told Lucy. He pressed a thumb against his throbbing temple. He had the midday shift at Hertz, and Hannah was meeting him down the street from the office at 3:30. He had to manufacture an excuse for leaving work for a few hours.

Before he left, he went outside and crossed the patio to his workshop at the rear of the garage. Keys rattled as he unlocked the door, and he was greeted by the scent of wood shavings. He was proud of the shop—it was one of the things he'd done right. Pegboard attached to the walls displayed his tools, arranged in ascending order of size.

The workbench had also been his project and now offered a spot at just the right height where he could saw, hammer, glue, grind, and polish. Not that he'd used the shop much in the last few weeks.

He unlocked a tall cabinet and moved aside a collection of power tools to reveal the crate containing the dynamite. A scale on the workbench showed that the twenty-five sticks weighed twelve and a half pounds. A bit on the heavy side but still in the ballpark. He drilled a small hole into two of the sticks, carefully attached the fuses, then bound the entire lot together with construction tape.

His watch read 9:45. The work shift began at ten. He packed the dynamite back in the crate, slid it into the cabinet, and locked it, checking the fastening twice after turning the key.

At work, the Hertz office bustled with customers, many of them turning in cars they'd rented for the Oldsmobile convention. Jack was at his best, working quickly to inspect the cars for damage, record mileage, collect payment, and send customers on the Hertz shuttle bus to Stapleton.

As he worked, he read the customers' meeting badges still clipped to their shirt pockets. Using their names, Jack made conversation in a flow of casual, knowledgeable chat. He'd made sure when he dressed this morning he looked sharp: suit, green-and-blue-striped tie, white shirt, and his black oxfords polished with the care he'd been trained to use in the Coast Guard.

About 1 o'clock, his boss, who'd come in early, turned the operation over to Jack. "Good job today," he said. "Olds is one of our Gold customers."

Too bad you pay me in chicken feed, Jack thought.

Once it was only he in the front and Eldon in the shop, Jack paced the office, moved a stack of papers, rearranged the chairs in the waiting area, clipped his fingernails. Finally, he spotted Hannah's VW creep by the large plate-glass window and park half a block down the street.

He poked his head into the back shop where Eldon was repairing one of the new Mustangs that had a factory defect. "Come up and cover the counter for a couple of hours. I've got a doctor's appointment."

"Sure, Boss." Eldon washed his greasy hands with strong-smelling soap in the employee restroom and joined him in the front.

Outside, the air felt cool in the low afternoon sun. Jack folded a red muffler around the neck of his topcoat. He crossed the street, passing his own car, and slid into the passenger seat of Hannah's VW. His legs were so cramped his knees nearly hit his chin, but it didn't bother him.

She radiated innocence, with her pixie-cut hair and big eyes. "Hello, Pretty," he said. "I've been thinking about you all day." Too bad about the birthmark—it really messed her up—but from this angle, it was invisible.

"What are we going to do this evening?" she asked. "Not Gaetano's, for sure."

She looked scared—no, shy—giving him a quick side look. It was understandable, a girl with an experienced older man like him. Perfect for what he needed.

"You like steak? How about we take a drive into the hills? We could have an early dinner at El Rancho."

That was just the right note. A fancy restaurant among the pines would make her feel like she was getting somewhere with him.

"That sounds . . ." Her voice trembled a little. ". . . that would be so romantic."

"Great." He touched the back of her neck, sliding his thumb over the soft skin beneath her collar. She shivered.

"What's the matter? You weren't so touchy that night on Lookout Mountain."

"I'd had something to drink then." The corner of her mouth twitched. "I was feeling braver."

"Hornier?"

"Maybe." She dropped her eyes to her lap. "I have an idea. Let's take two cars. Then I won't have to come all the way back here to pick up mine. If I'm late, my evil stepmother will ground me."

"Maybe a little fooling around in the parking lot?"

"I'll think about it." There it was again, her tremulous smile.

"Whatever works for you." He kissed the corner of her mouth.

Hannah's scent in the warm, close car made his skin tingle. This was going to work just as he'd planned.

"Before we go up to the El Rancho," he said, "I need to run an errand. You can follow me. Would that be okay?"

"Will it take long?"

He could tell she was nervous again. His fingers stroked the back of her soft hand that clutched the wheel. "No big thing. It'll only take a few minutes."

"I guess."

On the way downtown, evening traffic was approaching its peak. He took deep breaths, forcing himself to drive slowly so they didn't get separated. After they crossed the Platte, he turned toward downtown to a district of brick warehouses and building supply stores.

Here it was. Rimer Electric. He cruised along another half block, and she parked behind him, lights reflecting in his rearview mirror. He climbed out and ducked into the VW's passenger seat again. Excitement and fear raced through him, creating a bit of a stiffie. He had to do this right.

"Could you do me a really big favor and make a purchase?" He tucked ten dollars into her hand. "Here's the money."

"You've got two good feet and a ten-dollar bill." Her voice was sharp. "I don't know anything about electrical stuff. Why do you need me?"

"I'm really sorry, Hannah. I know it's an inconvenience. It's just that, well, last time I bought an item from this outfit, it was defective. Rimer wouldn't refund my money. I'll admit, I got pretty testy with him. Gave him a couple slaps."

"So go somewhere else." Her face had a mulish cast, the look Lucy got when she was spoiling for a fight.

"Rimer's is the only store within fifty miles that carries this particular device, an electronic on-timer."

"So it's for, what?"

His thoughts whirled, contriving a way to divert her off this train of thought. "I'm organizing Christmas lights at the church. They were lousy last year, and I told Kellems I'd do the whole thing: colored spots on the entrance, small Italian lights on the shrubbery, and a big manger scene with the three kings, shepherds, Joseph and Mary, the manger, whole deal."

"And you need the switch to turn off the lights during the late hours," she said slowly.

"Exactly." He chuckled inwardly at his elaborate story. "You're a smart and pretty, both." He ran a finger around the shell of her ear.

She wiped her palms on her skirt. "Okay, the electronic on-switch. Is there more than one brand?"

"An on-*timer*, remember that. A timer. And be sure it's the on, not the off-timer. The one I need comes from a supplier in New Hampshire. Rimer'll know the one." Excitement was making his heart beat fast.

"What should I say?"

"Tell him you're buying it for your uncle, who's too busy to come into town. He works as the church custodian and can't get away."

She climbed out of the car. The sun was low enough that her small figure cast a long shadow as she scurried across the street, dodging the evening traffic.

Minutes ticked by. Tension wound him up until he climbed out of the VW and paced up and down the sidewalk, keeping out of sight of the store windows. He plunged his hands into his suit coat pockets to warm them. Cars rushed past, their headlamps probing him for a few seconds, like searchlights, then passing on.

Finally, he saw her emerge from the store, a brown paper sack in her hand. She hesitated, waiting for a break in the traffic, looking like a sexy girl from a magazine in her short pleated skirt and tight sweater.

This was his lucky night.

"Here it is." She handed him a brown paper bag and a handful of change. Her chest rose and fell after running across the busy street. "Sorry it took so long. He had to hunt for the right one."

"That's great, Sweetheart." He tucked the bag under his arm, then leaned over to kiss her on the lips. He couldn't remember kissing a woman who tasted this good. His hand slid down the back of her soft sweater and skirt to cup her ass. "Are you ready for dinner, or should we forget food and go to Lookout?"

"I can't, Jack." Her body slipped out of his grasp. "By the time we drive there and back, it'll be late."

"Come on, Hannah. I think about you all the time." That wasn't true, but at this minute, he definitely needed her. "I can't make love to Lucy because she's not you."

She backed up, the motion of the passing cars swirling her skirt to mid-thigh. "I'll call you. Maybe this weekend. We'll have more time then." With a wave of her hand, she ducked inside the VW and started the engine.

Up ahead on the cross street, a fire truck and ambulance raced by, and traffic was at a standstill. Jack climbed into his car. He listened to the siren for a few seconds, then jerked the package from under his arm and ripped it open.

The box was clearly marked. It was the off-timer. Had she done this on purpose, or was she just stupid? Did she suspect something? Maybe she was scheming with Young Eugene.

The bitch. His lips curled back in a snarl. The conniving cunt. He'd show her.

17

Another fire truck and two ambulances roared by, sirens blaring and red lights flashing. Impatient drivers in the traffic lanes ignored Hannah's desperate attempts to wedge the small VW into the line of full-sized cars.

Meanwhile, the high beams on Jack's car in her rearview mirror stabbed her eyes. His car crept closer until it was inches from her rear bumper. He must have discovered right way that she switched the timers. Her anxiety escalated until she wanted to scream. She was trapped.

What would he do if he caught her? Beat or kill her? Clearly, he was capable of erupting into violent rages; Lucy's bruised and swollen face was evidence of that. But he was also sly. Alonzo said Jack was shopping for a cache of dynamite. Was the timer connected to his plan for the explosives?

Even at the electrical shop, she'd felt scared. The clerk hadn't sounded suspicious. In fact, she was overly helpful, as if she were sorry for her, a clueless young girl doing a favor for her uncle. Hannah had played up the subterfuge, acting a bit confused while wracking her brain for a way to derail Jack's plan, whatever it was.

"You need an on-timer? Are you sure? The brand you want comes both ways, either an off or an on." The clerk was a tall, dark-haired woman whose high heels tapped on the floor as she scurried back and forth between the counter and the rows of shelves in the storage area.

"Oh, gee," Hannah said, "I think—no, maybe it was the—oh, golly." She looked up at her pleadingly. "He didn't give me enough money to buy them both."

"Then I'd definitely recommend the off-timer," the clerk said. She slowly counted the change. "Where do you go to school? At Woodlake? I bet you have a boyfriend." Hannah shook her head. "No? You're kidding."

"Could you put it in a bag?" Hannah asked. Maybe, if the timer were covered, she could get away before Jack discovered the switch.

As she'd opened the door, package tucked under her arm, the clerk said, "Bring your uncle with you next time, Dear."

***

The scream of sirens faded. Hannah aggressively nosed the VW between two cars in the traffic lane, leaving Jack trapped at the curb. A driver honked furiously, but she refused to yield. Once the line of cars began moving, she exhaled a shaky breath.

In a few blocks, she swerved right onto Sixth Avenue, only to see the dark green sedan barreling after her. Tires skidded as she changed lanes, trying to shake him off, but Jack followed relentlessly through the evening traffic, cutting off other cars.

Her heart thumped wildly, and her sweaty hands stuck to the wheel. Home was less than a mile away now. As the turnoff approached, she slowed until the light changed to yellow, then accelerated through at the last moment. Her relieved sigh arched into a scream. Jack's car ran the red and pulled alongside, so close his mirror scratched against her metal, forcing the VW south, away from the route home, toward the dark rise of the hills.

Hannah jammed the accelerator to the floor, racing into the low foothills, but the VW's small engine was no match for his V-8. The road narrowed to two lanes, rocks looming on one side, a canyon yawning steeply on the other. She hugged the hill, her car rushing past the tracks of dinosaurs preserved in the vertical slabs of rock.

Driving inches from her back bumper, he flicked on his brights again, the beam blurring her vision. She forced her eyes to stay open, smelled the sweat on her clothes. *Please*, she said to the retreating glimmer of the city. *Please.*

She imagined her beloved car plunging off the road, being bent and broken. Windows smashed, headlights shattered, tires flattened, wheels torn off, fabric fluttering in the wind. Pieces—from jagged metal to thumbnail screws—flung onto the rocks.

With a neck-snapping jolt, the sedan hit her rear bumper. She screamed, the sound blending with the howling of the brakes and squeal of tires as the car skidded across the pavement. It slid, grinding on loose stone, until she could see only the lip of shoulder, then the sickening drop to the bottom of the canyon. Sweat dripped off her face as she shifted into reverse. Wheels spun. The horizon tilted sickeningly.

The car jolted backward away from the edge, and, hardly aware of what she was doing, she shifted gears again. Jack's sedan idled on the shoulder, ready to nose her to the precipice again.

The flood of terror receded, leaving a sharp edge of determination. Her tires spun as she wheeled uphill. In the rearview mirror, she saw his headlights swing to follow. The town of Morrison was still a few miles away, and the road was deserted. Around the next turn, her headlights illuminated a sign for Red Rocks Amphitheater, a quarter-mile ahead.

Last summer she, Rosemarie, and Paulette had driven there in Paulette's pickup. They'd bought tickets to see singer Rosemary Clooney, who was appearing at the amphitheater's stage, a famous venue tucked among natural sandstone obelisks.

Hannah veered into the amphitheater park as final rays of sun illuminated the tips of the rocks. At the entrance, she pounded the wheel in frustration. The road up to the amphitheater was blocked by a stout chain. Behind her, she spotted Jack's car passing on the highway, then slowing and backing up.

The entrance hadn't changed; an information booth stood between the In and Out lanes. She studied the barrier. Steel posts secured the chain, but on one side a gap opened between the post and the rocks, just wide enough for a VW to bump across the gravel and squeeze past.

As Jack roared up behind her, she coaxed her car with maddening slowness around the post. When she emerged back on the pavement, she turned off her lights and drove slowly in the dark, listening to the roar of the car's engine. Creaking and clashing sounds careened among the rocks, signaling he was butting the station wagon into the chain.

Without headlights, the landscape of looming rocks and branching roads seemed unfamiliar. Last summer when the parking lot had been full, Paulette had found a place to leave the truck in a small, sandy niche shielded by a pair of tall rocks. Hannah rolled down the window to see more clearly, feeling the cold night air on her face. Jack's engine roared as he took another run at the chain.

This seemed to be the spot. Hannah tried to back in, but realized she the space was too small. Below, a squeal of tires broke the stillness. She cruised slowly now, to keep the engine sound low.

She almost missed it, a barely noticeable gap between a pair of tall sandstone slabs. The VW fit perfectly, able to squeeze even farther back in the recess than Paulette's truck. In seconds, she had cut the engine, which ticked as it cooled.

Beams appeared on the road, probing the mesquite and twisted pines clinging to the sandy soil at the base of the rocks. Jack zoomed past, the V-8 engine seeming to keen in frustration. Sitting in the dark cove, her body shook, her trembling arms pressed against her sides, her breath came loud and ragged.

A half hour passed. An engine sound approached, and through the cleft she saw Jack's car flash by, driving downhill at high speed. Somewhere down below, his tires squealed on a turn.

Hannah feared for Lucy when Jack arrived home. He would be blazing with anger.

What was his plan? And what was she going to do?

18

Terror clung to her as she drove back to town from the dark pocket of the hills. Headlights from oncoming cars, neon lights on the stores along Colfax, street lights, none reassured her that she was safe. Her foot pressed the accelerator, but her hands shook as she gripped the wheel. She imagined her body parts scattering like leaves in the wind.

Who could she tell about what happened? No one would believe her story. Her eyes hurt, swiveling constantly from the road ahead to the rearview mirror, checking whether his car skulked behind her.

Deep inside, her bones seemed to quiver. Once before, she'd felt like this, when she was twelve and her mother was dying in the hospital. No one had told Hannah the truth, but as soon as she entered the room, she knew. Chantal was propped up with pillows, face as white as a full moon.

Back then, Hannah's legs seemed to dissolve under her and she fell on the tile floor. Chantal had raised one thin hand a few inches off the coverlet, and tears glistened in her eyes.

What made her think of her mother now? Maybe Hannah, too, was on the verge of dying. Jack had almost succeeded tonight.

Her own street finally came into view. Should she turn here, or drive farther to divert Jack away from her house if he was following her? Anxiety to be home safe outweighed diversionary moves, and she turned off Colfax, past the homes of buff-colored brick, weaving from this charming street to that one, bare tree branches arching over the road, warm yellow light streaming from windows, winter-brown lawns as welcome as spring flowers.

She pulled into their driveway, parking the VW on the far side of the detached garage where the scratches and dents wouldn't be visible from the house. Clyde, when he was a senior in high school, had parked in this spot to hide his late arrivals home.

She slipped into the house through the rec room's sliding patio door. "Name That Tune" was on the television screen. It was Nancy's favorite show, but she wasn't watching. From the kitchen, Hannah heard snatches of Nancy's telephone voice, the whiny tone she used when Beau called from the road.

"Hannah's worse than no help at all," Nancy was saying. "Today, she never even showed up after school to babysit the boys. I couldn't grocery shop, get my hair done, or pick up your suit from the cleaners."

The twins, corralled in front of the TV in a playpen, stopped throwing their toys over the side as soon as they spotted her. Marcus stretched his arms, crying "Up, up," while Jasper gave her a drooling smile that displayed a new front tooth.

On TV, George Dewitt conducted the orchestra as the band played the Mystery Tune.

The well-worn familiarity of home did her in. Tears began to dribble down her cheeks, then flowed. Her nose dripped. Her throat ached from stifling the sounds. Barely able to see, she groped her way downstairs to the basement. Light from upstairs was the only illumination. The pool table, her father's office, a guest bedroom, and the darkroom where she developed and printed her photos were dimly visible.

She entered the darkroom, locked the door. When she snapped on the safelight, its strange red illumination amplified her alienation, making everything unfamiliar. She was no longer a good girl, helpful daughter, responsible student, faithful friend, or law-abiding citizen.

Nancy rapped on the darkroom door. "Hannah, where have you been? I about went crazy today, what with Jasper's diarrhea and Clyde's telephone calls begging for money."

Hannah sank to the floor and buried her face in her hands.

"Are you crying? Has something bad happened? Are you in trouble?"

"Nothing. Leave me alone."

"Come on, Hannah, unlock the door and talk to me." Nancy was clearly irritated, but her voice also carried a note of concern, something Hannah hadn't heard before.

"Go away." So what if Nancy was trying to be nice? The last thing Hannah wanted was a girl-talk session with her stepmother.

The door rattled against the lock. "You're not going to hurt yourself, are you?"

"Don't be stupid." Hannah's throat was thick and sodden with tears. "Leave me alone."

"Suit yourself, but if you want to tell me something, I'll be available after I get the twins in bed." For Nancy, the twins always came first.

"Right." She heard Nancy climbing the stairs, and a few minutes later from overhead the boys' muffled footsteps as they raced around in their footed pajamas.

Sounds diminished until only the groaning and crackling of the cooling house remained. Crouching on the concrete floor, Hannah felt the chill as it crept up from her toes to her butt, her fingers, and finally the tip of her nose. Her teeth rattled.

She looked up at the safelight and the chemicals stored on the shelves. Strung on a makeshift clothesline were two rolls of negatives from film she'd snapped a year ago when Boomer was home on leave. They'd driven to places their mother'd loved like Lookout Mountain, City Park, Pikes Peak, and Red Rocks. She also shot several pictures of the bird feeder right outside the kitchen window that Chantal had set up.

Hannah unclipped one roll of developed negatives and held it up to the safelight, the dark images pale and the pale images dark. On the negatives, tiny juncos fought the large, aggressive crows for seeds and suet.

Hannah set the negatives on the counter. When she opened the darkroom door, the safelight spilled into the shadowy basement. She skirted the bulky pool table in the center of the room and went to her father's home office.

He kept it locked, a habit from the years when Boomer had used it as a private sanctum to drink booze. She retrieved the key from inside a swimming trophy Clyde had won when he was in junior high and went inside. The small room was piled with paperwork now that Beau worked for the truckers. The phone with her father's private line sat on his desk. Years ago, he didn't use it much, but now he was there every weekend completing reports on his out-of-town trips and talking on the phone to Roger Quint about the upcoming week.

She sat on the edge of the swivel desk chair, fingers pulling out strands of her hair. Hannah had no doubt now Jack was scheming to set off a dynamite blast. It was real, not just an informant's unsubstantiated whispers or Jack's bizarre fantasy. He was an angry, twisted man. Could he be scheming to bomb Fitzsimons?

Jack had made it clear he hated Ike. If a bomb exploded at the hospital, the president would die, along with many others. Ike was the most powerful leader in the word, even more so than Stalin or the pope. Hannah couldn't let him be blown to bits by a crazy, twenty-four-year-old failure of a man who beat his wife and tried to seduce a high school girl.

She must—she simply must—alert someone, even if it meant putting herself in Jack's path again. The clock on her father's desk showed it was after 11, but she knew Paulette was a night owl.

Her shaking hand misdialed twice before she connected with Paulette.

"It's me."

"What's the matter?" Paulette sounded wide awake.

Hannah inhaled a deep breath. She had to be brave now. "I'm calling the FBI tomorrow for a meeting."

"What the heck's happened?"

"It's bad. Give me a ride to school, and I'll tell you everything," Hannah said. "And when I can get ahold of an agent and set up a meeting, could you come with me?"

"On the assumption two misfits are better than one?" She sounded like the old Paulette from before the dinner at Gaetano's and the meeting at the lake.

"Something like that." A dizzy wave of relief washed over Hannah. They were friends again.

***

The next afternoon, the sun had dipped toward the mountains while the two of them waited at the Morse Park baseball diamond. Lumps of crusted ice lingered in dugout beneath the bench where they sat. Hannah shivered.

"It's not so bad." Paulette infused her words with fake positivity. "We're doing the right thing."

Hannah hunkered down on the bench and dug her hands into her coat pockets. "The agent's not coming."

They'd arrived right after school for the 3:30 meeting, but had seen only a few junior high kids, smoking under the bushes. In this lonely shaded place, the hands of Hannah's watch crept toward 5.

"Let's wait another fifteen minutes." Paulette munched on a bit of leftover Hershey's bar from her coat pocket.

The dusky light accentuated Paulette's long thin face and prominent nose. Hannah felt the comfort of her friend's presence. Gratitude filled her. Paulette was here for Hannah. Who else would freeze their behind in the dusk for a strange meeting? Kenny, maybe.

Hannah missed him.

She blew on her hands, then tucked them into her armpits. "Do you think we'll ever get away?"

"From Denver?" Paulette threw the candy wrapper into the frozen grass. "I've marked 212 days, more or less, on my calendar. I can't wait."

"No, from him."

"He's a petty criminal asshole, not John Dillinger," Paulette said. "We're going to leave this whole shitty town behind, including Creepy Jack. The last note of 'Pomp and Circumstance' will barely be over."

"Where *is* the FBI guy?" Her anxiety felt like a squirrel running laps in her gut. "What if he doesn't come?"

Paulette shrugged. "Everybody in law enforcement sucks except Alonzo, and even he's not all that great."

"I'm tempted to go home and forget all about Jack, but what if it's the real thing? Dynamite. Oh, my God, the president!" Hannah tugged at handfuls of her hair.

"Come on, Hannah, Graham's not that smart."

"Yes, he is." Certainty made her voice fill the small space. "He knows construction and mechanical things. He told me he had a construction job in Alaska where they used dynamite."

"So, maybe—"

Twin beams of a car's headlights streamed onto the baseball field, then stopped. Hannah peered over the dugout's roof to see a man climbing out of the car. He wore a topcoat and a snap-brim felt hat. Although shorter than she'd expected, he looked like an agent from the movies: good posture, clean-shaven. He strolled through the gate in the fence.

"Hello, girls." He tilted his head, peering down into the dugout. "I'm Agent Finch."

Hannah and Paulette stood awkwardly in the narrow space. "We were afraid you weren't coming. I'm Hannah, the one who called. This is my friend, Paulette."

"I was on my way home for dinner, so I thought I'd stop by."

His casual air disturbed her. "Didn't the secretary tell you what this is about?'

"Something about TNT. Somebody wanting to bomb some-one." He raised his eyebrows as if it were a joke.

"It's about a man we know who's going to set off a dynamite bomb." She hated the sound of her voice, high and breathless.

"Well," he said, folding his arms across his chest. "That sounds pretty darn serious."

Hannah shot a worried glance at Paulette, whose eyes had narrowed to slits. Should she trust this guy? He obviously thought Hannah was an empty-headed fool, yet what was she going to do? She couldn't ignore warning signs that a disaster was in the making.

Hannah inhaled a long breath, then spilled everything she knew about Jack, not sparing herself or her mistakes: Young Eugene, Alonzo, and the purchase at the electric shop.

"Jack hates the president," she concluded. Agent Finch's face looked vacant, as if he were contemplating what his wife was fixing for dinner.

"What if . . ." Hannah was desperate now, "what if he tries to hurt Ike?"

"And you, young lady?" The agent turned to Paulette. "What do you know?"

"She just told you all of it, *Sir.*"

"And the story about your brother?" The agent pursed his lips. "He heard something from someone, but now he's sick and in the hospital? That's true?"

"Absolutely."

"Please, please listen," Hannah said. "Jack's dumb, but smart. Something's going to happen. If not Ike, then someone."

"How come you're only contacting the bureau now, after some time has passed?"

"Because I thought it seemed farfetched, until he asked me to buy the timer," Hannah enunciated clearly and slowly, as if the agent were a child. "Jack was very anxious about it."

The agent rubbed his chin with his hand. "And why was it you who purchased the timer? It was because you were infatuated and wanted to see him again, right?"

"No, that's wrong!" Outrage twisted in her chest. "I didn't want to see him. He's a dangerous man, but I promised Alonzo I'd help.

When Alonzo got sick, I had no one to confide in, so I spied on Jack myself."

"Sort of like Nancy Drew." The agent crossed his arms across his chest, like a stern father with a small child.

The effort to stifle her anger nearly bent Hannah double. "Please, see Alonzo. Question Jack about what he's doing. Check with the informant or the dealer to confirm Jack did buy the dynamite. You don't need to believe me or trust me. Just find out what his plan is."

The agent extracted his car keys from his coat pocket. "Girls, an extremely interesting story, but I'm late for dinner. I'll give it some thought."

Hannah couldn't contain herself. "You condescending asshole! Get the hell away from us!"

They listened as his car door slammed, watched as his car pulled away, tires screeching as he wheeled onto 20th.

In the houses behind the park, lights snapped on. They seemed small and distant, inadequate to pierce the night.

"Do you think he was a real FBI agent?" Paulette asked.

"I don't know." A bitter taste filled Hannah's mouth.

19

Jack loaded .30-06 cartridges into his Winchester. The click of metal seemed as loud as a shot in the shadowy forest.

The three of them—Jack, Daisie, and her friend, Dr. Otto Blaine—had set out from Denver at 3:30 a.m. It was nearly dawn now, and they were gathered in the gleam of headlights from Otto's station wagon, organizing for a deer hunt.

Daisie'd hunted here, south of Toponas, during the years she was married to Earl King, and Jack had joined them when he visited her as a teenager. He usually enjoyed the beginning of a hunt, which seemed to unfold like a Technicolor movie, stars fading, indigo sky turning to pale yellow and then to blue. This morning, however, tension wound through him like a bad fish dinner. Two time-outs in the bushes hadn't relieved his stomach cramps, and his leg muscles twitched.

The red-letter day was coming. As the hours ticked down, he was unable to keep from obsessing about it. Was the bomb—dynamite, fuses, wiring—going to work? Would the timing be right? Was that little bitch, Hannah, still unaware of his objective? What if the cops stopped him?

Unable to contain his fidgeting, he zipped and unzipped the quilted Army jacket he'd bought years ago at an Army surplus store, stained now with dirt and deer blood from long-ago hunts. The bushes rustled. Headlights caught the glittering eyes of small animals creeping in the undergrowth.

"One more for the road?" Otto asked. They'd finished the ham and cheese sandwiches they'd brought along, and Otto poured another round hot coffee from his thermos into their tin cups. Wisps of scented steam rose in the air.

Otto and Daisie'd grown up in the same southern Colorado town and hunted together since they were teenagers. He was a big, good-natured guy—overweight, which was strange. You'd think a heart surgeon would take better care of himself. Good shot, though, able to put a bullet in a deer's neck at two hundred and fifty yards.

Jack liked having him along, because Otto flattered Daisie and sweetened her mood. From time to time, Jack had wondered if Otto was plugging her, but he didn't care one way or another. It was enough that Daisie's old friend deflected her anger from Jack when she was on one of her rampages.

"How are we going to set up the hunt?" Jack tugged his orange cap to position the ear flaps. Wind, blowing briskly when they first arrived, had died down, but the temp had to be twenty degrees or lower. He stomped his feet in the heavy boots, ready to move out.

"How about Daisie and I are on the stand, and you take the chase?" Otto said.

"Sounds good." Jack tossed the dregs of his coffee into the bushes.

"Absolutely not!" Daisie slapped her gloves against her thigh. "Jack's fidgety. Look at him, he can hardly stand still for a second. What if he takes a shot, and it goes bad? He'll ruin the hunt."

"You don't know anything." Jack felt a flash of the familiar pain over his eye. "I'm calm, for God's sake, I'm calm."

"See what I mean?" Daisie's lip curled.

"You're crazy, old woman." He raised his hands in the air, palms out, reminding himself not to get physical with her.

"You shit, I'm not old! Fifty-five and perfectly sane."

Unfazed, Otto stepped between them. "If you two don't shut up, the bucks will skip breakfast and hunker down. Come on, Daisie, we're too old for the chase. Let Jack do the hard work. He's solid."

Jack didn't mind being the chaser. It would give him a chance to get his mind straight.

"You'll see, Otto." Muttering, Daisie picked up her Remington and shouldered a knapsack. Her hunting expertise was legendary, and she bragged about it at every opportunity—how her father'd taken her on hunts for pheasant, ducks, and rabbits beginning when she was five.

Long ago, Jack had gotten sick of his mother's stories. She pretended she was the great white huntress, but she was getting old, unable to climb steep slopes anymore. Her bragging about going caribou hunting on her upcoming trip to Alaska was wishful thinking. Nonetheless, she'd packed cartridges in her luggage. Her suitcases were lined up in the basement apartment in anticipation of her flight.

"Here's the plan." Otto knelt on one knee and used a stick to draw a map in the dirt. "Daisie and I'll take the station wagon on that little dirt track that crosses the stream and winds up to the hilltop, here. We'll walk down a ways, but not too far—Daisie, you'll be at this location, and me, right about there."

Jack nodded.

"You got your knife?" Daisie paused, her hand on the door handle of the station wagon. "And don't forget to put 6-12 on your neck and ankles—mosquitoes are gone, but ticks and fleas are still out."

As if he didn't know. There she was, making him look like a stupid fool again.

The station wagon pulled away, tires crunching on the gravel, headlight beams bouncing as it rolled over the ruts. When it disappeared around a turn, the engine sounds faded. The silence seemed to swell with meaning.

Jack adjusted the Winchester's scope. A pat on his coat pockets confirmed he had another ten cartridges in addition to four in the rifle. He climbed over the road's berm and began a moderate traverse uphill, through a grove of Doug fir and past a thicket of bushes. The land here was still in shadow, but off to the southeast, the sun rose, shining on the tips of the snow-covered peaks.

Shit, he was out of shape, leg muscles screaming, breath coming fast. His eyes scanned the hill, watching for movement and darker shapes among tree the trunks and tangles of fallen branches. He made no effort to move quietly, instead throwing rocks, hitting branches, and barking like a dog. His job was to push deer upward toward Otto and his mother.

After half a mile or so, he switched his trajectory, recrossing the hill on a faint deer trail. As he climbed steadily upward, his body seemed to stretch, like a dog released from a cage.

The plan for tomorrow churned through his mind, pieces clear one moment, scrambled the next. Yesterday he'd checked the bomb. The fuses, battery, timer, and dynamite were loosely wrapped in brown paper. The only tasks remaining were setting the timer and secreting the package in the proper location.

Doubts crept in. It might not go off. Maybe Hannah had figured out what was about to happen and called the cops. Even with all his planning, would he have the guts to go through with it? Granted, the impact of his plan was terrifying. Maybe he should back out. Reverend Kellems would call what he was planning a deadly sin, something that gave him chills in the middle of the night. But Jack couldn't stand the life he was leading, slogging in a soul-killing job where no one respected him, scrimping for money when his mother was swimming in cash, It galled him that a depraved scumbag like Young Eugene Smalldone lived the high life.

Jack knew he was smart enough. In high school, he had sneaked out of his algebra and geometry classes because they were ridiculously easy for him. The innards of cars were as simple to read as the lines on his palm. And he was a good talker. The car dealership would be the perfect match for his talents.

As he skirted a rocky outcrop, memories of his father, William Graham, churned in his head. In one of Jack's few recollections, he was riding through the mountains beside his father in a beat-up truck. He couldn't have been much more than three or four. Sitting in the front seat, Jack had leaned against his father's side, feeling the movement of his father's gaunt, bony chest as he shifted and the wool of his father's coat scratching his cheek. Where had Daisie been on that trip? He had no recollection of her from back then.

Stopping in a clearing, he unclipped the canteen from his belt and took a long drink of water. Sun peered over the Divide, illuminating the tops of the trees on the slope above.

His breath came faster. A red-tailed hawk huddled at the top of a lodgepole pine, while goldfinches and juncos arrowed from one tree to the next. He could feel his thoughts speeding up, pricking him like spears.

After his father had died, Daisie never spoke of him nor told Jack what happened. Instead, one spring morning, she'd taken him to the Clayton College Orphanage.

"Be good," she'd said. "See you soon."

As a four-year-old, time meant little to him. He'd waited all day, but Daisie didn't return. At night, a thin woman with a stained front tooth handed him a pair of ill-fitting pajamas that drooped off his butt. He was given instructions to lie on his back in a dormitory bed and not turn over. The other orphans lay in rows like dead rabbits after a hunt. He'd been certain he was going to be killed.

It was five months before he saw Daisie again. That became her habit during those years—months between visits. A breath of tremulous hope would flutter through him when she arrived. She'd hug him against her skirt, where he caught her familiar scent, or kissed him on the forehead.

But after a couple of hours, her mood shifted. She became irritable, slapping his hands if he bit his nails, mocking him when he stuttered.

The sound of a hoof striking rock wrenched him away from his black memories.

"Oh, fuck!" He broke in to a run, dodging brush piles and stumbling over rocks as he tried to circle in front of it, but the buck had a head start. If he followed, it would be iffy whether he could change the animal's course toward Daisie or Otto. He turned back, focused on locating another quarry. His ears strained to pick up sounds through his thick wool cap, but birds offered the only sounds of life.

He climbed rapidly, breath coming fast and painfully; working the office job at Hertz had reduced him to a pile of flab. To calm himself, he focused on a quick mental image of his name on the dealership signboard. He'd be selling high-end cars to Denver's high rollers at a big markup. His bank account would be flush. The stucco-sided box of a house where they lived now would be rented out, and they would move into a fine home in Cherry Hills.

Not long now. Everything was in play.

Off to his left and a little above, he heard rushing water. A small, fast-moving stream. Deer would be stopping there to drink. Although ice had formed on the edges of the muddy bank, a shaft of sun penetrated the trees, and, in a small patch of soft earth, he saw fresh hoof prints.

He crossed the water, balancing on a half-submerged log. Above him, a flash of brown, then a second one, moved up the slope. With a shrill whistle, he signaled Daisie and Otto. Sweeping uphill, he threw a rock at a tree trunk above him, then uttered his best barking dog imitation.

Suddenly a young buck, a three-pointer maybe, crashed through a clump of bushes, too low to be in Daisie or Otto's line of vision. Jack raised the sight on his scope, but his uneven breathing moved the rifle just a hair. He missed. A second shot went wide. With a flash of white rump, the buck disappeared.

Fuck, fuck. He was too tense and nervous about tomorrow to bag anything. Sweat collected in his eyebrows, and he scrubbed at them with his sleeve.

When his gaze returned to the slope, the other buck trotted some distance above Jack, as beautiful as a vision from a dream. Its haunches moved in supple rhythm under the dark, rich coat, gleaming in the early light. He caught a glimpse of a proud neck arched beneath a head carrying a ten-point rack.

A crack from Daisie's Remington echoed among the hills. The buck didn't fall but leaped over a fallen log and began to run diagonally downhill.

Without conscious thought, Jack glued his eye to the scope, held his breath, and slowly squeezed the trigger. A second shot from Daisie's Remington came just after his, close enough that they could have been Irish twins.

The buck staggered a few steps and fell onto the thick carpet of pine needles. By the time Jack reached it, the deer's eyes were wide and unmoving. It was the best shot he'd ever made, exactly the right spot in the neck that immediately dropped the animal.

Daisie slid the last few feet down the slope, out of breath. "God, what a shot!"

"Yeah. Call me Deadeye." He patted the buck's still-warm body, feeling a surge of pride. What a trophy the antlers would make.

His mother's eyes blazed. "What are you talking about? I made that shot."

"You're crazy, you old bat." The forest seemed to darken, as if a filthy haze had spread over his vision. "I put that one down so fast he never took another step."

Daisie's lip curled, showing her teeth. "I've been hunting since I was five years old. There's no way I would've missed the shot. You're just pissed because you messed up, like you always do, ever since you were a kid."

Otto strode along a faint deer path to join them, rifle slung over his shoulder. "Good job, Daisie, he's a beauty." A big hand patted her shoulder. "What I wouldn't give to have that rack on the wall in my den."

"Goddamn, it isn't Daisie's kill. It's mine—you can see that, can't you, Doc?" Jack could hear himself pleading, as if he were, indeed, still a child. "The angle is wrong; she couldn't possibly have dropped it from where she was."

"Well, I've been hunting with this little lady for a lot of years, young man." Otto shifted from one booted foot to the other. "If she says she hit it, I assume she did."

The area over Jack's eye throbbed as if something in his head was trying to kick its way out. "You gut it and carry it out yourselves, then. I'm done."

Soon, he thought, *you'll get yours.*

20

Hannah surreptitiously wiped her sweaty palms on the white linen tablecloth. Dinner was on its way, but she'd never felt less like eating.

"Okay, Hannah Marie." Her father leaned across the table, fixing her with a hard-eyed stare. "What the hell's going on?"

They sat in a secluded corner of Stapleton Airfield's Sky Chef Restaurant. She'd come with him to drive the family station wagon home—a father-daughter dinner before he boarded the plane for Portland. At a nearby table, a dark-haired woman with a long, silky ponytail fed crackers to a squirming baby boy in a high chair. Her husband, a red-haired man covered with freckles, sat across from her, browsing the menu's daily specials. At the floor-to-ceiling windows, two men in business suits tossed down drinks, sure to be sloshed before their flight.

Hannah wished she were old enough to drink. It would make this conversation easier. Her father's cheeks flushed with repressed anger while the waitress slid the dinners in front of them, but she'd left, and his voice rose again.

"The great car I bought you, cherry condition, not a dent, looks like a junker." His voice rose. "In a matter of weeks! I can't believe I trusted you."

The mother turned to stare, a bit of cracker in her upraised hand. One of the businessmen rolled his eyes and made a face.

Hannah glanced over her shoulder. "Dad, be quiet. People are noticing."

"And tell me about Friday night. Where were you? Nan was awake until all hours, but you," he took a long drink of his bourbon, "never came home."

She leaned across the table and whispered, "I stayed over at Paulette's, but forgot to call."

"'Forgot to call?' That's an outrageous lie." His fingers tightened around his steak knife. "You're seventeen, not seven. You didn't forget to call; you did it deliberately to upset your stepmother."

Actually, she *had* forgotten. After failing to prod some action from the condescending FBI agent, she'd taken refuge with Paulette and Rosemarie at Paulette's house. As Hannah and Paulette replayed the disastrous meeting with Agent Finch, frustration consumed her, making her limbs twitch and her brain endlessly replay the meeting. She welcomed the diversion of the other two girls. Paulette had tired of rehashing the meeting and switched on the TV. Hannah had fallen asleep on Paulette's living room floor, awakening at 5 a.m to the test pattern on the screen.

"And speaking of the telephone, someone's been ringing us five times a day, then hanging up when Nan answers. You're doing something fishy, Hannah. It smells to high heaven."

She wished she were five again, when she'd run to her father to console her over jeers and teasing, but the nice little girl from back then was lost. Now she was the ugly bad girl no one would believe.

If she ignored Jack's scheming, what would happen? Ike was still recovering at Fitzsimons. Hundreds of others came and went from Fitzsimons daily—employees, patients, and service workers. A terrifying vision of broken windows, collapsed walls, and torn bodies threatened to choke her.

"There's this guy . . ." The words wouldn't come.

"A guy? You mean a man?" His voice cut like broken glass. "An adult?"

"Yes." She dug her nails into her palms. "Twenty-four or something. I've gotten to know him."

His hand whipped across the table, grasping her wrist. The silverware rattled. "Are you pregnant?"

"Ouch, you're hurting me!" She snatched her hand away.

A gray-haired woman at a nearby table stared in wide-eyed alarm.

"Tell me." His lips pulled back from his teeth. "If you are, I'll kill the guy."

"Dad, it's nothing like that." Her cheeks heated at the thought of the night in her bedroom with Kenny, of afternoons after school in the back seat of his car. Of the condoms he'd taken from his pocket.

"Don't lie to me, Hannah. God, I wish your mother were here." He leaned across the table, his face damp with perspiration. "Listen, if you are pregnant, I know someone who can take care of things."

"Dad, I'm not pregnant," she whispered. "Just let me tell you."

"Okay, say it." He wiped his forehead with his napkin. "What the fuck are you up to?"

Her chest was tight, as if her body wanted to hold back the words; nevertheless, she pushed ahead, relating the encounters with Jack but editing details of the night on Lookout Mountain.

"All this, the whole thing, was going on without my knowledge?"

His look of astonished betrayal gave Hannah a second's cynical pause. Had he been this blind when Boomer and Clyde were her age? Even she, in grade school and junior high, knew about their participation in clandestine beer busts, reefer parties, and nookie nights.

"Your story sounds as though it's been lifted from a dime novel." Beau retreated into skepticism. "Jack Graham, though he's a rather strange fellow, is nevertheless the son-in-law of a pillar of Woodlake Methodist Church. His wife was the honored queen of the Job's Daughters when she was in high school, same year as Boomer."

"I'm telling the truth!" Her fingernails dug into the tablecloth in frustration. "The Comet *did* have a gas explosion. The incident with the train *was* in the paper. Alonzo really *did* tell me about the dynamite."

He shook his head. "I've been an attorney for a lot of years, Hannah. You say there were no charges in the drive-in incident, and only a fine for the train/pickup collision. Alonzo Merrick was depending on the word of a criminal informant that Graham was in the market for dynamite. None of it adds up to a massive conspiracy of the scope that you're suggesting."

The threat failure loomed before her. "You've got to believe me, Dad. I'm a lawyer's daughter, and I'm not a fool."

"Hannah, I know life's been hard for you the last few years. If this is a fantasy you've concocted to get attention, tell me what's really bothering you. I'll listen. Promise."

"I'm not making it up." Her throat contracted with the effort to hold back tears. "The damage to my car proves Jack was trying to kill me."

She was interrupted by the roar of propellers as a plane pulled away from the gate, passing the Sky Chef's windows. Dining conversation trailed to a halt. Rapt customers traced the plane's looming silver bulk and blinking wingtip lights as it swept onto the runway through the falling snow.

Beau checked his watch. "Jesus, it's 6:20. My flight boards in ten minutes." He tossed his napkin onto the table. "I've got to pay the tab and get my suitcase from the locker."

Hannah stared. His focus had completely shifted to the business trip. Was he only interested in her story if she were pregnant? "What about Jack Graham, and the dynamite, and the timer?"

He signaled the waitress, then turned back to Hannah. "I'm not ignoring you, but if what you say about Graham is true, the guy's a thundering whacko. Ike's Secret Service men are tough and highly trained. If Graham were actually serious about killing the president, they'd be all over him."

"Why would he trick me into buying a timer, and lying about what he's using it for, if he's not serious? Maybe it's not Ike, but he's got a plan. I'm absolutely sure of it."

He sighed and tossed a twenty on the table. "Okay, I'll try to get back Friday morning and talk to a friend at the Department of Justice. See what he thinks."

Her heart knocked against her chest, and sweat popped out on her forehead. Why did people ignore suspicious behavior until *after* a tragedy? She remembered the two Puerto Ricans—known terrorists—who plotted to shoot President Truman but were stopped after wounding one of his bodyguards. Why hadn't the Secret Service sniffed them out?

"Please, Dad! I'm begging you." She grasped his coat sleeve. "Do something now."

He pulled away. "Hannah, stop it. I've got meetings I absolutely must attend."

"Friday might be too late." She could tell it was useless now; his eyes were avoiding hers.

"Stop worrying; I'll take care of it," he said. "Come on, walk me to the gate."

Her stomach was churning. "I have to visit the restroom. Meet you there." She scurried down the stairs to the lobby and half-ran to the Ladies'. For a few moments, she leaned over the toilet. Her nausea subsided.

When she emerged, a woman wearing glasses turned from the sink. "Hannah, how funny to see you here!" Lucy Graham shook water from her hands and dried them on the roller towel. "Where are your travels taking you?"

Jack's wife looked better tonight. Either the blue-green bruise around her eye had faded, or she'd added another layer of makeup. Her hair was curled, her eyelashes darkened with mascara.

"I'm not going anywhere; it's my dad. He's traveling to Portland." In the mirror, she saw her own white face.

"What a coincidence! Daisie's on the same flight but continuing to Alaska. She's taking a ton of luggage, which Jack had to haul in from the car."

Hannah leaned closer to the reflection. Her birthmark as vivid as blood on snow.

"Are you coming?' Lucy held the door open.

"What? Oh, not for a minute."

"Well, Daisie's already on the plane. The gate attendant said it would be a few minutes late taking off." Lucy's fingers fluttered. "Goodbye, see you in church."

The door whispered as it closed. In the mirror, her image seemed thin and insubstantial, as if at any moment it might fade away altogether.

Daisie King on the flight to Portland. Jack's mother, whom he hated, on the same plane as her father.

Suddenly, dinner rose from her stomach in a sickening heave, spilling into the sink. She wiped her mouth on her sleeve, then sprinted for the door. She scanned the lobby as if she were peering through her camera's wide-angle lens. At the front door, a policeman guarded the airport's main entrance. Just outside the revolving door, a group of picketing flight engineers huddled on the snowy sidewalk. In the center of the terminal near the ticket counters, a coin-operated vending machine offered flight insurance policies. Jack Graham was bent over the machine signing paperwork.

Farther on, the mother she'd seen in the dining room carried the baby in her arms, the child's red cap a spot of bright color near the gate. The woman, ponytail swinging, handed her ticket to the United Airlines attendant. She kissed her husband, and mother and child moved through the gate.

Standing beside the podium was Beau, waiting to say goodbye to Hannah, last of the passengers to board United 629 to Portland.

He waved.

Of all the years she'd known him—the man who'd carried her on his shoulders when she was tiny, taught her to ice skate, grown thin and desperate when her mother was dying, found another woman whom he'd never loved in the same way, the man who looked with wonder at his two little sons—in all those years he'd never seemed more vulnerable than at that second.

She ran, her feet slipping on the polished floor.

PART TWO

21

Hannah darted around suitcases, past clusters of departing families. She wasted only a brief flicker of attention on Jack Graham, who was scurrying toward the main exit, his upturned coat collar half-covering his face. Her father was the only person who mattered now.

Beau, briefcase in hand, spotted Hannah as he stood at the gate. He waved and pointed to his wristwatch, signaling the scant remaining time.

"Dad, don't go!" she shouted across the waiting area.

Ticket in hand, he was showing it to the attendant when she reached him, panting. Her hand clutched the back of his coat.

His face darkened with anger, and he pushed her away. "What the hell's the matter with you?"

The attendant drilled her with a narrow-eyed stare.

"You can't take the plane!" She screamed in his face.

Beau's cheeks flamed. "Stop acting like a damn spoiled child! I told you I'd be back at the end of the week. Weren't you listening?"

"Dad, I just saw Lucy Graham in the restroom. Daisie King's taking this flight." She struggled to catch her breath.

"You tell me an outlandish story at dinner, and twenty minutes later you've suddenly discovered a conspiracy? Involving this very flight?"

"He was here, Jack was just here, buying insurance. The bomb's in her suitcase. "

"This sick fantasy has gone far enough." Fists squeezing her shoulders, Beau shook Hannah until her head bobbed and her eyes crossed.

"Papa, you can't get on—what will happen—if I lose you, too?" Tears ran down her face.

Despair flooded her, as if her very foundation was dissolving. Her father's tall frame and strong chin, the wrinkles at the corners of his eyes and the mole on his neck—he was the only person on earth who mattered. She had no one besides him. Her mother was gone, brothers moved away, a grandmother living a thousand miles distant.

His face twisted as he released her. "You're embarrassing me and making us both look like fools."

The airport's loudspeaker crackled. "Passenger Beaumont Brightman. Doors for Flight 629 to Portland will close in one minute. Passenger Brightman."

"What about the others on the plane? They're in danger, too!"

"I've no time for your fucking histrionics." He pushed her toward the exit. "Everyone's perfectly safe. Go home."

She knew as surely as she knew the lines in the palm of her hand or the aftertaste of vomit in her mouth, that the bomb was not hidden anywhere near Fitzsimons Hospital. She'd been wrong. It rested like a coiled viper in the hollow of the plane in Daisie King's suitcase.

And she knew another thing: words were useless.

She inhaled a great gulp of air, so much that her lungs felt they would burst. With head thrown back, her first scream scoured her throat like sandpaper. She screamed with her mouth wide, lips stretched tight. She screamed mean, desperate screams never uttered in her sheltered life, where girls like her uttered cute, self-conscious screams for touchdowns at Friday night football games.

She screamed, her brain pulsing and throbbing.

Her father's face crumpled like wadded tissue. She'd seen him look like this only once—when she was thirteen, the day her mother died in the cancer ward at St. Anthony's.

He pulled Hannah to him, pressing her cheek against the stiff wool of his topcoat. "Hannah, I'm here, so stop, please." His trembling hand patted her head. "Come on, let's go home. We'll talk to someone. I know a good doctor."

But now she couldn't stop. Screams scoured her lungs, strained her gut, shrieks that seemed to pierce the ceiling, the windows, the seats. All consciousness of her plan faded until she felt only tremendous fear and loss—Jack's mother Daisie, the infant and mother from the Sky Chef Restaurant—they would join her own mother, dead these five years.

***

It had been only Hannah and Beau at her mother's bedside. Her brother Clyde, the planes of his face as sharp as broken glass, was unable to bear seeing her suffer. He stared out the window of her private hospital room watching gray clouds massing over the mountains. Boomer fled to the parking lot where he spent their mother's last hours huddled in the car.

Hannah remembered every detail: the smell of alcohol, medicines, and dying flesh. This vibrant woman, her mother, who hiked the mountains painting landscapes, could scarcely lift her hand off the white sheet. Dark, curly hair that once brushed Chantal's shoulders now lay thin and flat against her head.

The shock surrounding her cancer diagnosis had hit the family hard. For some reason none of them understood, Chantal had kept the knowledge of her tumor a secret. She'd spurned any medical attention or treatment so late in the course of her cancer until nothing could reverse its deadly course.

***

On the runway, propellers revved and roared. A plane gained speed. The sound of its engines faded as it rose into the air. Hannah's cries stopped, her raw and swollen throat could endure no more. Beau's hand closed over her elbow and he guided her away from the gate, her back bent like an injured old woman.

As they passed the ticket counters and approached the exit, an airport policeman, uniform jacket unbuttoned and food stuck between his teeth, intercepted them.

"What's up with this kid? The United gate agent called me."

Beau shrugged, as if throwing off his embarrassment and shame at her performance. "She's my daughter. Thinks there's a bomb on the Mainliner."

"Bomb? In Cuba, maybe, but not here in the U. S. of A." The agent brushed a crumb from his cheek. "She crazy or something?"

"Hannah's been very upset lately." Beau jiggled her arm, an unspoken warning to stay silent. "Unfortunately, I think she's read too many stories about the Medicine Bow crash in the *Rocky*."

"Very upset, is she? Sounds like female trouble. My mother used to go bonkers at that time of the month."

"Did anyone ever tell you that you're rude and stupid?" her father asked.

"Listen, Sir, Stapleton doesn't need crazy people getting our passengers upset." He hooked his thumbs in his duty belt. "Get her out of here. If she was my daughter, I'd put her in the nut house."

Beau held the door with one hand while escorted Hannah out onto the sidewalk. In front of the terminal, picketing flight engineers had built a fire in an empty oil drum near the driveway. Falling snow glittered in the headlights of approaching cars. Hannah, only dimly aware of where she was, slipped and fell on the icy pavement. Her father leaned over to lift her to her feet.

In the station wagon, Beau heaved a great sigh. Hannah huddled against the passenger door. Wipers thumped as they cleared the windshield. Beau clicked on KIMN. Traffic thickened as they turned right from Quebec Street onto East Colfax. KIMN took a break for a 7-Up commercial, then launched into "Autumn Leaves."

The song stopped, followed by a second or two of silence. "KIMN Radio interrupts our Sunday night Top 40 Show to bring you an important news exclusive." The announcer's deep voice was rushed. A little unsteady.

"A United Airlines flight from Stapleton Airfield has crashed near Longmont, spreading wreckage over a wide area, according to sources close to the disaster site. Burning wreckage can be seen over a wide area, but it's unclear whether there are any survivors. KIMN will bring you more information as soon as it's available."

Hannah snatched at the radio knob, turning it off with a snap of her wrist.

Her father stopped at a corner phone booth to call Nancy, then cranked the steering wheel in a sharp turn toward the road to Longmont.

22

There was no need to search for the crash site. From a distance, Hannah watched in horror as towering gouts of flame leaped into the night sky. Fires climbed upward as if to invade the heavens, lapsed for a few moments, then rose again as they consumed new fuel. Bare fields and an occasional lonely farmhouse or barn were revealed in bursts of hellish detail.

Could anyone still be alive? Hannah sank her teeth into her thumb to keep from crying out. Was there a chance someone could survive such a trauma? It had been nearly two hours since the radio announcement of the Mainliner crash, but their car was still creeping along the highway, trapped in a capsule of onlookers' vehicles.

This wasn't another Medicine Bow disaster high in the craggy mountains of Wyoming. Instead, the downed plane had crashed into flat farmland planted in wheat and sugar beets only forty miles north of Denver.

The car radio aired continuous coverage as they drove. The plane had been in the air a scant eleven minutes. Tonight's crash occurred just three weeks after the tragic loss of another United Airlines passenger plane. Officials had released a preliminary listing of thirty-nine passengers and five crew members aboard tonight's doomed flight.

Beau veered off Highway 66 onto a dirt road. A line of cars and pickup trucks in a funerary cortege lined the plowed fields for over a mile, headlamps reflecting off horrifying debris. Hannah longed to keep her eyes squeezed shut, but they would not remain closed. If she turned away, for even a second, she feared she'd miss some small movement, a face, a hand raised, a faint twitch.

The car slowed, but she didn't wait for her father to park. She swung open the door and jumped out. Leaving the road, she stumbled into the field over lumps of frozen earth and into furrows left by a farmer's plow. Her knees and palms were quickly scraped raw.

A hundred yards ahead, a massive crater held the twisted carcass of a plane engine, flames clawing the sky. Another engine burned in an adjoining field. In the distance, more fires dotted the horizon.

She scrambled to her feet. Fumes tore at her lungs—aviation fuel, greasy smoke, plastic—and something she'd never encountered before but recognized from some primitive knowledge as the odor of burning human flesh.

Behind her, Beau levered the car into a narrow space among the parked vehicles. A flashlight in one hand, he caught up to her, grabbing her arm. "Don't. You mustn't see this!" His strong, handsome face was twisted in horror.

A great force seemed to grow inside her, to impel her to stay and search. Fire engines had pulled onto the field. Firefighters were setting up lights and establishing a grid. Streams of water doused auxiliary fires.

She tore herself from her father's grasp and plunged into the flickering half-light. Where were Daisie King and the young mother with the ponytail? They could be alive. And the baby wearing the knitted red cap—the little boy who ate crackers in his high chair at the Sky Chef, he could be easily overlooked by searchers. Terrible images of the child lying torn or broken in the frozen ruts impelled her into the chaos.

The field around her was bare of its sugar beet crop but sown with the shards of people's lives: their small needs, their huge machines. She passed a dark bulk the size of a house, a twisted metal carapace that might be a remnant of the fuselage. It smoldered in a yawning pit. Farther into the dark, a complete airplane seat sat upright, as if ready for a passenger. A purse lay open like a gutted fish. Mud was clotted on a single glove, and a book's pages fluttered in the wind.

It took every scrap of will to scan places where the dirt was littered with torn and burned flesh, scattered like the devil's planting.

Her legs beneath the hem of her wool skirt were numb. Ahead of her, a pumper truck was lumbering over the littered, uneven ground. Firefighters unrolled a white canvas hose and shot an arc of glittering water toward the burning engine in the pit. Onlookers began bringing small searchlights, flashlights, and even kerosene lamps as they scoured the area for survivors.

Among the chunks of twisted metal, Hannah spotted a swath of white envelopes on the ground, fluttering occasionally in the wind. Stooping to retrieve one, she saw it was a letter that had floated down from the plane's shattered hold. The letter was addressed to a woman in Salem, Oregon, and the sender had written Air Mail in dark blue ink in the lower right corner of the envelope. It was smeared with dirt now, with a small tear near the top. She slid it in her coat pocket.

From afar, a massive explosion rent the air.

"Hannah!" Her father caught up with her. "You shouldn't be seeing this. It's too terrible." He gripped her again, not angrily, she realized, but determined to lead her away.

"We don't know," she cried. Her eyes burned from particles of black ash swirling in the air. "Someone . . . there might be someone."

"There's no one," he said. "You know it; no one could possibly have survived. The tail of the plane is lying in the dirt."

His hands reached to cup her face, but then fell at his side. She caught the sharp scent of sweat on his clothes, soaked despite the chill. He seemed to want to comfort her, but since Chantal's death, no longer knew how.

"You saved me, my girl." His eyes caught hers, brimming with unbearable gratitude amidst the shattering horrors of the moment.

"I had to choose you." Tears ran down her cheeks, wetting her lips. "God help me, I couldn't save the others."

She felt a fierce, sharp pain in her side. If she hadn't bought the timer, maybe the plane would've flown safely. Mothers and fathers with hopes and dreams, and children full of youthful joy might have been stepping onto the tarmac in Portland by now, kissing their loved ones on the cheek, heading to a hotel bed for the night, or, like Daisie King, flying on to other places.

Over her father's shoulder, she saw the silhouette of a man, carrying a sack, stoop to pluck something from an unmentionable mound in the dirt. Stealing belongings from the dead.

Consolation was impossible. Her urgency swelled until she thought she'd burst.

Flashlights and lanterns fanning out from a white clapboard farmhouse bobbed across the field. Perhaps with the lights, searchers could find signs of life. With Beau trailing behind her, she scrambled across the furrows.

A man in his thirties wearing a tattered coat and hat with ear flaps waved at them. "I've searched the area to the southwest. No sign of anyone alive." He ran a hand over his sooty face. "Heaven help us."

"What can we do?" Beau asked.

"If you want to help, take the area east to the fence."

They trudged past a farmyard with two barns, sheds, tractors, trailers, a fertilizer spreader, and a ripper with sharp metal teeth. Beyond, hay bales lay scattered next to a cattle herd tightly clustered in a fenced field. Three cows lay dead while the remainder of the herd bellowed in pain.

Debris studded the area: a pair of glasses with intact lenses, shards of glittering steel, a long piece of rubber hose, the smashed remains of a cockpit radio. Hannah circled the barns while her father walked ahead with the flashlight. Smells of cow shit, earth, and airplane fuel were stronger here. She trembled in the face of the cold wind that whipped between the buildings. It had to be well below freezing.

She drove herself on, legs and fingers aching fiercely. The ground seemed to quiver under her feet, and distant fires left dark spots in her vision.

"Hannah, please, please, let's go," her father said. "There's nothing else we can do. You're about to collapse."

"Not yet—" More words crowded into her throat, but she was unable to force them out.

"Ten minutes, then we're headed home." Beau aimed his flashlight toward an unpainted wooden storage building alongside a scattered haystack and cattle pen.

Hannah headed for a haystack. With an eerie chorus of deep-throated lowing, animals in the pen skittered away from them, forming a tight huddle on the far side. Wind kicked up, scattering hay from the top of the stack.

The flashlight flickered unsteadily, then went out. "Come on, dammit!" Her father shook the flashlight and slapped the barrel.

As she turned to leave, the moon emerged from a scrim of cloud. The landscape leaped into focus, bathed in luminous silver, the scattered debris gleaming, the midnight blue sky shimmering, falling particles from the crash winking like fireflies.

Tipping her head, Hannah glimpsed a scrap of red lodged halfway up the haystack. She screamed and broke into a run. Pawing at the stack, she couldn't reach the scrap, which sat two or three yards above her head. Her shoes fell off, and feet slipped out from under her.

Beau joined her. Gasping and sweating, they clawed on their knees up the dry stalks, dislodging them and sliding the small bundle closer until it slipped into Hannah's hands. It was the baby boy from the restaurant, the red cap still tied in a bow under his chin.

His eyes were open, smooth and glassy as brown marbles. Wisps of black hair peeked out from under the cap. He seemed unhurt, almost weightless in her arms, small fingers curled against his chest. But the child was dead, his skin an icy blue in the strange light.

Gently, she closed his eyelids. Beneath the searing tragedy of the moment, she felt an overpowering envy. The baby and his mother lay separated in death but not grieving for one another. They'd be joined forever in the afterlife.

23

Jack's hands shook as he turned into their driveway and parked Daisie's Buick behind the dog of a sedan he'd been driving. He checked his watch again. It was 7:10.

"What's the matter?" Lucy stubbed out her cigarette in the passenger-side ashtray, never one to smoke around the kids. "You're acting strange."

"I'm relieved, that's all. Thirteen days having that woman around was twelve days and twenty-three hours too many."

"She's bossy and a bit overbearing, but she's your mother. That's the way mothers are." Lucy gathered her purse and headed for the house.

Better watch his tongue. In another half hour, the plane would be in fragments on the slopes of a Wyoming mountain, and the shitstorm would begin. His hands still trembled. As he stepped out, he dropped the keys on the floor mat. He reached down to retrieve them, cracking his cheekbone against the door.

Cursing, he snatched the keys, touched a jacket sleeve to his head, and entered the house through the back door. Serena sat at the yellow chrome and Formica table, eating a bowl of Cheerios.

"Hi, Daddy." She studied him from under her brows with a frown that reminded him of Daisie. "You've got blood on your head. Are you going to die?"

He dabbed at it with a paper towel. "Not anytime soon," he said irritably. In the living room, Lucy held Albert on her lap while she chatted with the gray-haired neighbor woman who'd been watching the kids. He walked the old gal down the block to her apartment. She was a nice woman, about sixty with sagging chin and wispy gray hair. His mother was about the same age but avoided such hallmarks of age with expensive skin creams and weekly beauty shop visits.

"That'll be a dollar," the sitter said, hands folded at her waist.

"Right. Thank you so, so much." He patted her shoulder and extracted an additional five from his wallet, which was damn generous, considering her hourly rate was $1.05. No worries. Before long, he'd be rolling in cash.

As he walked home, he shoved his hands into his jacket pockets and tipped his head back to look at the moon. It was nearly full, illuminating the frozen grass and leafless trees until they were nearly as bright as day. Excitement surged through him, and suddenly his heart was pounding. He was free of Daisie at last. He gulped mouthfuls of cold, pure air as if it were Black Label. He still had to deal with Hannah, but he'd fix that problem soon. Meanwhile, his plans—the dealership, a fine house in Cherry Hills, the respect of the powerful men in Denver—all of it hovered at his fingertips. He just needed to play it right. Get through the next few days without screwing up. He patted the flight insurance policies in his coat pocket.

When he returned, Serena nestled on the couch, pretending to read a storybook upside down while Lucy nursed Albert. His gaze lingered on her exposed, swollen breast. Lucy's nursing didn't usually excite him, but in this hyper state, he felt his cock harden.

He went to the kitchen and poured a glass of cheap whiskey. Ice clinked as he returned to the living room and switched on the new Motorola television, the one piece of decent furniture in their living room. Daisie'd bought it so she could watch the daytime soap opera, *Guiding Light*.

The Perry Como Show was just beginning on KBTV. Settling into the overstuffed armchair, a castoff from Lucy's parents, he settled back, legs stretched out, to ease the tension zinging through him. His wristwatch read 7:40; probably another thirty minutes before the disaster report from Wyoming authorities broke into programming.

"What's the matter with your cheekbone?" Lucy asked. "It's got blood on it."

"Hit it on the car door. It's nothing." A touch told him the bump was beginning to scab.

Como appeared, crooning with the band, but almost immediately zigzag black lines flashed across the screen, dissolving to the KBTV news desk. Jack swung upright in his chair.

"We are interrupting our regular programming to bring you a news flash." A grim-faced newscaster read from a written script rather than the teleprompter. "A United Airlines DC6, which took off from Stapleton Airfield shortly before 7 p.m. tonight has crashed northeast of Longmont. Emergency personnel are at the scene of the burning plane, which is scattered over an estimated two-mile area. A Civil Air Patrol spokesman told KBTV News it's unknown if there are any survivors."

"No! Oh, my God!" Jack rose unsteadily, spilling his drink onto the rug. His face felt as if it was falling off his skull. Fucking plane never made it to Medicine Bow Peak. Somehow, it had been behind schedule, and the bomb had detonated too early. Mainliner 629 was lying not on a rocky, inaccessible mountain peak but in some farmer's open field about forty miles from Denver. Investigators would have little trouble collecting and inspecting the wreckage.

Jack's brain felt as if it, too, had exploded. In his plan, he'd envisioned himself completely in control inwardly while at the same time playacting grief for everyone else.

Lucy pulled Albert away from her breast. "Is it her flight?" A few seconds passed, milk dripping from her nipple, while she watched the image of fires burning in the dark. She laid the fussing Albert on a couch pillow, but her hands trembled so badly she had difficulty buttoning her dress. Serena gazed with wide eyes over the top of her book.

"I . . . Jesus Lord, I think so." Authorities would be here in the next few hours. In the interim, he had to get himself together. Play the grieving son.

Summoning enough tears to send them down his cheeks, he dialed the United Airlines Denver office. The line was busy. Two more tries yielded a busy signal; then on the fourth, a man answered.

"My mother, my sweet mother, Daisie King, was on Flight 629. That's the one . . . please tell me . . . were there any survivors?"

"I can't comment on specific passengers," the airline representative said. "I'm only authorized to say all those aboard expired."

"Expired?" Jack shouted. "All you can say is they expired? What the hell happened?"

"I have no information as to the cause of the crash," he said. "Someone will visit you personally later tonight."

Lucy lifted Albert, crushed him against her chest, and began to sob. Serena curled into the corner of the couch to suck her thumb. Digging into the scheming deftness he'd always told himself was his best quality, he paced in front of the TV, crying and pulling his hair.

The station swung into full-bore coverage, cancelling *Arthur Godfrey* and *I Love Lucy*. Film rushed from the crash site to the station showed flames leaping into the air from the burning tail section.

He wiped tears—unsure if they were real or feigned—off his cheeks with the back of his hand while he and Lucy watched wide shots of the scene and interviews with firefighters, the National Guard, airline officials, and eyewitnesses.

"Oh, my God, Gretchen." Lucy clutched his arm, while on the screen a mob of reporters clustered around Mayor Quigg Newton. "Your sister's probably leaving for the airport about now. You've got to call her."

Jack's thoughts darted frantically. How would he explain he'd forgotten her? He misdialed and entered the number again.

"Jack, what's the matter?" Her voice was tight and stiff. "Has something happened? When I called to check if the flight was on time, they said it had been cancelled."

"Thank the Lord I got ahold of you, Gretch. There's terrible news." He cleared his throat. "Daisie's plane has crashed just north of Denver. We waited to be positive before we called, but it was just confirmed on TV a minute ago. No one survived. I can't believe it. Our poor, poor mother."

That sounded good, he thought.

"I just finished making her bed and putting a fresh towel in the bathroom." Gretchen, a strong, independent woman who trained sled dogs, spoke in a strange, childlike voice. "I have the car keys in my hand."

"She's gone, Gretch. It's a bad deal." Jack cried a few tears that weren't entirely fake. "Come down tomorrow and stay in the basement apartment. That way, you can go through her things. We'll need help making arrangements, and you were the one who knew her best."

"I can't . . . I can't believe it. She wrote me a letter, saying she planned to hunt caribou while she was here. The girls decorated her room with pictures they drew in school." His sister finally lost the stoicism that had characterized her relationship with Daisie and began to cry.

"She died instantly, Gretch. That's what they said on TV." He felt angry. Naturally Gretchen would cry. She was the favored child who received all the attention and praise.

He heard Gretchen cough and blow her nose.

"I'll be there as soon as I can get a flight," Gretchen said.

As he hung up, Serena began to cry. "Honey, what's the matter?" Lucy rubbed Serena's back with her free hand.

"I feel sad. Can Grandma come back?"

Lucy closed her own red-rimmed eyes. Albert continued to fuss. "This is just too much," she said. "I'm going to call my mother and have her take the kids for a few days."

Jack nodded. His mother-in-law hated him, but he also needed fewer distractions to keep his brain sharp during the funeral services and all-important crash investigation. Not having the kids underfoot would help. Lucy called her mother, Mary Englehardt, who arrived twenty minutes later.

Her car brakes squealed as she stopped in the driveway. She rushed inside, not bothering with the doorbell. "Do we know for sure it was her flight?"

"It was the only one on that route at this time of night." Lucy's voice was weak, and she began to cry again.

Mrs. Englehardt gave Jack a hug. "Such an amazing woman, so full of life and love! What a tragedy." He tolerated her gesture for a few seconds, then untangled himself from her suffocating grip. His mother-in-law'd never liked him. In her estimation, he was a failure—not finishing his stint in the Coast Guard, dropping out of DU, needing Daisie to front the money for the Comet and even the house they lived in.

"Daisie wasn't the best mother in the world, God rest her soul," he said, "but she was the only one I had." It was a good line, but the words created an unexpected quiver in his chest.

The kids were sleepy and fussy as Jack carried them to his mother-in-law's car. The air was icy cold, down in the teens, according to the news. Back in the warmth of the house, the TV had returned to regular programming, assuring viewers it would break in as more film arrived from the scene. Lucy stared transfixed, barely moving her head to look at him, fearing she might miss something.

Jack paced. He tossed down a couple more quick shots of whiskey. Hard to tell how long before officials arrived for the notification. Hours maybe. Meanwhile, he needed to hide the flight insurance policies until he was calm enough to forge Daisie's signature. They had to look as if she'd bought and signed them.

A stairstep creaked as he descended to Daisie's basement apartment. He paused in her sitting room, sniffing the hint of cinnamon potpourri scenting the air. She'd used it everywhere she lived, and it made him feel strange, as if her ghost were hovering at his elbow.

He switched on the desk lamp. Above it on the wall hung the photographs of his mother with her three husbands, like a rogue's gallery of her mistakes. The middle husband, his father William, wore a flannel shirt. Judging by the drooping collar, jutting cheekbones, and dark smudges under his eyes, the poor guy must have been sick already when the picture was taken.

He jerked open her filing cabinet and pawed through manila folders, which were plump with documents detailing the extent of property Daisie owned, including Earl's ranch in Toponas and the Comet Drive-In. More money for him—he was one of the heirs, along with Gretchen.

The insurance file would be the best place to stash the policies. Tomorrow, when he wasn't so off balance, he'd forge the signatures. He flipped open the file. The top document was a surprise—another flight insurance policy, bought by Daisie three days ago. Sweat gathered under his shirt. She'd never bought flight insurance before. He thumbed through the pages and uttered a sigh of relief. He and his sister, Gretchen, were the beneficiaries. He slid the new policies from his jacket pocket into the manila folder and crammed it back into the drawer.

Why had Daisie bought insurance for this trip? Had she suspected something? Sweat popped out on Jack's forehead. Drops trickled from his hairline to the broken skin on his cheek, making it throb. He shoved the drawer to close it and caught his finger. Cursing to himself, he climbed the stairs, nursing his finger against his chest.

In the kitchen, Lucy talked on the telephone while she wiped tears from her face with a dish towel. "It's Gretchen, confirming she'll be here tomorrow."

***

A few minutes after 11 that night, the knock on the door came. Jack put on his sad, scared face. The two men on the front step wore pressed suits, not like the dog-ugly local cops who arrested him in Texas for bringing liquor into a dry county.

"Mr. Graham? We're from the United Airlines. We regret to tell you that your mother, Mrs. Daisie King . . ."

Behind him, Lucy began to wail. As Jack summoned his own tears, he could tell, in that calculating corner of his brain, the difference in sound between his wife's genuine grief and his own manufactured sorrow.

Lucky no one else could detect the fake.

24

Hannah stumbled into the car and slumped wearily against the door. The dash clock showed a few minutes before midnight. Beau slid behind the wheel and started the engine. She'd never seen him look so hopeless, even after Chantal's death. Through the windshield, she saw towering fires, still alight, fueled by gasoline-soaked ground that underlay the shattered plane.

From the passenger window was a landscape of small lights winking on-off, on-off, like lost souls. Each beam was, in fact, a flashlight held by a police officer or sheriff's deputy marking the location of a victim. The law officers waited, like caretakers at the gates of heaven, until the United Airlines recovery team arrived to chart each body's location and cover it with a canvas tarp.

One light, barely visible in the far distance, marked the spot where a Longmont policeman guarded the dead baby.

"No, I'm not leaving!" Hannah had told the young officer when he arrived at the haystack where the tiny body lay. The loneliness of the child, abandoned to the oversight of a stranger, filled her with desperation.

He was adamant. "The scene is closed now. Authorized personnel only." His voice sounded a little shaky despite his officious words.

Beau had gently taken her arm and guided her away. Now, she heard choked sounds from the driver's side, as if he were crying softly. After a few minutes, he scrubbed his cheek with the back of his hand.

He switched on the car radio. The news was reporting forty-four believed dead. As they drove away, her father maneuvered around barriers set up by the National Guard to stop onlookers from driving toward the crash site. Guardsmen were also clearing out those already crowding the dirt tracks, so Beau was able to retreat quickly onto Highway 66.

Hannah's shoulders sagged. Her feet and her scratched, bleeding legs warmed up under a stream of air from the heater. The engine hummed, but her eyes refused to close. She was afraid. Sleep might invite horrors that would suck her life away.

A stream of police vehicles, National Guard trucks, and heavy-duty cranes passed them northbound as their car sped south toward home. When they finally pulled into the driveway in Woodlake, Nancy rushed out the front door and down the driveway. Beau, barely moving in his weary hopelessness, opened the car door. Nancy stood in the glare of the headlights, not welcoming Beau joyfully after his narrow escape, but screaming at him.

"Where have you been?" She looked like an asylum inmate, her teased hair standing on end, face twisted in fury. "I've been going crazy! Crazy!" Her fist pounded the hood of the car. "My God, it's been hours since you called. Where were you? Why didn't you come home?"

Beau's eyes were bloodshot and his face smudged with soot from the fires. "We went to the crash site, Nan, but I'm here now. Home safe." His voice held a tremor of desperation Hannah'd never heard before.

"It's all over television," Nancy raced around to the driver's side and grabbed his arm. "The passengers on your flight—the flight you were going to board—they're dead. The ones that would've been sitting next to you, they're in bits. How come you didn't get on? Because somebody knew." She stared at Hannah with loathing. "It was her, wasn't it? The little slut knew something was going to happen to the plane."

"Nan, what's the matter?" Beau cried. "I'm safe, and it was Hannah who saved me. She somehow learned the truth about the flight at the last minute. Even then, I almost didn't believe her."

Rather than feeling grateful her father was alive, all Hannah could feel was the weight of the dead. She couldn't shake the feeling of the baby resting like a stone against her chest, his tiny fingernails neatly trimmed and blue in the cold.

Backing away from Beau, Nancy turned on Hannah. "You were up to something, and it stinks to high heaven. Those telephone calls, where someone hung up when I answered? The damage to your beautiful little car? The smirk on your face when you came home late from school?" Her breath roiled like smoke in the frigid air.

Beau tried to embrace his wife. "Listen to what I'm saying, Nan. I'm here with you now because of Hannah."

Nancy slapped his hands away. "What if she'd been five minutes later? I'd be a widow with no husband, trying to raise two fatherless little babies."

Hannah followed them up the walk, Nancy ranting as they went. Inside, Nancy seized Beau's arm and pulled him toward the bedroom for what Hannah knew was one of her "talks," but Beau shook off his wife's grasp. "Not now. I have to handle this." He half-guided, half-dragged Hannah down the stairs to the basement to his home office.

Before Chantal had died, when Beau was moving up the hierarchy at a private law firm, he'd used the office infrequently for a handful of private clients and for a variety of relatives seeking free legal advice. With the expenses of two more kids and Clyde's college fees, he'd opted for the trucking association's higher salary, but now he spent part of each weekend barricaded here.

Tonight he waved Hannah inside and closed the door with a firm click.

Hannah huddled under a blanket on the love seat. The raw skin of her knees seeped blood from falls in the rough sugar beet field. Her father settled at his desk and began making call after call to reach someone from the crash investigation team. Repeated attempts to contact an agent from the FBI's local office yielded a nonstop busy signal. An overnight operator at FBI headquarters in Washington, DC promised to pass a message to an old friend of Beau's at the bureau. When he tried to reach Alonzo, the night dispatcher said the Denver Police Department had called up all personnel to assist in Longmont.

Toward 3 a.m., Hannah heard the thump of the *Rocky* landing on the front sidewalk. In her mud-caked shoes, she took the stairs two at a time and scurried outside into the darkness to pluck the early edition off the concrete. Returning to Beau's office, she held up the tabloid's front page. The headline was accompanied by a photo of a flaming wing section looming against the night sky.

Her father's cheek twitched as if a tooth ached. "What have they learned? Anything?" His chin sagged with fatigue.

Hands fumbled in her haste as she opened to Page 3. She read aloud. "*Authorities are unsure of the cause of the crash, but theorize it may be the result of gasoline fumes accumulating in a closed section of the plane that were ignited by friction or heat.*"

Hardly daring to believe it, she looked up at him. "Is it possible Jack *didn't* do it?"

"I don't know, Hannah, but I'm expecting law enforcement to knock on the door soon. It's imperative you tell me all of it, every single detail about you and Graham. And do it right now. Leave nothing out."

"Please, Dad, no." She raised an arm as if to ward off another onslaught of the devastating truth. "I said it at dinner last night. I can't face it again." She sank onto the love seat. Her stomach churned, and saliva pooled in her mouth, as if her stomach rebelled against the retelling. "You're alive, isn't that enough?"

Thwack! His palm hit the top of the desk. "You damn well better spill it! Law enforcement from every damn agency in the country will be looking for the culprit. We can't wait, even for another hour, to develop our strategy.

"Don't you realize the danger you're in?" Beau asked. "They're so desperate to lock up the perpetrator they'll arrest everyone they can lay their hands on to capture the mastermind." He rose from his chair and walked around his desk to loom over her.

She pressed her hand against her mouth to control the rise of additional acid from her gut.

"Here's what we're going to do." He pushed his face close to hers. "I don't want you saying one word to law enforcement, not yes, no, or maybe. If you begin talking, they'll twist what you say and manipulate you. Every facial expression, every misstatement and emotion will be exploited. Each good intention will be twisted into a crime. In the end, you'll go to prison."

He folded his arms across his chest, looking fierce and determined, the way she remembered him from years ago. "Instead, *I'll* relate to them what I've heard from you. What you must do is say not one word to them, not even remain in the room. I'll share information, but they'll have no basis to arrest me or call me as a witness."

"They'll know it was me," she said. "I already talked to Stupid Ass Agent Finch."

"Yes, but if you refuse an interview now, they can't call you to testify in court based on what you told them weeks ago. It would make the agency look tragically incompetent by ignoring your warning."

For a moment, words wouldn't come. Closing her eyes, she took a breath, then began to speak. She'd told parts of it to Paulette and Alonzo, but here, in the face of tragedy, the story cut her throat like broken glass: she'd climbed into a strange man's car, driven into the mountains, drunk whiskey and touched his privates. He'd touched hers. She'd dined with him, knowing he was married man. She'd met known criminals, learned of a possible plot, and agreed to buy the timer.

"He tricked me," she said. "Jack told me the timer was for Christmas lighting at the church, but it sounded strange. Why would he be so anxious to buy the timer when Christmas was almost two months away? I didn't like it, so at the last minute I changed what he wanted from the on-timer to the off-timer."

Her father listened and took notes on a legal pad, his face flushing bright red when she related her narrow escape on the road to Morrison. Her hands twisted the blanket in her lap as she described her gnawing fear the president might be a target but could find no one to listen. When the final piece of her story came—her glimpse of Jack buying flight insurance—Beau's chin sank to his chest, either in relief at his escape or sorrow for the victims.

Her tale seemed like the capstone in a life of failures. She wasn't homecoming queen, top scholar, winner of the national spelling bee, or secretary of the science club, but even her smallest victories seemed grotesquely twisted. She covered her face with her hands and cried. Escaping tears dripped onto her shirt.

He handed her a tissue from a box in his desk drawer. "Hannah, let's go over some of this again. Did Graham at any time tell you he was going to dynamite a plane?"

"Never."

"Did he confide that he'd tried to blow up the Comet?"

She thought back to their strange dinner date at Gaetano's. "No. He said a gas leak had caused a small explosion at the Comet, and it had been closed for repairs. But I heard Young Eugene teasing Jack, saying his 'boom-boom deal' didn't get done."

"You're doing fine." Beau propped his elbows on the desk. "Now, here's a very important point. At the airport, how did you know to get me off the plane?"

"I knew Jack hated his mother; he said so several times. Then, when I talked to his wife in the bathroom, she told me Mrs. King was on the plane." Hannah struggled to drag up details from her memory as if they were a disinterred corpse. "I went into the lobby and saw him buying flight insurance at the vending machine. When he saw me, he ran away."

"That's good. Now, one more thing. If I recall, it's quite a distance from the restrooms to the vending machines. How far were you from him?"

"I don't know. A ways."

He walked to the office door. "This distance?"

"More."

"Here?" He opened the office door and walked toward the pool table.

"Maybe twice as much, like from where I'm standing to the far wall of the basement."

"How did you know it was Jack, his being at such a distance?" His voice was casual, but eyes searched her closely.

She sorted her memory, which was snarled in the horror of the crash. Jack had been standing at the vending machine, bent over as if he were writing. Then he straightened up. What was it?

"I don't know." Hannah rubbed her tired eyes. "I just knew it was him."

Beau sighed.

His desk phone jangled like a fire siren in the quiet house. He talked for some time while Hannah half-dozed. When his call was completed, he tapped her shoulder gently. "I talked to a friend who's a defense attorney. I think we're ready. Why don't you take a shower and change your clothes."

Her skirt, which had been freshly dry-cleaned when she dressed for school yesterday morning, reeked of smoke. Mud crusted her socks. She undressed and stepped into the basement shower, letting the spray pelt her head while she picked dirt and tiny bits of gravel from her bruised knees. As she finished toweling off and pulling a sweatshirt over clean jeans, the doorbell rang. She trotted up the stairs and moved quietly down the dark hall. It rang again.

"Somebody get that for God's sake!" Nancy shouted, ignoring the fact the twins were asleep.

"I'm coming," Beau called.

Hovering close to the door, Hannah peered through the narrow sidelight. In the glow of the porch light, two men stood on the step. She recognized one of them immediately: Stupid Ass Finch, the FBI agent who'd kept her waiting in Morse Park, then treated her with condescending disbelief.

Her father's hand touched her shoulder. "This is normal operating procedure," he murmured. "They arrive in the early morning when suspects least expect it." He opened the door.

"That's the girl," Stupid Ass said. He was dressed in the same topcoat and snap-brim hat, but the casual cockiness of their last meeting had evaporated. His eyes slid over to his companion, as if for instructions. The other man also wore a snap brim but was older, with a heavy jaw and sinewy body. His stature reminded her of aggressive boxers she'd seen on TV.

"Special Agent Grimwalt, FBI." He pulled a leather case from an inside coat pocket and flipped it open, displaying his identification. "And this is Special Agent Finch. Sir, we've received an alert that your daughter may have vital information concerning last night's United Airlines crash."

Beau studied the identification carefully. "What makes you think my seventeen-year-old daughter would know anything about some monster who committed mass murder?"

Finch opened his mouth to speak, but Grimwalt cut him off. "My colleague interviewed your daughter ten days ago concerning a person of interest in this tragedy."

"Come in." Beau hung their coats and hats on the hall tree, then ushered them downstairs into his office. Nancy, who'd been watching from the kitchen, clattered down the steps behind them. She confronted Beau just as he was closing the door.

"There will be no meeting without me." Leaning into the office she said to the agents, "I'm Hannah's stepmother. She's a secretive girl, and I damn well deserve to know what's going on in my own home." Soft flesh around her eyes was purple, as if Beau's narrow escape had hit her like a fist.

"This is a criminal matter of utmost importance," Grimwalt said. "You have no business being here." He closed the door in her face. Beau directed the agents to straight-backed chairs in front of his desk like job applicants. Hannah returned to a corner of the small couch. When Beau leaned back in his leather desk chair, he looked somber yet confident.

Grimwalt let a silence ripen, gazing at the office wall displaying Beau's diploma from the University of Chicago Law School and various commendations from his service in the JAG Corps during World War II.

"I want to make it clear," Beau said, "Hannah will have absolutely nothing to say. I will relate to you details concerning her brief encounters with a possible suspect in this horrendous crime."

Grimwalt's eyes flared with anger. "Your daughter talked to Agent Finch less than two weeks before last night's crash. At that time, she had information that may at this point help us catch the perpetrator, yet you won't allow us to question her?"

"That's correct."

"Hannah," Grimwalt pleaded, "it's really important you talk with us. We desperately need someone to help us, and you can be that person. There are families, like the father and sisters of a small baby boy, who are crying out to know why their plane exploded, and if it was intentional, who did it."

Her fingers closed over the scratches on her palms that came from climbing up the haystack where the baby lay. That little boy had sisters who would grow up like Hannah, without a mother. No one else in the world had her knowledge about Jack Graham's actions. Shouldn't she help? Wasn't that what good people did?

The sound of fretful crying came from upstairs. She heard Nancy's voice trying to calm one of the twins, probably Jasper. At the desk, her father sat so still he might be holding his breath. Stupid Ass's eyes gleamed.

Slowly, she shook her head, lips tightly closed.

"So, Mr. Brightman, you're determined to impede our investigation." Grimwalt's words sizzled with anger. "Be prepared for the consequences."

"On the contrary," Beau said, "I'm ready to provide you with valuable information that will brief you about a dangerous individual. He's certainly a prime suspect in the bombing. And, as you probably know by now, his mother died in the crash."

"You and your daughter should be prepared to face charges for obstructing justice," Grimwalt said.

"Nonsense. My daughter will not be present or give you one single word. If you call her to testify in a court trial, she'll reveal the shocking news that she confided to the FBI well before the crash that Graham was planning a criminal act. Despite her courage, you ignored the warning."

Beau leaned back in his chair. "The FBI is in deep trouble. In the early morning hours, I talked to one of my contacts at the Department of Justice in DC. He told me Ike is extremely upset about the crash. One of his senior Department of Health executives, Dr. Harold Sandstead, was on the plane."

Color drained from Finch's face. He gazed straight ahead, avoiding his boss's icy stare.

"J. Edgar Hoover and the FBI will be lucky if they survive such a scandal," Beau said, "or at the very least, you two will be out of a job. However, I'm offering you a thorough briefing of my daughter's limited but meaningful contacts with the suspect."

"Leaving out pertinent facts that might lead to her being charged as an accessory to murder," Grimwalt snarled. "Wait until the prosecutor gets you on the stand. You'll be lucky if you retain your license to practice law."

"Don't mess with me," Beau said. "My information is offered to help you catch Graham and convict him. As you well know, it's hearsay, and as such, is not admissible in court."

He turned to Hannah. "Please leave the room and go upstairs. I'll handle it from here."

Straightening her shoulders, she walked out, meeting the agents' angry gaze with her own look of contempt. Rather than obeying her father, she tiptoed into the adjoining bathroom and sank down on the floor next to the hot air register. Sound filtered clearly through the grill, and she listened, legs pulled up to her chest. Like a sow bug hiding under a rock, she thought.

Beau took more than an hour laying out the bones of her story. Grimwalt returned to each piece of information several times, to snare any discrepancies, but it was a futile effort. Finally, her legs cramped and trembling, Hannah heard him tell Beau, "That's all—for today."

Once the agents had retrieved their hats and coats and left the house, Hannah climbed the stairs and peered out the sidelight adjacent to the front door. It was dawn. The rising sun had turned streamers of clouds blood red.

25

Hannah, Beau, and Nancy watched as Finch backed the gray, government-issue sedan out of the driveway.

How could their street look so normal? Hannah watched Craig, who lived across the street, as he scraped frost off the windshield of his car, as he did every winter morning. From the brick duplex on the corner, a tiny old lady tottered down the steps one at a time, her dachshund tucked under her arm.

None of the Brightmans, clustered at the window, spoke; even the twins in their playpen were quiet. But Hannah felt the tension tighten around her chest.

Nancy grasped her arm. "What I want to know is this: who's been calling here ringing, eight, ten, fifteen times, driving me crazy, waking up the boys? Was it your friend, Jack the Ripper?"

Hannah tried to shake Nancy off, feeling the sting of her stepmother's fingernails.

"You and your boyfriend really scored big, didn't you?" Heat seemed to radiate from Nancy's stale-smelling clothes. "A multimillion-dollar plane in pieces and forty-four people dead."

"Nan, cut it out," Beau snapped.

She wheeled on him. "This how you raise a daughter? Your girl, who's the accomplice of a mass murderer?" A drop of spittle flew from her mouth.

Beau recoiled. "That's absolutely untrue, and you know it, since you apparently had your ear glued to the office door while the FBI was here."

"Oh, I should stop, should I? Well, think about what our friends going to say. And the parishioners at the church. And your boss. Do you think Roger-Dodger Quint will choose you as his successor when he finds out?"

Even during her mother's last illness, Beau had never looked this bad. His eyes were red and crusted, his jowls slack. He looked seventy, not forty-five.

"And the newspapers." Nancy advanced on him like a she-wolf. "It shouldn't take long for the *Post* and *Rocky* to connect us to the crash. We'll be lepers. No one will speak to us."

"Hannah's a confidential informant," Beau insisted. "The public absolutely won't know who she is, or what she's confided to law enforcement."

"Something that big will never stay secret. I guarantee you, someone will blab." Nancy crossed her arms tightly across her chest.

Hannah felt herself slipping toward a dark abyss of worthlessness. She was a nobody at school, a failure as a girlfriend, and a despised outsider at home. How could she survive? Longing flooded her. She wished she *had* died when Jack forced her to the edge of the canyon with his car. There was no point in living now, because any kind of normal life would be over. If there were such a place as heaven, maybe she and her mother would be reunited.

All at once, she remembered how it had felt when the lip of the canyon yawned just feet in front of the VW's windshield. A burst of energy had transfixed her at the last second. She'd jerked the wheel enough to squeeze the car past Jack's and onto the road again.

She whirled to face her stepmother, words seeming to spring to her lips unbidden. "You're forgetting, Nancy, I saved him. Your precious Beau would be dead if it weren't for me. I pulled him back from boarding the plane." Her voice gained strength. "Me, terrible Hannah, saved your husband, the father of your children."

Nancy's eyes widened, and she retreated a few steps.

Hannah stepped closer. "You should be kissing my feet, Miss Beauty Shop Skank, who got herself pregnant so she could land herself a husband."

Nancy's gaze wavered. "You liar, that's not true!"

"I can count to nine, even if you can't."

"Hannah, stop." Beau inserted himself between them. "Nan, back off. We can't exist in this state of warfare."

Words stifled for years sprang from her lips. "Admit it, Dad. Nobody wanted her here, not me, not Boomer and Clyde, not even you. You married her because she was pregnant."

Beau's face reddened with anger. He opened his his mouth to respond when Jasper began screaming in the playpen. Marcus was beating him with a wooden block. Her father's chest rose and fell with a ragged sigh. He went to the playpen and lifted Marcus into his arms, then turned slowly, tears glistening in his eyes.

"Hannah, you've got to move out. I can't take it."

The floor seemed to tilt under Hannah's feet. In the midst of death and chaos, he was kicking her out?

"I'm sending you to Chicago," her father said. "I'll call my mother and let her know."

***

In her bedroom with the door locked, Hannah sat cross-legged on her rumpled blankets, the telephone handset pressed to her ear. While she waited for Paulette to answer, she heard Beau and Nancy shouting in their bedroom.

"What?" Paulette answered, sounding out of breath.

"It's me." When she heard her friend's voice, relief filled Hannah like a fresh wind.

"Was your phone out of order last night?" Paulette said. "I tried for hours to get you. Alonzo called me at 4 a.m. You'll never guess what happened."

"Can I come over to your house?"

"We're going to be late for school—but let me tell you . . ."

"I already know, Paulette."

"What? No, you don't. Alonzo said . . ."

"Jack Graham's mother was a passenger on the plane that crashed last night." Each word felt like a stone dropping from her mouth.

"My, God, how did you—"

"It's a long story. Please, can't I come over? There's nowhere else I can go."

"Of course. Are you in trouble?"

"Maybe. I don't know." She gathered her resolve. "Yes. I need a place to stay for awhile; things are bad here."

"The ass-wipe slut kicked you out? I thought my alkie mother was bad, but kicking you to the street?"

"Not exactly the street. Beau wants to send me to Chicago to live with Grandma Brightman."

"You poor, crazy dope. You can stay with me as long as you want."

White noise whispered on the line as Hannah fought to hold back tears.

Finally, Paulette said, "He did it, didn't he?"

***

She pulled her suitcase from the bedroom closet. It was too small to hold all the skirts, sweaters, jeans and underwear she needed, but there was nothing to do about it. A few essential clothes would have to suffice. At the last minute she added a picture of her mother as a young woman and another of the five of them during the good times. She slipped her fifty-dollar babysitting cache into a side pocket.

It was quiet as she tiptoed to the bathroom past Beau and Nancy's bedroom door. Their bitter quarrel must be over. Were they wrestling under the blankets in the throes of make-up sex?

Hannah loved her father, but she felt the gap between them widening even farther. He had a new wife and new children; Hannah was a hangover, a reminder of the woman whose death had caused him unbearable pain.

In the bathroom, she collected her hairbrush, makeup, and a pair of pearl earrings her grandmother'd given her. When she had everything wedged into the suitcase, she leaned on the top to engage the latches. It was heavy, and she set it down for a moment beside the hall table, where a bowl of candy still sat, left from Halloween trick-or-treating.

Jasper and Marcus were scooping up blocks and throwing them over the rim of their playpen. They seemed older this morning, not laughing at their own antics, but quietly intent on creating a mess. Jasper squatted down to retrieve a plastic truck from the playpen floor and offered it to her.

Despite with their food-streaked faces and dirty-diaper smells, leaving these two little brats was hard. They'd upended her life, no question. Initially, she'd hated them, but, frustrating and loveable as puppies, they'd ended up winning her over.

Hannah accepted the truck from Jasper's grimy hand and gave each of them a kiss, inhaling the scent of their baby shampoo. Suitcase in hand, she slipped the toy truck into her coat pocket.

It took Hannah several tries to start the VW, as if the car, too, was reluctant to leave. As she backed out, a fender scraped the battered elm beside the driveway.

26

Jack slept only an hour or two. The wave of erotic pleasure that had arisen with news that his plan had succeeded didn't last until bedtime. Rendered sleepless by a raging sea of emotions, Jack turned his back to Lucy. One moment, dizzy feelings of freedom and joy consumed him, and moments later he roiled with fury and hopelessness.

In the morning, his sister Gretchen would arrive from Alaska. He'd be driving to Stapleton to pick her up, a reminder of the perilous danger he was in. Would the bomb's early detonation have left clues that TNT was responsible for the plane's destruction?

To make matters worse, Gretchen would stay in the basement apartment. After weeks of enduring Daisie squatting down there like a Halloween goblin, he now would have to put up with Gretchen. She'd been Daisie's favorite child, the one lavished with all her attention.

At breakfast, he pushed aside the bowl of oatmeal Lucy slid in front of him. Her eyes were ringed with dark circles. She'd already smoked two Kools, filling the kitchen with its sweetish menthol smell.

There was none of their usual morning conversation, which suited him just fine. While he was spooning sugar into his coffee, someone knocked at the front door.

"Get that, will you?" He wasn't in the mood for visitors.

"What if it's a reporter?"

"Tell him to get off our property," he snarled, "or I'll punch him in the face."

Lucy peered cautiously through a gap in the kitchen curtains. "It's Otto Blaine."

Jack didn't want to see Otto, but it would look bad to ignore his mother's oldest friend. He opened the front door, feeling a rush of cold air on his bare ankles.

When Otto saw him, he began to cry. "I'm so sorry, my friend." Otto's tears fell on a bouquet of chrysanthemums in his hand. He stepped inside and gave Jack an awkward hug, the damp petals of the bouquet brushing the nape of Jack's neck.

While Lucy put the flowers in a vase, Otto and Jack settled on opposite ends of the sofa. "A horrible, horrible tragedy," Otto said, fishing a handkerchief from his jacket pocket and blowing his nose. "Can't believe the three of us were hunting together day before yesterday. She got her deer, just like always."

Jack ground his teeth. Daisie'd lied, of course, as she always did when Jack was in the way of something she wanted. He'd bagged the deer, but his mother hoarded the credit.

"We'd known each other since we were eight years old," Otto said, "Daisie and me, growing up in Buena Vista. It was barely on the map back then."

Resigning himself to more of Otto's recollections, Jack settled back against the couch cushions.

Otto rambled on. "She was a little bit of a thing, but hell on wheels. I remember, she'd say, 'Let's hunt pheasants,' and then, she'd open her dad's gun cabinet, load up the shotgun, and off we'd go."

The old man wasn't such a bad guy—good to have along on a hunt—a person who'd always treated Jack with respect. Too bad Daisie'd fooled him all these years.

Lucy brought them coffee, and Otto talked for awhile. Finally, Jack looked pointedly at his watch. "Thanks for coming, Otto, but I've got to leave in about five minutes to pick up Gretchen at the airport."

Time to trade one annoyance for another.

***

Gretchen was easy to spot as she descended the stairway from the plane, a tall woman, five-nine or so, with a red scarf tucked in the neck of her parka. Her hair was twisted into a lumpy knot on the crown of her head. Never, as far as Jack could remember, had she worn lipstick. He wondered, with a stab of jealousy, how Gretchen, who trained huskies for Alaska's major sled races, had secured a mother's genuine devotion from Daisie, who'd faked the little woman role well enough to attract three husbands.

Dispensing with any spoken expressions of sorrow or sympathy, Gretchen set her suitcase down and gave Jack a bone-crushing hug. The scent of her skin was like his mother's. He felt the same frightening mix of satisfaction and unnamed sorrow that had kept him tossing all night in twisted sheets.

"Bad night, bad day," Gretchen said. "The girls were all set to see their grandma. Not sure they understand why she didn't arrive."

"How's Skipper?" Jack asked.

"Our divorce is moving along." She loosened the scarf tucked around her neck. "He's on rotation this week, so a neighbor is taking the girls." Her husband Skipper was an Air Force pilot, so seldom home that Gretchen's three daughters ignored him when he told them to make their beds or finish their dinner.

"Lucy's sorry she couldn't come to meet you." Jack picked up her suitcase. "Serena has a sore throat." It wasn't true, and Gretchen would find that out soon enough, but right now he couldn't tolerate the kids' oppressive neediness.

His and Gretchen's footsteps on the terminal's polished floor reminded him of the events here last night. He'd sent Lucy with Daisie to the gate while he got her remaining suitcase from the Buick. He hauled it to baggage intake. The dynamite had jacked up the weight to sixty-one pounds and cost him an exorbitant twenty-six bucks. He'd planned it correctly; his mother had boarded the plane, Lucy was on her way back to the car, and he slid right up to the flight insurance kiosk.

He'd had the fucking policies in his hand when he spotted Hannah near the restroom. Had she seen him? His footsteps as he ran for the north door, dodging passengers and luggage, had beaten a tattoo on the tile floor.

Today as they stepped outside, the picketing flight engineers marched in full force on the sidewalk in front of the terminal, causing a traffic jam.

"In Anchorage, we don't see this many cars in a month," Gretchen said. Despite rising wind and the beginning of another snowstorm, she removed her coat and carried it over her arm. How odd, Jack thought, he and his sister, walking without Daisie as the barrier between them.

When they arrived home, he put Gretchen's suitcase in the basement apartment. Lucy was already there, stripping the sheets off the bed Daisie'd slept in and making it up with fresh linens. Clean towels hung in the bathroom. Scent of the cinnamon potpourri Daisie always used was nearly gone, as though it had been months or years rather than eighteen hours since she died.

He returned upstairs and dressed for work. If he stayed home, spending twenty-four hours a day with his Lucy, Gretchen, and two kids, he'd end up in the nut house at Pueblo.

As he was about to leave, his boss called.

"Jack, it's Barny from Hertz. Listen, I heard on the news about your mother. I'm real sorry; please, take all the time you need off work."

"It's tough, but I'll be in today as usual." Jack thought he did a good job sounding sorrowful. "Work will help me take my mind off it."

Barny cleared his throat. "I have to tell you, man, I think you should stay home."

"Really, I'll be okay."

"The thing is," Barny said, "we're doing a shitload of additional business, pardon the expression, but most of it's from reporters arriving in town to cover the crash. Not a good scene for someone in your situation. Stay home. Be with your family."

Jack left the house anyway, driving the mother's Buick. Irritable and jumpy, he traveled west on Colfax, then north to the quiet neighborhood where Hannah lived. Leaves had dropped from the huge trees that lined the meandering streets. Clumps of hard, brown earth heaped the gardens where daisies and zinnias had bloomed during the summer.

The Buick coasted slowly by Hannah's large, tan brick house. A station wagon occupied the driveway in front of the garage, but there was no sign of the VW. Through the wide picture window in front, he spotted someone in the living room. A bedraggled blonde running the vacuum cleaner.

He parked half a block away. With the car idling, he flipped from one radio station to another. A half hour passed. A high school boy driving a customized red Ford pulled into the driveway of a house further down the street, but no sign of Hannah. Was she hiding out? He needed to get to her. Tell her to shut her mouth.

He drove to the high school and skimmed past the student parking lot. The VW wasn't there, either. With nothing else to do, he cruised up and down Federal Boulevard, past the boarded-up Comet each time. With his mother dead, he and Gretchen would inherit the property. Not that it was worth much now. Thinking of Daisie left him with an empty feeling. Alive, she seemed to smother him so he could hardly breathe, but with her dead, he was hollow as a rotten log.

Depressed and restless, he drove home through late afternoon traffic, dodging among delivery vans, construction trucks working on a road repair project, and men driving home for dinner.

When he stepped inside the house, he saw Gretchen sitting on the couch. She barely looked up from reading the huge black headlines of the *Post* and the afternoon Extra edition of the *Rocky*.

In the kitchen, Lucy was spooning pablum into Albert's eager mouth. "Oh, God, I'm so glad you're here!" She stopped feeding the baby—who began to cry—and retrieved a slip of paper from the desk. "An FBI agent called. He said to contact him no matter what time you got home."

Jack dialed, his finger trembling.

On the second ring, a man picked up. "Finch here."

After Jack had identified himself, Finch said, "I appreciate your getting back to me, Mr. Graham. I want you to know that teams investigating the crash of Mainliner 629 have located several items we believe belonged to your mother, Mrs. Daisie King. We'd like to have you come down here and identify them."

"What items?" Jack asked.

"Things of a personal nature," the agent said. "Can we expect you within the hour? We're located downtown on Stout Street."

Jack rebuttoned his coat, and Gretchen tossed the newspapers aside. "I'm riding along. Maybe they'll have an idea what went wrong with the plane."

He shrugged. "Not likely. Feebs wrote the book on locked lips, but come if you want."

Downtown streets were nearly deserted by the time Jack parked the Buick on 19th Street in front of the United States Customhouse, where a cluster of regional federal offices, including the FBI, were headquartered. Lights shone brightly from second-floor windows behind the building's ornate marble façade.

As they approached the entrance, Jack straightened his tie and sucked in his gut. Enough law enforcement types had interviewed him that he knew how they worked. He had to be alert and confident. On his game.

Agent Finch met them in the lobby of the FBI's offices, and Jack introduced Gretchen.

"That didn't take long," Finch said. "We appreciate it. I know this must be a difficult time." Although Finch was neatly dressed in suit and tie, he smelled of cigarettes. Dark circles ringed his eyes. He led them down a long, brightly lit hallway where telephones rang and the rumble of men's voices could be heard behind closed doors.

"Here we are." He opened one of the double doors and gestured them inside. Laid out on two long, polished conference tables were islands of personal items—a man's shoe, a toothbrush, a tiny blue child's coat—many burned or twisted. At Jack's side, Gretchen inhaled a guttural breath.

Only one other person was present, a sinewy agent who resembled Rocky Marciano in a suit. "Special Agent Grimwalt, Mr. Graham." His handshake left Jack's fingers aching.

Grimwalt walked to the second table at the far end of the room, stopping in front of what appeared at first to be trash, laid out like a still life.

"Holy Jesus, it's her purse." Gretchen's hand trembled as it hovered over the scratched, beaten leather. "I recognize this. It's made from the hide of a buffalo she shot herself. Remember that, Jack?"

"No," he said. But he *did* remember. Daisie'd been invited to a special hunt years ago to thin the southern Colorado buffalo herd. She'd told him the story numerous times.

"These items were found inside," Grimwalt said. "Go ahead. You can touch them."

Jack picked up two keys he was fairly certain opened her safe deposit boxes at Colorado National Bank. Her last will and testament was probably stashed in one of them. He opened her wallet and riffled through a thick stack of traveler's checks. A thousand dollars—worth months of salary at Hertz.

"Here's a letter from her sister," Gretchen said. "She lives in Missouri. I'd forgotten about her. We've got to call."

Grimwalt folded his arms across his chest. "Is there anything unusual among the items? Something unexplained?"

Jack didn't answer; he was leafing through her address book.

"Oh, no, look at this." Gretchen picked up something off the table and showed it to the agent. It was a gold ring, prongs surrounding the empty space where a large gem had rested. "It was the diamond ring—at least six carats—that Earl King gave her when they were married. See? Their initials are engraved on the inside curve."

Grimwalt inspected the ring, then nodded, looking regretful. "Looters apparently arrived before law enforcement had the scene secured. I'm sorry."

Tears glistened in Gretchen's eyes. "She thought this marriage would be the one that would last, but he died too soon. Jack, look." She held the ring setting in her hand.

"It's a shame," he said.

With a slight movement, he fingered a thin newspaper clipping from between the leaves of the address book and slipped it in his pocket. Grimwalt didn't seem to notice. Instead, he spent half an hour asking him questions about Daisie's state of mind, their drive to the airport, baggage check-in, and final goodbyes.

"She was a remarkable woman and a fine mother." Jack knew he had to say the words, but they left a bitter taste in his mouth.

He and Gretchen were silent on the way home, a wide space between them on the seat as each leaned close to their own car door. Although Jack thought he'd played the interview with Grimwalt well, he ached from the tension in his muscles.

The hidden paper in his pocket—a newspaper clipping—actually seemed to have weight. While Grimwalt studied Daisie's ring, Jack had delicately unfolded it and glanced at the headline. It was the *Post's* story about his arrest years ago after the forgery incident at the car parts store where he worked.

Where did Daisie get it? She hated the *Post*, preferring the *Rocky*. Probably from Mary Englehardt, Jack's mother-in-law. It would be like her to point out to Daisie what a failure he was.

At home, Jack trailed Gretchen wearily into the quiet house where Lucy had tucked the kids into bed. "We all need a little something," Lucy said. She poured three tumblers of whiskey, and they gathered in the living room.

Gretchen took a large swallow. "Jack, do you think she ever loved us?"

"Daisie never loved anyone, except maybe you, three days a month." Jack crunched a bit of ice between his teeth.

"I doubt she cared much for me, although she might have loved my girls a little bit." Gretchen untied the band around her hair and let the heavy, dry strands fall to her shoulders.

"She was hard. Changeable," Lucy said.

Gretchen swirled the liquid in her glass, her eyes distant. "I remember one time when I was ten or eleven—she was married to your dad then, Jack—they were having a terrible fight about something. She was furious and slapped him in the face. Her, five-foot-one. Him, he must have been six-two, a bit taller than you are now."

Jack rubbed his cheek, remembering the whack Daisie'd given him a few weeks ago. "I know how my dad felt. She had a vicious arm on her."

"Your father wasn't usually a mean guy," Gretchen said, "but I think the mining project he'd been working on had just gone belly up. Anyway, he hit her back. Knocked her to the floor."

Lucy gave Jack a sidelong glance. After the last time he'd hit her, she told him she'd pack up and leave with the kids if he ever did it again.

He looked away. Lucy'd deserved it, but hitting her had been a sort of cowardly thing to do. "Maybe it taught Daisie a lesson," he said.

"What I remember was, it knocked Daisie on her ass," Gretchen said. "She lay there on the floor for a few seconds, then scrambled over to him on her hands and knees. I'll be damned if she didn't sink her teeth into his ankle."

A smile creased Gretchen's tanned face. Tilting her head back, she swallowed the remainder of her whiskey, throat muscles working. "It's been a long day. I'm going to get some sleep." She set the glass on the side table and went downstairs to the apartment. In a few minutes Jack heard the clatter of the pipes as she took a shower.

"Thank God this day is over." Lucy gathered the glasses, put them in the kitchen sink, and went to bed.

It was after midnight when he slipped under the covers beside her. He fell asleep and dreamed his mother'd returned to life, teeth cracked and broken, and bitten off his nose. When he awoke, his skin was drenched in sweat.

27

Hannah knocked on the Merricks' front door about 7:30 in the morning. On the street, a lone car passed by, headlights bobbing as it hit a pothole, tires crunching on frozen snow. She dropped her suitcase on the doorstep, slid the camera bag off her shoulder, and blew into her cold hands.

Hurried steps approached from inside. The door swung open. "I was worried." Paulette was out of breath. "I thought you'd be here earlier." She was dressed in a wool jumper and white blouse, ready for school.

"There was a free-for-all. Dad, Nancy, and me." Hannah's shoulders sagged, exhaustion leaving her almost unable to move. Paulette gave Hannah a hug. Even though Paulette's bony clavicles dug into Hannah's cheek, it didn't matter. Here, at last, was a place of safety. Relief flooded her like a warm bath on a snowy night.

Paulette grabbed Hannah's suitcase and dragged it into the entry, dodging piles of magazines, muddy shoes, and wrinkled, unread newspapers. "Come on up. I've put sheets and a blanket on the other twin in my room."

In the years they'd been friends, this was the first time Hannah'd been upstairs at the Merricks'. Paulette's room was Spartan: two single beds against opposite walls in the modest space, a scratched lamp table set between them. A small dresser occupied a corner.

"It's not much, sorry." Paulette folded her arms across her chest, eyes focused on the toe of her saddle shoe.

A single picture of the Golden Gate Bridge served as the only wall decoration. San Francisco had been Paulette's dream destination since the two of them shared a locker in grade school. "After we graduate, it's the city by the Golden Gate." She'd said it dozens of times.

Hannah sank down on the narrow bed. "I'm so tired, it's like heaven." There was no bedspread, but she shed her clothes, crawled under the thick blanket, and had fallen asleep almost before Paulette had left for school.

***

When she awoke, the low afternoon sun crept between the slats of the venetian blinds. The alarm on the lamp table read 4 p.m. She pressed her thumbs into her eye sockets, trying to banish the remnants of a dream that swirled in her mind like an evil mist.

She dressed in a sweatshirt and jeans from her suitcase and smoothed the blanket on the bed. On her way downstairs, she clung to the banister to steady her shaky legs. The smell of greasy frying food hovered in the air. She found her way to the kitchen, where curtains were closed, and a single bulb remained aglow among the dead soldiers in the overhead fixture. Unwashed dishes were stacked in the sink. Mixed with the odor of grease was the faint odor of an overflowing garbage pail. A yellow-striped cat stalked the kitchen counter sniffing for scraps.

Paulette's mother, Delilah, stood at the stove, frying bacon and eggs.

"Want something to eat?" Delilah forked a slice of bacon out of the pan and laid it on a plate. The afternoon was nearly gone, but she still wore pajamas, slippers, and a ragged sweater. Her short gray hair stood up like quills on a porcupine. Within her reach on the kitchen shelf was a half-filled highball glass.

"Not yet, thanks." The thought of runny yellow egg yolk made Hannah want to gag, but Delilah sounded cheerful and unapologetic.

"There might be coffee left over from when Paulette made it this morning." Delilah said.

Hannah plugged in the percolator and found a clean mug on the drainboard. "School's out. Where is she?"

"Some FBI agent called about 2 o'clock. Wanted to talk to her, so I left a message at school. She drove the pickup to meet him as soon as classes were over." Delilah slid a spatula under the egg and laid it atop the bacon, then refreshed her drink with a splash of vodka.

Paulette had become Hannah's best friend in grade school, but it took a year or so before Hannah realized why she was hardly ever invited into the Merricks' house: Paulette was ashamed of her mother. When Beau drove Hannah to pick up Paulette for a game or sleepover, Paulette slipped quickly out her front door and nearly ran for the car, time enough to allow Delilah only a wave or brief hello. If Delilah brought Paulette's forgotten textbook or brown bag lunch to the classroom, Paulette kept her head down, cringing at her mother's unkempt clothes and messy hair.

But Hannah knew that Delilah, years ago, had been a champion tennis player. One of the highlights of her amateur career had been a win against the famed Alice Marble at the US Championships in the 1930s.

Sitting down at the table, Delilah said, "Make yourself some toast and come talk to me."

"Not right now, Mrs. Merrick. I'm talked out." Despite eight hours' sleep, last night's events threatened to break her into bits.

Delilah slapped her cheek with her palm. "Sorry. I'm not much of one for tact these days." Ice clinked in her glass as she gulped down a swallow. "You got a boyfriend?"

"Sort of. I mean, not really."

"What happened? He dump you?" Delilah's brown eyes glinted with congenial curiosity.

Hannah shrugged. "I've gotten myself in a lot of trouble, which makes it hard. On boyfriends."

"I can understand that." Delilah spread strawberry jam on her toast using broad knife strokes. "My preference for liquor has had the same effect on potential husbands. Not many candidates knocking on my door these days."

Boomer, who'd gone to high school with Alonzo, had told Hannah that when Delilah was young, she'd married her coach. Delray Merrick was an ambitious and driven opportunist who'd latched onto Delilah just as her tennis career was gaining momentum. He pushed her relentlessly—even after Alonzo and Paulette were born—to succeed on the professional tournament circuit. But Delilah hadn't possessed that last bit of talent necessary to mount the top tier like Marble or Althea Gibson. In the face of his wife's failure, Delray'd become abusive.

"Why don't you stop drinking?" Hannah poured the warm coffee and stirred in a spoonful of sugar.

Delilah's mouth twisted in a half smile. "Drinking keeps me entertained, and it's much more satisfying than kowtowing to some asshole man who thinks he's king of the castle." The yellow cat nosed among the dirty dishes, rump in the air and front paws in the sink. If this house were a castle, then Buckingham Palace was the Kingdom of Heaven.

"Paulette says you're going to be staying with us for awhile," Delilah said.

Hannah realized she needed to make nice if she were going to impose on the Merricks. "That's right," she said. "Thanks for taking me in. I can give you money to help with groceries." *Until I run out,* Hannah thought

"Call me Delilah, and don't worry about it. I've got alimony, and in the summer, I teach tennis at the country club." She rotated her glass on the tabletop, leaving a damp circle.

During the silence, Hannah realized the television was broadcasting unwatched in the living room. The KLZ reporter was in the midst of updating the names of the local and prominent crash victims, one of whom was Dr. Harold Sandstead, top health expert in Eisenhower's administration.

Hannah cocked her head to listen to the news anchorman.

"Dr. Sandstead was the last person to board the doomed plane due to the late arrival of his flight from Washington, DC," the newsman said. "This was the second tragic crash in a month of a United Airlines plane out of Stapleton Airfield, following the crash of Flight 406 into Medicine Bow Peak in Wyoming, killing all sixty-three persons on board. Cause of the crash has not been determined due to the inaccessible terrain."

Her stomach churned on Delilah's stale coffee. It was clear to her now what Jack's evil plan had been, and how it had gone awry. The pilot had delayed takeoff—another ten or fifteen minutes even past the time when Beau would have boarded—waiting for Sandstead. Meantime, the timer was ticking in Daisie King's luggage. When the Mainliner rose into the air, it was nearly half an hour behind schedule.

The bomb had exploded as the plane flew over the field north of Denver rather than high in the Wyoming mountains as Jack had planned.

The odor of bacon grease seemed to grow stronger as the broadcast continued. Reaching across the table, Delilah took Hannah's hand in hers, cold from the icy glass. "Don't worry, Sweetie. Paulette told me. You saved your father. That's the important thing."

Even slightly slurred, Delilah's words brought tears to Hannah's eyes. How strange, that this sad, unrepentant alcoholic was the first person to offer a measure of consolation. Everyone else had scoffed, questioned, interrogated, or condemned. Her mother, she was sure, would have done the same as Delilah—offered sympathy.

The cat jumped down from the shelf and climbed into Hannah's lap. The animal's warmth felt pleasant. At home, they hadn't had pets because Clyde suffered sneezing fits from animal hair.

The front door slammed. "Everyone decent?" Paulette called out from the hallway. "I've brought company."

"In here." Delilah wrapped the cardigan more closely around her chest.

Paulette appeared, with Rosemarie and Kenny trailing after her. "These guys asked about you at school, Hannah. They wondered if you were sick. After I finished the interview with Finch, the FBI guy, I asked them to come over."

It was an unlikely place and an unusual collection of friends, but at this moment they felt like treasure to Hannah. Tears filled her eyes.

Kenny's face was drawn with concern. "Paulette told us. I'm sorry, Babe." Hannah reached out, took his hand, and touched it to her cheek. She hadn't spoken to him for . . . what? Seventeen days and two hours, since their afterschool date at Berry's.

Rosemarie, wearing the orange and black cheer club uniform, seemed to waver between sympathy and fear, as if Hannah, who'd been close to such a tragic event, might be contagious.

Paulette unzipped her car coat. "It's not like we're at a funeral. The crash happened to other people. We're all okay, and none of our mothers, fathers, brothers or cousins was on the plane."

A lump rose in Hannah's throat. "I knew Daisie King, and *she* was killed. And I held the body of a baby, younger than the twins, in my hands." She wound the tablecloth in her fingers. "When I picked him up, his eyes were wide open, as if he were looking at me and saying, 'What happened?'"

Kenny looked stricken. He pulled up a chair, sat down beside her, and reached out to enfold her hand in his. "The crash wasn't your fault, Hannah."

In her lap, the cat began to purr, a soft, soothing vibration.

Kenny rubbed Hannah's palm with his thumb. She began to cry. Rosemarie, who'd been twisting a loose button on her coat, pulled a handkerchief from her pocket and handed it to her. "Here, it's not bad. Only used once."

Hannah dabbed her cheeks, then tucked it in her pocket.

"Maybe, possibly, Graham wasn't involved at all," Paulette said quickly. "A busted fuel line might have caused the crash, not some plot by that crazy son-of-a-bitch."

"It was no frigging accident," Delilah said. "My Alonzo is smart, and if he says Graham was looking for dynamite, you know it's true."

"We're not going to talk about this anymore," Kenny said firmly. "Do you have anything to eat? I'm starving."

"Just like Alonzo when he was your age." Delilah rubbed her cheek in concentration. "Let's see, the eggs and bread are gone. We've got hot dogs, bacon, creamed corn—that's about it. I was going to make a run to the store, but I woke up late."

Paulette looked pointedly at Delilah's glass, then stared at her mother with loathing.

"Hot dogs aren't kosher," Rosemarie said. "Or bacon."

"That's not so bad," Hannah said quickly. "We can broil weenies wrapped in bacon for us and heat up the corn for you."

Kenny wrinkled his nose in disgust. "Forget that. I'm treating all of you to pizza at Sole Mio." The Italian restaurant on Colfax was one of the only places in Denver other than Gaetano's that served pizza, the popular new Neapolitan food.

It took Delilah half an hour to brush her hair, wash her face, and dress in a skirt, even with Paulette yelling at her through the closed bedroom door to hurry up. Delilah finally emerged to see four impatient, hungry teenagers waiting.

"There." Delilah knotted a headscarf under her chin. "I hope they have wine."

28

When Hannah awoke, she saw with one open eye that Paulette's bed was already neatly made. This was the fourth day after the crash, and Hannah hadn't yet attended school. If she skipped classes again, the attendance officer would begin an investigation.

Tuesday's outing at Sole Mio had gone badly. The family restaurant was small, featuring, eight wooden tables and an open kitchen with two wide ovens. Smells of tomato sauce and oregano might have been lovely if the slightly burned smell of wood-fired pizza crust hadn't tightened Hannah's throat until she couldn't breathe.

She'd taken refuge in Kenny's car until chef Luigi slid the pies from the oven and packed them in flat white boxes. Back at the Merricks', the others gathered around the kitchen table, but Hannah hadn't been hungry.

During her isolation, Hannah had propped herself on pillows in a corner of the bed against the wall and tried to divert herself with Delilah's collection of Reader's Digest Condensed Books. Fall selections included *Marjorie Morningstar*, a novel about a naïve young woman who aspires to become an actress. Marjorie becomes entangled with a self-centered singer and composer, gives up her virginity to him, and wastes years enduring his erratic attentions before leaving him, marrying someone her parents approve of, and sinking into suburban mediocrity.

Hannah closed the book, haunted by its nightmarish feeling. Marjorie Morningstar had wanted to escape, just as Hannah dreamed of doing. Marjorie's faithless lover, Noel, was a self-delusional failure like Jack. Hannah could see herself in Marjorie, yet Hannah had been entangled in something a hundred times worse. What scathing words would the author write about her, a young woman who, even for a few short encounters, had been involved with a monstrous murderer?

The sun had just risen. She pulled the blankets more closely around her. Gazing up at the window, she studied a row of long, pointed icicles hanging from the eaves. She roused herself and unzipped her camera bag. The shutter of the Rolleiflex clicked as she sat cross-legged and shot five or six takes of the icicles, which had begun a slow, dripping thaw.

"How are you feeling?" Paulette came in naked after a shower, twisting her damp brown hair into a ponytail. "My alarm didn't go off. If we want to make first period, better hurry."

The trip to the bathroom over the cold floor left her feeling depressed and tearful. She wiped the fog from the mirror. Her birthmark seemed darker this morning, the color of dried blood. She fixated on the birthmark's tiny color variations. Finally, she stumbled back to the bedroom and pawed through her suitcase for something to wear. The few skirts and blouses she'd packed seemed to belong to another person. Time was short, so she pulled on a pleated skirt and saggy wool sweater.

"Are you ready? It's time." Paulette shouted up from the front hall.

Hannah grabbed her coat and books and clutched the stair banister. Her legs felt shaky. When she stepped out onto the sidewalk, Paulette already was waiting at the wheel of the pickup, idling in the circular driveway.

Paulette revved the engine, startling a German shepherd doing its business in the junipers. "Come on, get your sweet ass in the car!"

Panic rose in Hannah's throat. She walked unsteadily to the pickup and leaned in the open window. "Not . . . not today. I can't do it."

"You're not so bad you might swallow pills or something, are you?" Paulette was only half-joking.

"I promise, no pills, no head in the oven. Maybe I'll go to school tomorrow."

"Okay, Hannah Banana. Have a good day with my mother."

Hannah retreated to the warm, silent house. Delilah was still sleeping off last night's alcohol. In the girls' shared bedroom, Hannah extracted the exposed roll of film from her camera. She lay back on the pillow, and was nodding off to sleep again when Delilah's yellow-striped cat poked its head around the half-closed door. It jumped onto the bed and began a string of mewling complaints regarding the scarcity of food.

Hannah roused herself and went downstairs. She rummaged in the kitchen cupboards and pantry until eventually locating a sack of dry pellets in the laundry room. While she was shaking the hard bits into the animal's bowl, the wall telephone rang. Fifteen rings, maybe, but she hesitated to pick up. It was Delilah and Paulette's phone after all, not hers. After a few beats, ringing began again, so she answered.

"This is the police! I want to speak to Hannah Brightman." The caller was her brother, Boomer, his voice sending a wave of static over the line.

She laughed, and it gave her a sense of relief, that she still had the capacity for joy. His real name was Dennis, but their mother had often told the story of how Boomer, at age two, used to shout from his crib with enough vocal power to blast Beau out of the sheets. He'd been Boomer ever since. At Woodlake High, Boomer became a legendary quarterback, famous for his passing game. He'd joined the Army soon after graduation. After a tour in Korea, he was assigned to Fort Ord, California where he was whipping Army recruits into shape as a drill sergeant.

"I understand there's a hobo girl living in the neighborhood, no home, carrying all her worldly goods in a burlap sack," Boomer said.

"Get with it, you hopeless oaf." She propped her elbows on the counter. "Women aren't hobos, we're wo-bos." A brief lightness crept over her. Boomer had always been able to make her feel better. "How'd you know to call here?"

"Alonzo. He called to brief me, but when I tried to get ahold of Dad, no one answered the phone. Wait a minute, it's 7:30 there. Why aren't you in school?"

"I can't face it, not now, maybe never. Does the US Army have jobs for seventeen-year-old girls with no high school diploma?"

"There might be ironing in the base laundry or washing dishes at the officers' club. Both have great potential for advancement," he said.

The beginnings of either a laugh or a sob lodged in her throat. "I'm not feeling so great, Boomer."

"What's up, kiddo? You saved Dad's life." His voice thickened with emotion. "For that, Clyde and I owe you our eternal gratitude."

Her momentary rush of happiness ebbed, and she felt tendrils of fear wrap around her again. "That's nice of you to say, but I'm scared all the time, and my dreams are something out of a horror movie. If I'm so great, why I can't go anywhere without falling to pieces? What's happening to me?"

He fell silent. The cat's sharp teeth crunched on the pellets.

"I wish I was there to give you a big hug, Kiddo, because I know exactly how you feel." He sounded unspeakably sad. "It happened to me in '51 after Heartbreak Ridge. I couldn't eat or sleep, and believe it or not, I cried a lot. What you're going through is called shell shock."

"How could I have shell shock? I wasn't there when the plane crashed. I didn't see any shells fired from cannons or dropped from the sky."

"You saw things, same as I did on the battlefield. Landscape scraped to the bone, equipment twisted and shattered. People . . . people torn apart, burned. You can't experience such terrible things and not suffer."

A hard rain of tears dripped down her cheeks, sorrow, but also a tremor of relief. "No one else has understood, not the FBI, Dad, or my friends, but you did, Booms."

"It's lonely, Kiddo, I know. If you want my advice, I'll give it to you, for what it's worth."

"I'm listening."

"First, get Dad to call the school and tell the counselor what's going on. Set up home study or something."

"Are you kidding? He kicked me out. We aren't even speaking." She waited a moment until the lump in her throat subsided. "I thought you were going to say come to Monterey, California and lie on a beach towel for a year."

"Smart-ass," Boomer said. "What worked for me after Korea was tackling one thing a day, a hard but doable task, then listing it in a notebook. I'd go to a movie, or walk a mile at sunrise, or visit the Army hospital and chat with a patient."

"I don't know. Maybe. I guess it's better than the state crazy farm."

He chuckled. "Call me doctor."

***

Hannah took Boomer's advice and walked a mile around the lake at Crown Hill Cemetery. Cold air pinched her face, but the intense blue sky seemed to suck away some of her depression. It was a weekday, and the only people she passed were a couple of gray-haired men, one pushing the other in a wheelchair.

Back at the Merricks', she scooped up the *Rocky* from the lawn. When she stepped inside, the scent of fresh coffee greeted her like a reward for her effort.

"In here. I'm cooking pancakes."

Hannah peered into the kitchen, surprised to see Delilah at the stove. She wore a soiled bathrobe and ragged slippers, same as always, but her hair was slicked back as if she were ready for the tennis court.

"You were up and about early, so I thought we might as well eat a nourishing breakfast. That's what my ex-husband used to say, a nourishing breakfast." Delilah flipped a pancake with the spatula, landing it neatly in the pan. "Not that he was necessarily wrong."

Hannah poured herself a cup of coffee. "I walked around the lake," she said absently, not looking up from the newspaper. "You can come with me tomorrow if you want to."

"The snow has to melt and the trees get leaves before I exercise," Delilah said. "Any news in the *Rocky*?"

The cup trembled in Hannah's fingers. "United Airlines and the Civil Aeronautics Board announced they're putting the Mainliner back together. They're taking the wreckage to an empty warehouse and assembling the pieces. It's supposed to tell them where in the plane the explosion happened."

29

Midafternoon, Grimwalt called. "Hannah, I need to talk to you."

After her long distance call from Boomer, Hannah'd been determined to catch up on the stack of neglected homework Paulette had brought her yesterday from school. The American history text and her notebook lay on the kitchen table, open to a chapter on the Articles of Confederation.

At the sound of Grimwalt's voice, she penciled NO in large letters on blank notebook page. "I'm not telling you diddly-squat." It felt good to throw the request back in his face.

"It's vitally important that we meet."

"I bet. Call my father."

"He's out of town and not responding to my messages." A cacophony of rough voices and metallic pounding at Grimwalt's end of the line nearly drowned out his voice.

"Where are you?" Hannah asked.

"I'm at a warehouse out near Stapleton."

"Oh, my God, you're at the place where they're putting it back together?" For a moment, memories of the crash site blotted out the kitchen, Delilah's cat, and a dying ivy plant on the window sill. Her heart pounded against her breastbone.

"How did you know about that?"

Even over the phone line, she felt his anger. She took a deep breath. "It was on Page One of this morning's *Rocky*, Mr. FBI."

"Fuck. The Civil Aeronautics Board didn't clear it with me before releasing that information."

"Anyway, I'm not coming. I've had enough." The words came out louder than she'd intended, but it felt good.

Grimwalt ignored her refusal. "United and the CAB are getting the operation set up, bringing in pieces of the Mainliner and its contents. I need you to identify something."

She wound the black telephone cord around her finger. "What can I tell you? The only thing I ever saw was the . . . no, I'm not coming."

"The timer is a vital piece of evidence. You're the only one who's seen it and connected it directly to Graham."

She pressed the pencil into the paper, breaking off the point. "So ask him."

"We'll be conducting another interview with him very soon, but right now, we need you."

"My father told you I wasn't saying anything. Get somebody else."

"Miss Brightwell," he said, "if you don't meet with me, I'll be forced to call in your friends—Miss Merrick and Miss Stein—for extended, in-depth interviews. See what information we can glean from them."

"You piece of garbage! You're going to manipulate and threaten my friends, even though they don't know anything. How low can you get?"

"The coroner is collecting the bodies of forty-four people. I'll do whatever's necessary to apprehend the person who did this." An undercurrent of panic tinged Grimwalt's voice. An agent under his command had committed a fatal error. The mistake certainly would cost Finch his job, but Grimwalt's position was in jeopardy as well.

She thought of Paulette's small, bare room with two blankets, one of which Paulette had used to make up Hannah's bed. Her friend had sacrificed her bedding and much more to provide Hannah with refuge. Paulette didn't deserve to be threatened and harassed on Hannah's account.

Grimwalt wasn't going to back down, she could tell. "I hate you, you and your pathetic sidekick. It was your fault. The crash could have been prevented if Finch had done his job."

"Be here before 5 o'clock." Grimwalt was taking her outburst as admission of defeat, which it was. She owed her friends, who'd been her only support when family turned her out. He sounded unrepentant as he gave her directions.

She propped her elbows on the table and pressed her fingers against her closed eyelids. What was she going to do? Her father knew the legal system. When he refused to allow her to talk to Grimwalt, he was protecting her from possible criminal charges.

The cat scratched at her leg, begging for food again. Hannah shook more dry kibble into its plastic bowl, but the cat refused the offering, instead yowling for its favorite, canned tuna. Hannah shooed the cat outside, where it clawed fruitlessly at the back door.

You had to admire the annoying animal, Hannah thought. It didn't settle for what's dumped in its bowl, but held out for the best outcome.

The clock on the wall above the sink read 3:30. A plan was forming in her mind. She dialed Kenny. He'd be home from school about now.

"Hey, Babe. Are you feeling better?" he asked.

She liked his voice, grown mostly deep, but with an occasional small break, reverting to the way she remembered him sounding in junior high.

"I'm doing okay, but could you, that is, would you drive me somewhere?"

"Umm, are we talking, like the hospital, or Lookout Mountain?"

"Don't even mention that place." The topic of Lookout Mountain made her feel nauseated, as if she were a child riding in a car on a twisty road.

"Sorry," he said, "just kidding."

"Anyway, the FBI agent called," Hannah said. "He wants me to meet him at a warehouse near Stapleton."

"Jesus, the old hangar on Cherokee Street where the plane's being put back together?"

"How did you know that?"

"My dad talked about it at dinner last night. He has a friend who owns property near there. It's actually a leftover from the days when the military operated out of Stapleton. When do you want to go?"

"As soon as you can be here."

***

Kenny parked on the street. When she climbed into the Model A, the heater was on, circulating the scent of his warm body beneath a crewneck sweater. As soon as she was beside him, she felt better, not so alone and scared.

"Hello, you." She tilted her head up to kiss his cheek.

"I've missed you, Babe." His fingers massaged the back of her neck while the engine rumbled.

She twined her fingers in his hair and pulled his head down for a better kiss, this one stretching into a long wet one with lots of tongue. His hands roved lower, inciting a surge of heat in the soft flesh between her legs.

A raucous horn blast interrupted them. Paulette roared past in her pickup, squealing the tires as she swept into the driveway. Hannah laughed and straightened up. It seemed like a long time since she'd laughed, and it felt good.

Kenny licked his lower lip and put the car in gear. As they drove, the sun sank low over the mountains and shadows lengthened. A ribbon of neon signs blinked along Colfax. Headlights of cars heading home from work formed a continuous stream across the Platte River and eastward of downtown.

The car radio played number thirty-eight on the Top 40, "Pepper Hot Baby," but Hannah grew distracted. They passed Stapleton's runways, then into an area of dark, seemingly empty warehouses.

Goose-necked lights over the rolling doors were the only illumination. The keening noise of a departing flight screamed overhead. Dread tightened her chest and restricted her breathing.

Kenny steered onto a concrete auxiliary runway and shifted to neutral. "Holy God, look at that!" Ahead of them, a truck was backing through the yawning overhead doorway of a hangar. On its flatbed trailer rested the looming tail section of the Mainliner.

At least twenty-five feet tall, it seemed eerily free of dirt or damage. The word "United" on the vertical section gleamed against the white background, and the six-digit tail number was still readable. On the lower edge of the tail, the word "Mainliner" looked heartbreakingly jaunty. What robbed Hannah's breath was the precision of the break, as if fiendish giant fingers had snapped off the steel tail from the plane's body like a matchstick.

Kenny parked in the street behind a dozen other vehicles. They climbed out, buttoning their coats against an icy wind. The truck tractor's engine growled as it slowly maneuvered the laden trailer into the open hangar.

Air swirled with the stink of airplane fuel and charred metal. Her eyes stung. With the back of her hand, she swiped away tears. Kenny swabbed his dripping nose with a handkerchief.

Inside, steel beams crisscrossed the hangar's arched ceiling. Industrial lights poured surgical illumination down onto the floor. Here, the flight's terrible autopsy was in progress: burned and twisted pieces of the fuselage. Wires. Windows, empty of glass. Seats with extruded padding.

One of several security guards, weapon in his leather duty belt, strode toward them. "This is a restricted area. Leave at once."

Behind him, the hangar hummed with activity. A crew had set up a network of steel scaffolding two stories high and nearly one hundred feet long. It resembled a whale's skeleton Hannah had once seen in a museum. Huge broken and twisted exterior parts of the plane were being attached to the scaffolding frame. Workers unrolled steel netting and wired it to the scaffolding, allowing smaller pieces of the plane to be fitted into the gruesome jigsaw.

"We're—" She was about to respond when she spotted Grimwalt, wearing a khaki jumpsuit, emerging from a small office at the far end of the hangar, its windows overlooking the work area. He hurried toward them, clipping his FBI identification badge to his breast pocket as he walked. Without his snap-brim hat, the glossy shine of his bald head reminded her even more of a trim, athletic boxer. She waved to attract his attention.

Grimwalt spoke a few words to a thin wiry man in a hard hat, then made a beeline for her. "Miss Brightman, it's past 5. I was about to send Finch to bring you in." His face was gray with fatigue. "Who's this?" He drilled Kenny with a piercing stare.

"My friend, Kenny Nilsson. He gave me a ride."

"Over forty people are dead," Grimwalt snapped. "This is no place for sightseers."

"He's not a sightseer, Mr. Grimwalt." She met his gaze with a defiant stare. "He's my friend, and he will be staying beside me."

"Okay, okay. Stick with me, young man. You wander off, I'll have you arrested." Grimwalt rubbed his swollen eyes.

They'd taken a step or two when a nerve-shattering screech of metal made Hannah cringe and cover her head with her arms. Loud voices from the reconstruction crew echoed off the lofty ceiling. The truck trailer, loaded with the wrecked tail section, had hit the corrugated metal wall of the hangar while it was backing in. Grimwalt spewed a flood of profanity. The foreman in a hard hat ran to join him, and the two men crossed the hangar to resolve the disruption.

After a heated argument with the crew, the truck driver climbed into the cab and realigned the trailer, backing it into place alongside the skeletal support structure. Hannah trembled as she watched, thinking of the terrible force that had blown the airplane to bits.

When Grimwalt returned, he signaled Kenny and Hannah to follow him down an aisle alongside the scaffolding. Across the aisle opposite the plane reconstruction, crews had erected row upon row of fenced-off areas resembling animal pens designed to store and categorize debris. Some already contained blackened shards of metal, plastic, glass, clothing, shredded upholstery, even a single shoe.

Each piece was a story with a heartbreaking shape. After a quick glance, Hannah refused to look at them, instead staring straight ahead at Grimwalt's jumpsuit collar. When they reached the hangar's far corner, he navigated a path between the debris enclosures and stopped in front of one containing two pieces.

"Do these look familiar? Don't touch," Grimwalt said.

She dropped to her knees on the cold concrete floor, Grimwalt and Kenny looming over her. Two pieces of the timer lay there, a plastic knob and shard of white plastic, the number 40 printed on it in black letters.

"I don't know," she said.

"What do you mean, you little liar?" Grimwalt grasped her arm and jerked Hannah to her feet.

"Just a darned minute." Kenny stepped between them.

"I don't know," she said again.

The flesh covering Grimwalt's bald head turned fiery red. "You bought the timer that Graham exchanged for a different model. The two timers look virtually the same except for the number, and you're denying you saw it?"

"I told my father everything, and he relayed it to you. I have nothing more to say." She rubbed the spot where his nails had pressed into her skin.

Grimwalt's lip lifted in a snarl.

Hannah gathered herself, straightening her spine, her gaze boring into his eyes. For the first time, she wasn't afraid of him. "I did exactly what you asked me to. I looked at some pieces."

"Wait until I get your friends in here," he said. "You'll be sorry."

"They don't know anything and I don't know anything. You'd be wasting your time," she said.

Kenny straightened to his full height, taller than Grimwalt and muscled from his years on the hockey circuit. "Back off, mister. She's not your dog to kick around. Get Graham in here. Ask that son-of-a-bitch about those pieces." His usual sunny manner had turned dark, his broad shoulders tense and his jaw working with emotion. His big hand clasped hers and tugged her toward the wide entrance door.

The deafening blast of a warning horn echoed in the huge space, making them pause. A crew chief signaled, and the crane's great motor keened. Metal groaned as a thick steel cable winched the metal hulk of the plane's tail off the trailer toward the scaffold.

Grimwalt hurried to catch up with them. "Don't go, not yet," he shouted over the noise.

Shoulders raised to ward off Grimwalt, Kenny hurried on, sheltering Hannah in front of him. They'd reached the wide overhead door when the crane stopped. Voices rose over the rumble of the tractor truck's engine as the foreman and crew conferred.

"I'm sorry, I apologize, Hannah." Grimwalt arrived, out of breath. "I haven't slept for forty-eight hours. There's something else we need very badly. Tests have confirmed dynamite was used to blow up the plane, but we're at a dead end. Where'd the bomber get it? Agents have called all over—Denver, Colorado Springs, San Luis Valley, Western Slope—even neighboring states, to businesses that sell explosives. None have records of a sale big enough to destroy a four-engine plane."

"What about the Smalldones?" It seemed obvious to Hannah. "Have you questioned them?"

"We've interviewed several members of the family, and all of them told essentially the same story—they wanted nothing to do with Jack Graham. They thought he was a nut case," Grimwalt said. "Do you recall anything—a trip Graham might have made, a contact he mentioned—that would help us? At this point, it's a very large hole in our case."

Thinking about her time with Jack was like poking her nose into a garbage can. She wanted to clap the lid back on.

The warning horn blared again. The crane began lowering the tail slowly onto the support frame. It was an odd moment, as if the

Mainliner were knitting back together. What row had Daisie King been sitting in when the bomb detonated? Was the baby sleeping in his mother's arms?

Against her better judgment, Hannah closed her eyes and focused on each of her encounters with Jack, searching for some scrap of information. He'd never breathed a word about buying explosives in Denver or anywhere else. Yet there was a memory . . .

Beside her, Kenny moved restlessly. She opened her mouth to share with Grimwalt what she was thinking, then pressed her lips tightly together.

"What? Tell me," the agent demanded.

Instead, Hannah tugged Kenny with her across the remaining length of the warehouse and through the yawning overhead door.

"Wait, let's talk," Grimwalt called. "We can work this out."

When they were close to the Model A, out of Grimwalt's earshot, she leaned against Kenny's shoulder.

"What is it?" he asked.

"Be quiet." She blocked out the stink of the warehouse, and thought instead of her only visit to Graham's house: smells of diapers, Lucy's cigarettes, Daisie's potpourri. Hannah rubbed her forehead, in an effort to recover the memory. Daisie and Lucy had dressed up for their dinner out. Why did they need a babysitter? Jack was out of town, that was it! What was it that his mother had said?

"You're not going to tell him anything, are you?" Kenny whispered, his lips close to her ear. "He'll put you in jail."

"Shhh." Hannah could see Daisie in her mind, the small woman with a hard face in a soft silk silk dress. Jack, Daisie had said, was away, performing maintenance at her late husband's ranch.

Near Kremmling.

Hannah felt her legs shaking. *Careful, careful.* She held tightly to Kenny's arm to keep from collapsing.

Leaning close to his ear, she said in a tense whisper, "I'm going to tell you something, between us. When you're sure you understand all of it, I'll go to the car. You'll then relay that information to Grimwalt."

"No, no, please, Babe!" Kenny wiped a sheen of sweat off his forehead.

"It's okay. They can't use it in court. It's hearsay." Hannah kissed him on the cheek, then began talking in a low voice.

A few minutes later, she climbed into the Model A. In the cold darkness, she slid her hands up the sleeves of her coat. Every minute or two, she peered in the rearview mirror to see Kenny speaking to an agitated Grimwalt. Shouting pierced the air. Once, the agent stepped toward the car, but Kenny thrust out an arm to stop him.

Finally, she heard Kenny's quick footsteps. The Model A's door opened, allowing in the smell of exhaust from the trailer truck. Kenny slid behind the wheel.

"Well?" She said, and held her breath.

He grinned and gave her a long kiss, full of desire and satisfaction. "It's done. I told it just the way you said. He hurried off to contact Finch and put a team on it."

30

Jack flexed his cold fingers. It was frigid down here in Daisie's basement apartment. Even the thick carpet his mother had installed did little to keep the place warm. No one was staying here now that Gretchen had returned to Alaska, so he'd turned off the heat to save money.

It was nearly dawn. Joists of the floor above him creaked. In front of him on his mother's drop-front desk lay the paperwork for the flight insurance he'd bought at the airport.

He needed to forge his mother's signature. Catching sight of Hannah that night at Stapleton had rattled him so badly he'd bundled the unsigned insurance forms into his overcoat pocket and hotfooted it to the parking lot.

Taking the cap off the pen, he took a few practice tries on a piece of scrap paper. The signature had to be perfect. The three policies, one for $37,500, the other two for $16,000, would set him up in the car dealership, with plenty of spare cash.

This wouldn't be an easy job. Daisie'd been meticulous about her signature, writing cursive with carefully formed letters and evenly spaced words. You're no stranger to forgery, he told himself. He'd been only nineteen when he wrote those forty checks on the account of the auto parts store where he worked. The checks had carried excellent matches for the boss's signature. The fraud detective had told him so.

But tonight his hand trembled as he signed her name on the bottom of the first policy. Forming the letters of his dead mother's name gave him an eerie feeling, as if he were Daisie, approaching the last thirty minutes of life, unaware she was about to be blown to bits. He held his breath for what seemed a long time, then picked up the pen again. The second and third attempts looked pretty good.

Jack slipped them into a folder in the low filing cabinet next to her desk. If anyone asked, he'd claim that's where he'd tucked them away when he and Lucy returned from the airport. As if he'd had no reason to think his mother was going to die.

"What are you doing down here?"

He slammed the file cabinet drawer, rocking the china figurines Daisie had arranged on top.

It was Lucy, a cigarette between her fingers and pink rollers in her hair. "It's 5 a.m., and you haven't been to bed." She held the cigarette between her lips and tightened the bathrobe sash around her waist.

"I wasn't sleepy," he said. "The mattress is too hard. It gives me a backache."

"Before the accident, you thought the mattress was fine, but you've barely slept since. I'm afraid you'll fall asleep at the wheel on the way to church."

Her words contained an annoying whiny tone that made his palms itch to slap her face. "Go make coffee and stop bothering me." He sank down into Daisie's red leather chair, eyes wide and stinging with fatigue. The days since the crash had stretched out as if they were years.

The FBI'd interviewed him twice this week. The pile of horseshit he'd fed them appeared to have gone down well. Still, he had a problem.

Several drive-bys past Hannah's house hadn't netted any sign of her or her VW. Yesterday, a blonde chick holding a baby had stepped out of the Brightman house and stood on the sidewalk, eyeballing his progress until he'd turned left at the end of the block. He couldn't take chances on having the woman report him to law enforcement. He had also failed to spot Hannah's car at the high school parking lot and on cruises through Berry's Drive-In.

His toes were numb from the cold, so he snapped off the lights in the apartment and went upstairs to take a shower. As he passed Lucy in the kitchen, she narrowed her eyes, as if she knew everything. Jack felt a cramp in his gut.

The shower's hot water pelting his back, which usually helped relax him, didn't do the trick this morning. Finally, he stepped out and took his straight razor from the cabinet. The razor was one of the few things he still had of his father's. One of the FBI rats—the older one—was about the same age his father would be now.

He tested the razor's blade with his thumb found it to be sufficiently sharp. As he scraped the stubble from his cheeks and neck, worries continued to nag at him. If the Feebs got even a hint about the purchase of the timer, there'd be trouble, but he could claim he knew nothing about the purchase and blame it on Hannah. It might work.

The more dangerous possibility involved the dynamite. He'd bought the TNT from Brinker's Hardware. The store in Kremmling was perfect, off the beaten track, and Jack was pretty sure Brinker conducted a lively business selling dynamite under the counter to criminals and underworld types. The old guy wasn't likely to spill his guts to law enforcement.

Thing was, after he visited Brinker's, he'd returned home to find Hannah in the house. He'd been startled, and began babbling about having just returned from a trip to Daisie's ranch at Toponas, which was a lie. But he seemed to recall telling her he'd stopped overnight in Fraser. Would she remember? He couldn't take a chance.

She'd slipped by him at Red Rocks. Now he had to complete the job.

He finished shaving and folded the razor's bone handle over the blade. In the bedroom, he put on a suit while Lucy finished coaxing Serena into a jumper and blouse. Jack selected a necktie. Albert began to cry, the stink signaling that he needed his diaper changed.

Lucy, her hair still wound in rollers, struggled to zip her church dress.

"Fasten this," she told Jack, turning her back to him.

Tension made his hands clumsy, and the zipper caught in lace at the top of her slip.

"For goodness sake, you're no help. Now I have to fix my hair *and* find something to wear. I don't suppose you'll lower yourself to change the baby, will you?"

The familiar pain blossomed over his eyebrow. He stroked his forehead, but then felt his thoughts click, like a key turning in a well-oiled lock.

"It's okay, Sweetheart. You stay home, I'll go to church, then stop by Hertz on the way home, tell them I'll be back on the job tomorrow."

He settled the knot on his tie and buttoned his jacket. On the way out, he stopped in the bathroom to run his hand over his hair. The razor slid easily into his suit pocket.

***

When he arrived at the church parking lot, it was only half full. He'd driven his nondescript sedan rather than Daisie's newer Buick; the older car was less noticeable. He pulled into a space in the middle of a row facing the entrance. From this vantage point, he took a quick look. Hannah's VW wasn't in the lot. He sank lower in the seat, scanning the passengers as each car arrived.

Hannah'd attended this service for years. The first time Lucy had brought Jack to Woodlake Methodist, he hadn't paid any particular attention to Hannah; she might've been a sophomore then, but he did remember the older brother, a big guy in an Army uniform. He hadn't seen the brother again, but the rest of the family still sat in the same spot, several rows ahead of them, every Sunday.

Cars approached the church, parking on the street, wheeling into the lot. Carillon bells rang, signaling services were beginning.

He felt the familiar throbbing pain over his eyebrow. The little bitch wasn't coming.

His hand was about to turn the ignition key when a beater of a pickup bounced over a pothole, then pulled up in front. There they were, the two of them; the tall, scrawny chick at the wheel, and the small one with the shaggy haircut in the passenger seat. Jack hunched lower. It would blow his plan to hell if Hannah saw him while she still had a chance to get away.

31

In front of the church, Paulette shifted into neutral. "You're sure you don't want me to come along? This could give him another shot at you."

Hannah straightened the collar of her gray wool suit. She avoided scanning the crowd but kept gaze straight forward, as if she were sighting through a camera lens. "Nothing is going to happen with two hundred people around."

A week had passed since she and Kenny'd met Grimwalt at the hangar. The *Post* and *Rocky* had reported that workers were laboring feverishly over reconstruction of the Mainliner, and just days ago, Ike had been released from Fitzsimons Army Hospital. On TV, the president, surrounded by photographers, had waved to onlookers as he strode to a waiting car.

There had been news stories detailing the reconstruction of the plane. Achingly sad background details about the victims had also received many lines of print: the fourteen-year veteran United Airlines pilot; a grandmother traveling to Portland to visit her daughter and grandchildren; an Army officer on his way to a new posting. Also in the press were accounts of close calls, such as an up-and-coming actress who'd come down with an attack of stomach flu minutes before she was scheduled to board and had sought medical attention instead.

Hannah hadn't returned to school. She she felt strangely removed from the dramas, mean gossip, and class assignments. Who cared about author George Eliot's whey-faced Victorian heroines compared to the terrible dreams, guilt, and flashbacks she was experiencing?

All this, but not one word about the arrest of Jack Graham.

"Here at the church, I really miss Dad and the twins." Hannah's voice trembled. This was one of those times when alienation from family—people she'd lived with, played with, fought with, and loved—seemed to pull at her heart. "I want to see them, tell Dad I'm okay."

"And what will Nancy, the blonde bombshell say about that?" With a look of horror, Paulette clapped her hand over her mouth. "Oh, God, sorry I mentioned the word b.o.m.b. Me and my big fat trap. Anyway, I'll be back to pick you up, after."

Hannah stepped out, and the pickup pulled away, spewing smelly exhaust from its rusty tailpipe. She raised her gloved hand, about to signal Paulette to come back, then dropped it at her side.

She hurried up the sidewalk. A couple of handymen in overalls were stringing Christmas lights on the thick green junipers and around the tree trunks. The terrible poignancy of their work, after Jack's lie about the timer, made celebratory lights seem repulsive.

Before she opened the church's tall double doors, she stopped to wiggle her feet more firmly into the heels. The shoes and a black felt beret covering her pixie haircut were items Delilah had dug from her closet last night. Both were dusty and looked like the 1930s, but Hannah hadn't wanted to dismiss Delilah's offering of a church outfit. Dressy clothes hadn't been Hannah's priority when she threw things into a single suitcase and moved to the Merricks'. She couldn't be choosey.

Inside, latecomers crowded the lobby as they made their way into the sanctuary. Organ pipes trumpeted the opening notes of the processional, and the choir gathered in a swirl of blue robes and gold satin stoles.

Hannah slipped into a pew in the last row as churchgoers sang her favorite hymn, "Here I Am." This spot was safer, her back to the wall with a good view on all sides.

She checked the congregation. Stu Hinkle sat up front with his brother. Between the passing line of choristers, she caught sight of Beau and Nancy standing in their customary spot, sharing a hymnal.

During the nearly two weeks since the crash, Beau hadn't called Hannah or written a letter. Calls to his office phone had gone unanswered. What did his silence mean? She'd speculated about it repeatedly. Was he angry at her? Ashamed he'd kicked her out?

Her father and Nancy stood close, heads tilted toward each other, as though they were perfectly comfortable being a couple with twins stashed in the nursery, as if Hannah and her older brothers had never existed.

A hot, painful ache spread through her chest. Her feeling of loss, which had eased as she settled into life at the Merricks', arose again, until it was nearly unbearable. Tears blurred her surroundings.

When her vision cleared, she caught sight of Jack standing at the sanctuary entrance.

Her heart thumped against her chest as if clamoring to escape. She ducked her head and crouched behind the heavyset woman alongside her. Jack hesitated, chin lifted as he searched the crowd, before he slid into a pew directly across the main aisle.

Had he seen her? Getting up and leaving now would only reveal her presence, assuming he hadn't already spotted her. The service crawled along, through the readings from the Old and New Testaments and the recitation of the Psalm.

Reverend Kellems' interminable sermon was inspired by First Samuel: the Lord calls to the prophet saying, "Here I am." The passage seemed like a finger pointing directly at her as she huddled behind the fat woman, who began to eye her warily. Finally, the service drew to a close. Through the crowd, Hannah peered across at the spot where Jack had been sitting, but it was empty.

It would be foolish to assume that he'd left, or that he hadn't seen her. Rather than attempting to slip unnoticed through the lobby, she joined her father and Nancy. Beau's eyes brightened. Nancy, however, turned her head away with a muttered hello.

"How are things going?" Beau reached out to hug her. His strong arm made Hannah want to lean closer, rest against his shoulder. Instead, she pulled away.

"Why haven't you called? I tried to get ahold of you." The sting of his rejection hurt.

"I . . . things have been difficult. With Nancy," he said in an undertone. To his credit, he looked ashamed, cheeks reddening under his tan.

Hannah clutched his arm. "Dad, I saw him. He was sitting in the back row."

"What? A mass murder suspect, and he dares to show up in church? What the hell is the FBI doing? It's unbelievable he hasn't been arrested yet." A foot taller than Hannah, Beau stretched his neck to survey the thinning crowd. "There's no sign of him now."

"I'd feel safer if you'd walk with me to the front of the church. Paulette's picking me up."

Nancy snapped her head around to glare at Beau, but he ignored her. "Of course. We have to get the kids from the nursery first. The boys will be glad to see you."

The three of them took the back stairs to the basement. Hannah recalled the Sunday she'd seen Jack when he came to pick up Albert and Serena—could it have been less than a month ago?

Now, Jasper grinned from a playpen when he spotted Hannah, displaying a single tooth, new since she'd last seen him. He spread his arms toward her, saying, "Up, up!" but Nancy moved in front of Hannah to take him in her arms.

For an instant, the persistent knot of fear in Hannah chest was overshadowed by anger at her stepmother. To annoy her, Hannah leaned across Nancy's shoulder and tickled Jasper's nose, making him laugh. Marcus, however, sat alone in the playpen, fussing and rubbing his eyes.

"He's tired, Beau. Let's get them home." Nancy fixed Beau with a wintery stare. She handed Jasper to Beau, then hefted Marcus in one arm and a diaper bag in the other. She stalked ahead of them up the stairs, not looking back.

As they walked to the front lobby, Hannah's eyes roved constantly—into the youth minister's office, where a repairman was fixing the radiator, and the church library, where a couple browsed the shelves. Sticking close to her father's side, she watched the intersecting corridors and between the storage cabinets adjacent to the chapel.

As they descended the front steps, Hannah saw no sign of Jack, either among a cluster of adults drifting from the church or several waiting in parked cars. The handymen had apparently finished installing the Christmas lights.

"Where's Paulette?" Beau asked. "I don't see the infamous pickup truck. Did she forget?"

Hannah shifted from one foot to the other in the ill-fitting heels. "She said she'd be here as soon as the service was over."

Jasper sucked his fist. Marcus began to cry. Nancy jiggled Marcus to quiet him "Beau, it's past the boys' lunchtime, and they're hungry. We've got to leave."

"Hannah, come with us," Beau said. "I can drop you off." He'd hardly finished speaking when Jasper joined the unhappy baby chorus.

The air between Beau and Nancy rippled with anger. The twins seemed to feed each other's hunger, or sleepiness, or whatever it was. Jasper rained snot onto the sleeve of Beau's suit.

"It's okay, Dad, go ahead. Paulette should be here any minute." The last thing she wanted to do was increase the bitterness between them.

After they had disappeared around back to the parking lot, the boys still crying, quiet settled on the church grounds and surrounding neighborhood. A few blocks away, a dog howled. The stupid beret itched, so she plucked it off her head and stuffed it into her coat pocket.

No sign of Paulette. Maybe something had happened to the truck. She hesitated, looked around, then walked back toward the church. The youth minister's office had been open; she could use the telephone there to call the Merricks'.

With only a few remaining steps to the door, Jack stepped out from an alcove.

"Hello, Hannah. Sorry we didn't have a chance to talk after the service." He was dressed neatly in suit, tie, and topcoat, but his face was thin, almost skeletal, his eyes surrounded by darkened circles of flesh.

"Get away from me, you bastard, you murderer!" Her legs wobbled in the borrowed heels.

"Is that any way to talk to a friend? We're going to take a ride together. Maybe to Lookout Mountain. Would you like that?"

She turned to run, but he grasped her bicep, squeezing it in a painful grip. A scream died in her throat when his other hand emerged from his coat pocket holding a straight razor, its honed steel edge glittering.

"I wouldn't call for help if I were you." The cold blade caressed the unmarked side of her face. "It would be a shame if I had to slit your throat."

"Please Jack, you don't want to do this. Nobody knows but us, and I swear I won't tell." She hated the sound of her groveling, awarding him power over her as if she were a helpless prisoner.

"I'm sure you won't." He hesitated for a second, then seemed to gather himself. "Walk ahead of me. We're going to the right, behind the old Sunday school building."

She couldn't run, not in these stupid shoes. Maybe, once they were at his car, she could ditch the shoes and jump out. Think about your brother, she told herself. Boomer is brave. He'd rescued another soldier in Korea while they were under heavy fire. But she wasn't brave. Her legs wobbled, and she felt pressure, as if she might pee herself.

Jack shook her, so roughly her head flopped like a dying flower on a stem. He dragged her, stumbling at his side, around the sagging building to a field of dead, frozen weeds where a nondescript sedan was parked. They circled to the passenger side. "Open the door and get in," he hissed.

She fumbled with handle. "I can't; it's stuck and my hand is shaking." Tears, only partially fake, filled her eyes.

With one hand Jack leaned over to twist the chrome handle, while the other holding the razor dropped toward his side.

During that second of inattention, Finch rose behind the trunk of the car, lunged for Jack, and wrenched the razor away. Four other agents raced from the cover of the outbuilding, leaped on Jack and bore him to the ground pressing his cheek into the dead weeds and cuffing hands behinds his back.

"Are you all right, Miss?" One of the agents touched her shoulder.

Hannah nodded, recognizing him as the repairman fiddling with the heater outside the youth minister's office.

Grimwalt appeared and stood over Jack's prone body, eyes glittering with satisfaction. "John Gilbert Graham, you're under arrest for the murder of Daisie King." Agents pulled Jack to his feet, his overcoat covered with mud and dead grass. One cheek dripped blood from a scratch. He was led away, an agent on either side grasping his arms.

"Thank you, Hannah." Grimwalt stooped to pick up the razor with a gloved hand. "You did well."

"You were pretty damned slow," she said.

32

The photographs she'd taken from Paulette's bedroom window a week ago made Hannah a little dizzy—a row of sharp pointed icicles hanging from the eaves, glittering like daggers in the early morning sun. Jack's straight razor had glittered, not with the icicles' translucence, but with a similar unforgiving light.

She'd just picked up the pictures from Rexall Drugs, and they'd turned out better than she expected.

He's in jail, she reminded herself; he's behind bars, locked up. The FBI had released no word after detaining Jack Sunday, but a frenzied burst of television and radio news Monday morning announced the arrest of Jack Gilbert Graham after hours of intensive interrogation. Today, probably within the next hour, he was scheduled to be ushed into a courtroom for arraignment, his wrists locked in handcuffs.

Hannah'd screamed in her sleep last night, awakening both her and Paulette and leaving a frightening tremor of disruption in the thick darkness. From the other bed came the rasp of Paulette's breathing as it slowly returned to normal.

"I'm sorry," Paulette had whispered. "It was my fault. I decided to take a shortcut, but Wadsworth was closed. There was a detour. All the traffic lights seemed to be red. I'm a crap friend. A shitty fuckup."

Hannah couldn't remember when Paulette, so stoic in the face of her family's dysfunction, had come this close to breaking down. Reaching across to the other bed, Hannah touched Paulette's cold cheek. "You tried your best, but it wasn't your fault—it was Jack's."

Now, parked in the VW across from the drugstore, Hannah stuffed the photos back in the yellow envelope and started the engine, heading for the auto repair shop. She'd disrupted the Merrick household for long enough, depending on Paulette to drive her around town.

Years ago, when he'd lived at home, Boomer used a small body shop a few blocks away on Colfax. She dodged in and out of the morning traffic and bumped over a pothole into the dark, cluttered garage. Richie, the owner, squatted beside a Chevy sedan, buffing the fender. The place smelled of turpentine and evil-smelling cigars he smoked on his lunch hour.

Climbing to his feet, Richie recognized her right away, probably because of her birthmark. "Miss Brightman, what did you do to this pretty girl?" He patted the VW's dented passenger door. It took her a moment to realize he was looking at the VW, not at her.

"I had a disagreement with a moving van." It was easier to tell the casual lie about Jack's first attempt to murder her now that he was in jail.

Richie said he'd get the new door, replacement chrome, and side mirror from the wrecking yard. "You leaving it here?"

"It's good enough to drive in the meantime." Hannah scribbled the Merricks' telephone number on a scrap of paper. "Call me here when you get the parts." Paying for it was something she'd figure out later.

Berry's was a few blocks away, and she hadn't eaten breakfast. The prospect of French toast with maple syrup enticed her, but when the drive-in came into view, she didn't stop. She was still truant from school. What if someone at Berry's turned her in?

Instead, she drove to a doughnut shop on Federal Boulevard, near where Beau's law office had been years ago. She often tagged along with him to work on Saturdays, and they'd stop here for one doughnut with sprinkles for her and two with chocolate icing for him.

Hannah bought a glazed and a cup of coffee and drove to Sloan's Lake, stopping in the lot a few yards from where Jack had parked Daisie's Buick that first night.

Early snow had left the grass dead and brittle. Shallow edges of the lake were still frozen, but sharp-edged chunks floated in the center where the ice had melted. She licked sticky frosting from her fingers. Jack should be entering the courtroom about now, escorted by two policemen, each gripping an elbow.

What perverse impulse had driven her to climb into Jack's car that night?

She remembered feeling trapped, as if nothing would ever change in her shitty life. The new red skating skirt had brushed her thighs in a sexy swirl, but Odessa and her clique of popular friends had whispered comments, laughing at her and turning their backs. Kenny had asked her to the Friday night dance, but attending would've subjected her to more ostracism and snide insults.

Instead, Jack had looked at her admiringly.

Her camera bag lay on the floor of the VW, and on impulse, she unzipped it and took out the Rolleiflex. Climbing out of the car, she adjusted the lens, focused, and shot a picture of the lake, then the empty asphalt lot and the log divider where Jack had parked. The click of the shutter sharpened her memory. She snapped the weathered wood of the closed snack shack, the muddy footprints on the shore bridge where she'd walked with Alonzo, the split cattails spilling their plumes like entrails.

Wind brushed her cheek, cold but refreshing. Back in the car, blood seemed to rush through her veins. The route to Lookout Mountain took her west on Forty-fourth and through Golden, then up the steep road laced with hairpin turns. She stepped on the clutch, unused to shifting on steep roads. The car slipped backward; she toggled the shifter again, the gear taking what seemed like an interminable time to engage. She came close to peeing herself before it caught

In daylight, it was difficult to spot the turnout where she and Jack had stopped that night, so she settled on one where the view seemed to fit her memory. Outside in the wind, she held the camera close to her chest and peered into the viewfinder. To the northeast, she imagined she could see the farmer's field where the Mainliner crashed. The lens caught the city, downtown towers thrusting upward, houses marching east to open land where the blue-gray plains stretched to the horizon. She shot one roll, then inserted another. This was her world, not the seductive night view of artfully lighted high-rise buildings or the glittering necklace of highways.

She'd been dazzled. He was a tall, fairly good-looking man. Worldly, she'd thought. Ambitious. True, he was married, but he was someone who dined at fashionable restaurants and mingled with the powerful Smalldone clan. The painful dreariness of her everyday life—Nancy's jealousy, her father's abandonment, Clyde and Boomer's self-centered neglect, the school kids' cruelty—seemed to have the potential to change. Color and excitement seemed close enough to touch.

Or so she'd thought.

Wasn't there a fairy tale about a girl, or was it a boy, lured by the promise of an alluring new land where life was all candy canes and chocolates? Maybe it was Hansel and Gretel plucking goodies from the walls of the witch's house.

Cold numbed the tip of her nose. She peered at the camera's counter, which showed two shots left. She climbed back in the car.

The drive took nearly forty-five minutes, down the mountain, through Woodlake, and into southwest Denver. On the radio, KIMN played "Unchained Melody" and "Autumn Leaves" from the Top 40. The VW slid into an empty spot on the street across from the Grahams' house, a boxy white stucco sitting on a dirt lot. A pile of broken concrete lay in the front yard.

On the west side, the window wells of Daisie's basement apartment rose just above ground level.

Hannah thought of the dynamite, which had been hidden somewhere on the property. Jack had crammed it into a nondescript suitcase, probably two feet by three feet, containing enough explosive power to blow apart a plane the length of a football field, scattering the wreckage for fifteen miles.

The shabby Graham house radiated a disturbing energy, as if destructive forces lurked in its stucco walls. Daisie and Jack had been boxed inside with Lucy and two toddlers, the dangerous volatility of their twisted relationship building hour by hour, day by day until its terrible power exploded, ripping and tearing to pieces forty-four innocent people.

Lucy and the two children still lived there, in an atmosphere infected with lies, scheming, hate, and physical violence. Could they recover?

Hannah stepped out of the car. The street was empty, so she stood on the asphalt and snapped a photo of the window wells peering slyly at her. One shot left. Moving closer to the house, she knelt at the edge of the road to focus on the broken concrete. Her hands shook, and she had trouble adjusting the lens opening.

When Hannah looked up, Lucy was striding across the dirt. "Get out of here! I never want to see you within a mile of this house again." She snatched a chunk of concrete from the pile and threw it at the VW, smashing the driver's window.

Hannah stumbled backward, her shoes crunching on the glass lying in the street. At the last second before opening the car door, she shot a picture of Lucy in her dark clothes, a specter against the white stucco.

33

On the last Saturday in April, Jack Graham's murder trial was in its tenth day, and Hannah felt panicked about her dress.

"A quarter turn to the left," Delilah said, twirling her forefinger. She knelt on the living room rug, a pincushion attached to her wrist, adjusting the hem of the green velvet dress.

"What if we can't get it done? Maybe he won't like it." Her watch read 3 o'clock. Kenny was picking her up at 5:30.

She'd never been to a school dance before. Kenny's invitation to the prom was her last chance for what was supposed to be a high school tradition. The event seemed far above her status in the school's pecking order. Imagining herself in a tulle-skirted dress, hair teased into a bouffant 'do, toes wedged into pumps, seemed laughable. She'd refused him at first, but the disappointment on his face touched her. He was good-looking, easy-going, and people liked him, but most of all he cared about her. She was unsure whether her feelings for him were love, but she loved making him happy.

Glancing up at Hannah from the floor, Delilah looked worried. "If you'll stop fidgeting and stand still, I can finish pinning and stitch it up." Delilah's hand was steady, and her face had lost its puffy look. In the last three months, she'd only been drunk a couple of times.

"Sorry, Delilah, I'm just feeling nervous. Twitchy."

"Relax. That boy is crazy about you. He'd like it if you wore a flour sack." One additional straight pin anchored the hem, and Delilah sat back on her heels, assessing her efforts. She'd worn the dress decades ago, when she'd been a single up-and-coming tennis star who attended fancy parties, but for twenty-five years it had been packed in an attic trunk. When Hannah despaired of scraping together money for a dress, Delilah shook this velvet number out of its tissue wrapping and offered to make alterations.

The vampy, 1940s style was completely unlike Hannah's vision of herself. Nonetheless, it felt luscious, the ankle-length skirt hugging her hips and thighs, the neckline dipping to reveal her cleavage.

She shimmied out of the dress, then handed it to Delilah, who was threading the needle on her sewing machine, set up on the kitchen table.

"Are you worried about the trial?" Delilah asked.

"It's impossible to get away from it." She rubbed her temple, feeling the rigid tension beneath her fingers. "I dream about the crash at night, read about it in the *Rocky*, in the *Post*, and in *Time* magazine. I see it on TV and listen to it on the radio. All I want is for the jury to say he's guilty. Then I'll never, ever have to hear that evil man's name again."

"Alonzo is furious at the judge for allowing photographers in the courtroom," Delilah said.

Colorado vs. Graham had earned the dubious distinction of being the first trial in the nation that allowed a pool photographer and cameramen to document the proceedings. "He says there's no way the jurors aren't secretly reading the coverage and looking for their face in the newspapers or on TV."

Hannah changed the subject. "I'm going to shower and wash my hair before Rosemarie gets here. We're going to get dressed together. Kenny and I are double dating with her and Stu Hinkle."

"That's nice." A wistful smile crossed Delilah's face, perhaps saying goodbye to any hopes Paulette would be going on dates with boys.

"You're a sweetheart, Delilah." She patted the older woman's shoulder.

***

A flurry of activity accompanied Rosemarie's arrival. Hannah had already showered and ruffled her pixie cut to dry it when her friend swept upstairs, nearly invisible behind the billowing skirt of the prom dress she carried on a hanger.

"Oh, my God, take this, while I go back down to get my overnight case." Her face was flushed, her hair still twisted into pink foam rollers. Hannah laid the dress carefully on her bed. Once Rosemarie had retrieved her case, she set up across the hall in the bathroom to brush out her lustrous dark hair and apply makeup.

Shedding her robe, Hannah stepped into panties and bra, then very carefully slid stockings up her legs, anchoring them with elastic garters. The soft velvet of her dress whispered against her skin as she shimmied into it.

Rosemarie rolled a final swipe of mascara into her eyelashes. Since the bedroom was small and Hannah occupied most of the free space, she dressed in the hallway where ample room was available to accommodate the swirling pink skirt of her formal.

In the midst of the turbulence, Paulette sat cross-legged on her bed. A book lay open on her lap, but she glanced at it only occasionally. Instead, she watched them as if she were a bird, hungry for a bit of food. Hannah had known since they were eleven or twelve that her friend wasn't interested in boys. Although whispers had circulated at school, the three friends had an unspoken understanding nothing would be said aloud about Paulette's romantic interest in women.

Hannah hiked her skirt and peered over her shoulder to assure her stocking seams were straight. In the hall mirror, she hardly recognized herself. Her pixie cut gave her an Audrey Hepburn winsomeness, and the velvet dress clung like a baby to its mother. Nonetheless, doubt threatened to dampen her joy. Who did she think she was, a disfigured girl on the sidelines of high school life, attempting to be noticed? How dare she attend the prom with a sought-after boy?

Turning slowly, she studied herself. Even considering the boost from high heels, she still seemed to have grown taller in the last few months. Her spine was straighter, shoulders back. In some ways, it seemed right. No one her age had faced what she had: saving herself and her father from being killed, helping the FBI catch a notorious mass murderer. A hundred years of experience separated her from those shallow kids.

Delilah called from below. "Hannah, Rosemarie, the boys are here!"

"Tell Stu I'll be there in a few minutes," Rosemarie said. "My hair's not right."

Hannah peered down, catching sight of the boys, who waited self-consciously in the front hall, hair trimmed, cheeks freshly shaved, outfitted in their rented tuxes. Stu, who'd been a chunky kid since grade school, tugged at the constricting cummerbund. Kenny's feet looked huge in the formal black shoes.

She ran her tongue nervously across her teeth.

As she hesitated, Paulette appeared beside her. "Have fun. Remember everything so you can tell me. I want to know it all."

"I promise," Hannah said. "And when you go to California, you'll have your turn." She reached out, and they clasped hands.

With a deep breath, Hannah took the first step down the stairs. Her feet settled into the high heels, dress clinging to her thighs. As she descended in a silly Marilyn Monroe strut, she imagined a photographer was clicking the shutter. In the hall, she swirled to give Kenny a full view, laughing at his look of stunned wonder. "Come on, you saw me in the skating skirt. I can swank it up once in awhile."

"The skating skirt had nothing on this dress." Kenny stepped close, a white florist's box in his hand. "Here's a little something." Nested in white tissue paper was a delicate green orchid, petals accented with ruby red. Kenny lifted it out and slipped the elastic band around her wrist, his fingers lingering on her bare arm. His care in choosing a flower so perfect for the dress touched her. She stood on tiptoe and kissed his neck, just below his ear, catching clean and spicy scents of soap and aftershave.

A flashbulb popped. Delilah, using Hannah's camera, took several pictures of them in various poses. Rosemarie hurried down, her full taffeta skirt swirling around her ankles, hair curled in a pageboy. After Stu pinned a gardenia corsage to her shoulder, the four of them posed together.

"We'd better go. We have reservations for dinner at the Tabor Hotel," Stu said.

Outside, Kenny's restored Model A stood in the driveway like Cinderella's pumpkin, waiting to whisk them to the ball. He'd worked on it for nearly a year, scrounging replacement parts. The newly painted tan body and black fenders gleamed like new, but when he opened the passenger door for Hannah, she noticed blankets tucked tightly over the seats.

"Sorry, the upholstery's not quite done." He ducked his head and ran his hand over his flattop. "I didn't allow enough time."

Hannah kissed him on the lips this time, their mouths warm and soft. "It's swank enough for me."

Stu, who was accustomed to the cramped interior of his VW, slipped into the back seat next to Rosemarie, sighing with of relief. "Better than a Bug, right, Hannah?"

They wheeled out of the driveway, the Model A's engine rumbling.

***

The dining room at the Tabor Hotel perched at the edge of a decorative pool. The restaurant's large windows, which dipped below the pool's water level, offered a view of the underwater lights. Hannah remembered a dinner with her family here when Chantal was alive. How old had she been? Six, maybe, or seven. Back then, she'd sat with legs pulled up underneath her to peer at silvery fish in the pool.

The four of them felt awkward in their fancy clothes. Stu's stiff shirt collar pressed against his Adam's apple; Rosemarie struggled to control the layers of her petticoats. Hannah couldn't stop glancing down every few minutes to assure her plunging neckline hadn't shifted to expose a nipple.

The waiter arrived, bowing and acting excessively polite. "Would you like soup or salad, Miss?" and "Would that be medium rare, Sir?" He nodded frequently as they ordered the cheapest entrees on the menu.

While they waited for their salads, Hannah looked up to see Odessa Stamos sailing into the dining room. She wore a yellow floor-length dress with a voluminous tulle skirt that barely fit between the tables. Her fingers fluttered at them in a halfhearted wave. Following her like a trained spaniel was her date, Jake Oliver, and two other couples.

"Is that skag going to be crowned prom queen tonight?" Stu asked. "Wasn't being homecoming queen last year enough?" His sister Natalie, an early favorite in the homecoming contest, had lost in the voting to Odessa, who circulated rumors Natalie had sneaked out of state for an abortion.

"Odessa can be a prom princess," Rosemarie said, "but she can't be prom queen, because rules don't allow her to win two crowns." She sipped her Coke. "I hear she's going to Stephens College in the fall."

"Isn't Stephens sort of a finishing school?" Hannah held her glass of ice water against her cheek to cool her birthmark. "It seems sort of last-century, learning the social graces so you can marry some rich guy."

"Two years, and you're ready to be a debutant and marry the guy with the bucks," Rosemarie said.

"Poor thing." Hannah set her glass on the table. She was only half-joking. Such a life seemed to hold no promise of excitement or surprise, like being locked in a closet of other people's expectations.

The waiter served the salads. The pool's jets sprayed water into the air, tiny drops glittering in the beam of spotlights.

"I got my final acceptance to Minnesota State," Kenny said. "The scout says I'll play hockey for the frosh team this year and move up to varsity in '57 if I'm good enough."

Hannah looked at him in surprise. "I thought you were going to play for DU and live at home. Boomer always said they have the best team in the West."

"I'm thinking it'll be nice to get away. Not from you," he said, stroking the back of her neck, "but from the same old things."

Rosemarie looked wistful. Her father opposed her going to college.

The waiter arrived with their trout and chicken, steamed vegetables and bread. After the last bites of their desserts had disappeared and dishes were cleared, Stu and Kenny conferred over the check in low voices. They fingered bills from their wallets.

At a nearby table, Hannah spotted Odessa, Jake and their companions. The homecoming queen had removed her gloves. Her hair, piled in an updo, looked as plastic and brittle as a doll's wig. Hannah felt an unexpected sadness for Odessa, who'd rejected and made fun of her, yet seemed more lost than she was, more caught in a net.

34

It was midnight when Hannah tiptoed into the house. A lamp had been left burning in the living room, but other than that, the house was dark. But not silent. Music from upstairs told her that Delilah had left the clock radio on to help her fall asleep.

Hannah tucked her corsage in the refrigerator, then went upstairs and undressed in the bathroom to avoid waking Paulette. With her high heeled shoes and the velvet dress in her arms, she moved quietly into their small shared bedroom and laid the folded clothes on the closet floor. The prospect of bed, after the strange and unexpected events that accompanied prom night, seemed like heaven. She lowered herself onto the mattress with a sigh.

"How was it?" Paulette asked.

Hannah jumped.

Paulette was tucked under the covers, yet fully awake. "Eager fans are awaiting news of the big event." Paulette's voice was light, but Hannah caught a wistful undertone.

Hannah propped her head on her arm. "I can now tell my daughter, should I ever have one, that in all my years in high school, I never attended a school dance."

"What?" Paulette said up and hugged her knees to her chest. "After all the shampooing and makeup and dress alterations and corsage, did you and Kenny have a fight?"

Hannah laughed. "We're good. Actually, I'm crazy about him. What happened was, we had dinner at the hotel—"

"Yeah, yeah, did one of you swallow a fish bone or something?"

"The dinner was fine," Hannah said. Weariness crept over her, as if she'd been awake for several days. "The boys paid the bill, and we walked out to the garage to get the car. Oh, on the way out we said hello to Odessa, wearing a skirt the size of the Hindenburg. She didn't look all that great, considering she's the former homecoming queen."

"Come on, stop making it sound like *The Odyssey* or something."

Hannah rolled her eyes. "The dinner was fine. We walked out to the parking garage to Kenny's car, but it wouldn't start."

"Oh, my God, that's classic! So, what did you do?"

"Kenny walked back to the hotel and called his dad from a pay phone. His dad got in his janitorial van and drove downtown. Kenny went out to the street to wave him down, but it took Olof nearly an hour to arrive. He'd gathered jumper cables and other repair stuff, but when he tried to fix it, nothing worked."

As Hannah thought back, she could picture how silly the four of them must have looked, decked out in their fancy clothes: she with the orchid corsage on her wrist, Rosemarie in a poufy skirt, Kenny and Stu in patent leather shoes with pointy toes. It tickled her sense of humor: There they were, clustered in a parking garage with oil spots on the floor and exhaust from other cars tainting the air while Olof Nilsson delved beneath the Model A's hood. At the time, it had seemed like the end of the world.

"This is as good as the pioneers who crossed the plains in covered wagons getting delayed by an Indian raid," Paulette said. "Then what happened?"

"Olof doesn't know. He couldn't figure it out, and they won't know what's wrong until Monday when a mechanic gets his eyes on it. Anyway, he attached a chain to the Model A's bumper and towed it behind his van."

"So, I'm assuming you couldn't see the other kids whizzing by to the prom in Dad's Caddy while you guys rode in the windowless rear of Olof's van?" Paulette's mouth twitched, and Hannah felt laughter fizz inside her.

"It's kind of mean to make fun of Kenny's dad, but it was sort of like that. He's really a sweet guy, ready to drop everything to help. Anyway, we decided to take a pass on the prom. We went to Kenny's and made popcorn. Actually, it was kind of fun. We ate popcorn and danced to the radio."

"It doesn't sound half bad." Paulette propped her chin on her clasped knees. "Maybe someday I'll dance to the radio with somebody."

The longing in her friend's voice made Hannah feel guilty. Everyone needed someone to love. The fact that Paulette liked women shouldn't keep her from having love. Not that Hannah was exactly in love with Kenny. She loved kissing him and having sneaky sex, but she wasn't sure this was exactly love. She liked him—not just for the petting and other things—but because he was one of the few truly nice people she knew. The difference between Kenny and a man like Jack Graham was as wide as a continent and deep as the Grand Canyon.

"Only three months, and we'll have saved enough money to be on our way to San Francisco. Goodbye, Denver!" Color bloomed on Paulette's pale cheeks. "We'll get a room in a boarding house at first, then an apartment with a view. The wind from the ocean will be the best air we've ever breathed."

She smiled a true smile of joy, not the usual teasing, half-cynical twitch of her lips. This had been Paulette and Hannah's plan, even back in grade school, to go to California once they graduated. Since they'd been sharing Paulette's bedroom, they—mostly Paulette—lay awake many nights talking about swimming in the ocean and riding cable cars.

"I can't wait to go to Carmel and watch Carroll Shelby drive at the Pebble Beach Road Race," Paulette said. "Maybe someone will hire me for their pit crew."

As they talked, a knot of reluctance swelled in Hannah's chest. She'd felt it before but smothered her doubts, reluctant to taint Paulette's enthusiasm.

In years past, Hannah had shared Paulette's excitement of leaving Denver, yearning for a new life, something exotic and exciting. California had seemed to offer that promise. Brooks Institute of Photography was just a few hours' drive down the coast from San Francisco, and it had the reputation as one of the best schools of its kind in the country. Hannah had imaged herself there, learning from world-renowned photographers.

Recently, however, something was holding her here in Colorado. Not Kenny. Although he'd surprised her, announcing he'd accepted an offer from Minnesota, she didn't yearn to follow him.

It was as though the strands of her life were still knitted to this place, the people and the landmarks that made her who she was. Red Rocks amphitheater, where Hannah, her mother, father, Boomer, and Clyde attended Easter Sunday sunrise services wrapped in blankets to ward off the cold. Washington Park Lake, where she'd learned how to swim. Denver Bears Stadium, where she and the boys had thrown popcorn at each other while they watched the game. She wasn't ready to leave those places, filled with the essence of her life

"What's wrong?" Paulette asked. "The silence is pretty loud."

"Aren't you afraid?" Hannah asked. "What if we don't find work or don't like it there? We can't come crawling back to Denver to work at the telephone company."

"We've been talking about it forever, and now, in the eleventh hour, you're getting cold feet?" Hannah felt the heat radiating from Paulette's body. "What the hell's going on?"

Hannah had to speak up, but how could she say it? "I'm not coming with you, Paulette." Every word that fell from her lips landed like a stone. "I'm not ready. I don't know if I'm in love or not, but that's not why I'm bailing out. Kenny won't even be in Denver; he'll be in Minnesota."

"So what's the truth? You just strung me along all this time? That's low. I guess I don't know you as well as I thought." She climbed out of bed and rummaged in a drawer for a sweater to throw around her shoulders.

"I'm a shit friend," Hannah admitted. "I should've spoken up earlier, but I didn't want to disappoint you."

"I'm going to sleep downstairs on the couch," Paulette's mouth twitched with hurt. "If you'd said something back then, however long ago that was, it wouldn't have been so bad. Now, it hurts like hell."

In all the years she'd known Paulette, Hannah'd never heard her acknowledge how painful her life had been. Backing out like this was destroying Paulette's dream of better times ahead.

"I'm sorry." Hannah crawled on her knees to the end of the bed. "It would have been wonderful to leave the snobbish kids at school, my family, the FBI, and Jack Graham—all of it—behind."

"So why aren't you coming?" Each of Paulette's words seemed laden with pain.

Her teeth sank into her lip. If only the road ahead were clear, not vague and half-obscured. "Things here aren't finished yet. I don't know what needs to happen, but I can't leave. Not until it's done."

The sight of Paulette buttoning up the sweater, as if she were about to step out into the cold, wrenched Hannah's heart. "Don't go downstairs. Stay here. I need you more than ever." She climbed off the bed and wrapped her arms around her friend. They hugged, rocking in the embrace like two football players after a game.

35

In early May, a jury deliberated for only eleven minutes—the same amount of time Flight 629 was in the air—before declaring Jack Graham guilty of murder in the death of his mother.

Chaotic months of drama had followed Jack's arrest last fall. After initially confessing to the crime, Jack had recanted, claiming he possessed no memory of signing the document in which he admitted his guilt. In the ensuing days, he'd offered jumbled and wildly unlikely scenarios of how the dynamite might have ended up in his mother's luggage.

Weeks later, he tried to commit suicide in the county jail by hanging himself with socks tied around his neck, but an alert jailer revived him. A psychiatric evaluation determined he was sane and able to participate in his defense.

His publicity-seeking defense team contributed to a circus-like atmosphere at the trial, but in the end, court-watchers barely had time to sip water from the courthouse drinking fountain before the jury came back with its verdict.

The judge had imposed a sentence of death in the gas chamber, and Jack now awaited execution in the Colorado State Penitentiary in Cañon City. Despite his insistence that he didn't want an appeal, his legal team was filing briefs with the appellate court.

It was July now, nine months since Hannah had thrown a few clothes and a hairbrush in a suitcase and moved to the Merricks'.

Tonight, after eating Paulette's Cajun version of macaroni and cheese, Hannah, Delilah, and Paulette had set up the Parcheesi board at the kitchen table. Delilah's cat darted in and out through an open window, jumping easily from the sill to the patio and back. The girls laughed and told knock-knock jokes as they shook the dice and moved the tokens.

The phone rang and Delilah answered. As she listened, her eyebrows shot up until they disappeared under her bangs.

"It's Nancy," she said, covering the mouthpiece.

Hannah put down her dice cup and took the receiver. Not more than a dozen words had passed between Hannah and her stepmother since the move. After Jack's second attempt to kill her, Hannah had stopped attending church, and had only been at her childhood home to collect the last of her clothes and documents like her birth certificate.

"What is it?" Hannah asked. "Is Dad all right?"

"Beau is fine," Nancy said. "He's on a quick trip to Idaho."

Several months ago, Beau'd finally been appointed head of the trucking association's Western branch, replacing Roger Quint. Despite achieving his longtime goal, her father clung to a travel schedule that called him out of state several times a month.

"What I wanted to tell you," Nancy said, "is that a letter came for you today. From *him.*"

"Did you read it? What did it say?" Hannah assumed Nancy'd opened it.

"I wouldn't read a word that vile man wrote. The cyanide can't come quickly enough, as far as I'm concerned."

Hannah was torn. In some ways, she agreed with Nancy. She wanted Jack dead for the havoc he'd wrought, the frightful rending of metal and flesh that had caused so much agony to the survivors. Since the crash, she had days where every moment seemed to hold the menace of another tragedy. Her pulse sometimes pounded in her temples until she came close to fainting. At school, she'd climbed into the VW in the parking lot and wept.

But as the school year had drawn to a close, she experienced more good days than bad. Terrible dreams haunted her sleep less often. Her camera became a creative way to push away the trauma and concentrate completely on something creative. The bag with her photo equipment nearly always hung over her shoulder these days. The yearbook photos she'd taken won an A+ from Mr. Lockley, who thought this year's edition might win a prize at a competition.

The prom misadventure was retold often, amid jokes and laughter. She and Kenny had gotten summer jobs: Hers was waiting on customers in the tennis shop the country club, a position Delilah had engineered, while Kenny worked helping Olof wax the floors and repaint walls at the school.

In their spare moments, Hannah and Kenny took walks around the lake at Crown Hill Cemetery. Afterward, they sometimes climbed into the spacious back seat of his Model A. Kenny had finished reupholstering the seats, and as they shed their clothes, the soft mohair fabric caressed their bare skin. They slipped fingers to pleasurable, hidden places that had become familiar to them in the last months.

Each moment shimmered with meaning for Hannah as their time together slipped away. In a few weeks, he'd be leaving for college in Minnesota, while Hannah planned to stay in Denver, at least for the time being.

"Do you want Graham's filthy letter," Nancy said at last, "or should I burn it?"

"I'll come by. Are the twins still up?" Hannah missed the little brats, the scent of their hair, the clasp of plump, sticky arms around her neck.

"The boys will be in bed." Nancy's voice was scissor sharp. "Don't bother to ring the bell; I'll stick the letter under the doormat."

***

The old neighborhood seemed unchanged; the tree-lined street gleamed, wet and shining in the aftermath of the daily summer rainstorm. The brick homes were cradled in lush green shrubbery.

Through the open car window, she caught the scent of newly mown grass. Kids pedaled their tricycles on the sidewalks or darted between the trees playing hide-and-seek. Hannah wheeled into the wide driveway, past the elm, which had lost one of its thickest branches over the winter. Curtains were closed over the house's front window, but the porch light was on.

A toddler's fretful voice drifted from an open window somewhere around back. She knocked several times and waited, but Nancy didn't answer the door. Tucked under the mat beside Hannah's sandal was the letter. The twisted legacy of Jack and his family seemed to crawl up her leg.

Back in the car, she tapped the envelope against the wheel. The paper was battered and bore a smudge on one corner. It was addressed to Miss Hannah Brightman. Jack's name didn't appear on the return address, only his prisoner number, 29625, and the post office box in Cañon City.

Impatient with her own indecisiveness, she slipped the letter out. It was written in pencil, the lines angling downward as if sagging under their weight.

Hello Hannah,

As you have probably heard, I'm staying here in the finest lodging in Cañon City (ha ha). Food is pretty good, better than the jail in Denver, where I lost so much weight I looked like a Halloween scarecrow.

Warden Harry Tinsley is a good guy, I don't have any quarrel with him. I'm in a special cell block, which is pretty lonely. I've told my lawyers, no appeals. I'm tired and just want to get it over with.

Reverend Kellems visited last week, which was nice of him but he really didn't need to. The good thing is, he's seeing to Lucy when she gets down about things.

I'm writing to you because you need to come down and see me. There's something very important I need to tell you. It involves you and your family. Yours sincerely,
  John G Graham (Jack)

***

Back at the Merricks', Hannah and Paulette sat on their beds, smoking. For a couple of years, Paulette had sneaked smokes in the backyard or her pickup truck. After the plane crash, Hannah'd taken up smoking, puffing a Marlboro every once in awhile to reduce her anxiety.

"What do you think?" Hannah asked. In the car, she'd balled the letter in her fist as soon as she read it, but now it was smoothed out in front of Paulette on the bedspread.

"He's trying to hook you in," Paulette said.

"We don't have any connection. It's all over." Hannah took a long drag on the cigarette.

"It is for *you*. But he's going to die, and you were the one who ratted on him. Maybe he wants to get even."

A fit of coughing overcame Hannah, and it took minute to clear her lungs. "What could he possibly do? He's locked up."

Paulette tipped her head to one side, considering. "Every newspaper, magazine and TV station wants an interview with John Gilbert Graham, the convicted mass murderer, before he takes his final walk. He could be hinting that he'll tell stories about you if you don't visit, information that would ruin you and your family."

"But why in person?" With trembling fingers, Hannah ground out her cigarette in an ashtray on the lamp table. "He could do it without seeing me."

"He's a disturbed, vindictive man. I hate to say it, but he might be pleased to see your face when he tells you what he's going to do."

The next morning, Hannah called long distance to Cañon City. Visiting hours were Wednesdays and Saturdays from 10 a.m. to 2 p.m. For death row inmates, a request letter was required.

36

A week later she took a day off from work at the tennis shop. She drove a hundred miles south to Colorado Springs, then another fifty or so southwest toward Cañon City. The day was hot, and the interior of the VW seemed to sizzle like bacon in a frying pan. She stopped in a turnout and rolled down the windows. Back on the road, wind whipped her short hair.

As she neared Cañon City, the Sangre de Cristo Mountains rose behind the prison's gray stone walls and cellblock complex. The three-story watchtower, she thought, looked remarkably like a penis. At the gate, a guard checked her driver's license and the letter approving her visit. Once inside the visitors' building, she was searched. Her purse and car keys were locked in a bank of metal cabinets.

She followed a thin guard with an acne-scarred face across the prison yard, past two walls and a barbed wire fence, into Cellblock 3, which included the eight segregated cells comprising death row.

"Just four inmates on the row right now." The guard's leather holster slapped rhythmically against his thigh. "Besides Graham, only Archina, Bermudez, and LeRoy Leick, the guy who murdered his wife for the insurance money. Funny, Leick and Graham, the two guys who offed family for the insurance, now in adjoining cells."

In the hall outside the visitors' cubicle, an inmate with a bucket and mop whispered obscene words as she passed. Although the prison smelled of Lysol, Hannah felt as though a veil of filth was settling over her.

***

Half an hour passed while she waited in the visitors' room for Jack to be brought from his cell. The space was small, furnished with a table and two chairs, all bolted to the floor. Through the barred window, Hannah could see a slice of sky, almost white with heat and dust. Within minutes, the back and underarms of her sleeveless blouse were damp with sweat.

The date hadn't been determined, but the reality of Jack's coming execution made her feel a little sick. Strapping someone—even Jack—to a chair and suffocating them with cyanide gas seemed barbaric. Still, shouldn't a terrible punishment be imposed on someone who inflicted such terror and human slaughter?

Hannah thought about the ripple effect of the forty-four deaths on wives, husbands, children. Not just immediate family, but on the others: mothers and fathers, friends and lovers. She knew what it was like to live with loss.

Her thighs ached from sitting on the hard chair. She could hear the soft whirr of an electric fan circulating in the hall, inadequate for the scorching day. Faint sounds of clashing iron indicated the opening and closing of iron-barred cells.

It had been stupid to come. She was about to call a guard to guide her back to the main gate when the clanking of chains told her Graham was coming. A guard opened the door, and Jack appeared, shackled hand and foot. The guard used a key to remove the restraints on his wrists, then closed the door, locking Jack and Hannah inside.

"Hello, Hannah. You're looking good." Jack wore a pair of denim pants and a wrinkled white T-shirt printed with the letters CAP, indicating he was a resident of the capital crimes lockup. He was thin and pale, hardly recognizable as the tall man in a pressed suit, starched shirt, and necktie who'd taken her and Paulette to dinner all those months ago.

"How is life treating you?" His question sounded casual, as if they were friends who hadn't seen each other for awhile.

"I'm as well as could be expected, considering." She propped her fists on the tabletop, nails biting into her palms.

"It's pretty lonely here. Each of us on The Row gets half an hour in the exercise yard three times a week, but we never get to talk to each other. Lucy comes sometimes, and Reverend Kellems."

"So I should feel sorry for you after what you did? And now you're writing me letters? What the hell do you want?"

He gazed out the window, watching a crow land on the eaves of the cellblock's intersecting wing. "Lucy visited last week. She said awhile back she caught you in front of our house, taking photos. What are you going to with them? Sell them to *Life* magazine?"

Hannah had asked herself why she'd snapped photos: Lookout Mountain, the shuttered Comet Drive-In, and Graham's stucco house on West Mississippi. It hadn't been to harass his family or satisfy a morbid curiosity. She'd had the urge to see these places again in real life, not the horrifying dreamscapes that haunted her sleep.

The photos comforted her that those locations were commonplace. A pretty but everyday mountain view. A shuttered drive-in. An unimpressive stucco house.

"I didn't bother Lucy," she said. "I stood in the street."

"Stop taking pictures. Don't go there anymore."

"Why? You've been allowing photographers to shoot pictures of you all along. Eating dinner in the Denver jail, being interviewed here in Cañon City by the guy from the *Rocky*." Her hands curled into fists. "You think Lucy's off-limits?"

"She's an innocent person. Leave her alone." Jack's ankle chains rattled as he shifted his feet. He seemed only vaguely aware of the jaw-dropping incongruity of his request.

"You're worried about a few photos taken of your house when you killed forty-four people?" Hannah leaned forward, her voice rising in outrage. "Don't you worry about *their* families?"

Appearing in the window of the security door, a guard gave her a warning shake of his head.

"They should hang you," she hissed, "like they did in the old days." Heat in the small room seemed intense. With the back of her hand, she wiped sweat from her forehead.

"But I didn't do it." Jack picked at his fingertips, which were raw and bloody. "There was this guy, who asked me to buy him some blasting caps, that's all."

Her bitter laugh seemed to fit perfectly with the grim surroundings. "You're a raving liar. Have you told the truth, even once?"

As if closing the cover on a book, he changed the subject. "You remember the night we went up the mountain in my car?"

"We never did that." The lie seemed as big as an orange in her mouth, but she was sick of regretting the whole evening. She wanted it gone.

"What I remember vividly," he said, ignoring her denial, "was what you said about your stepmother."

"What are you talking about?" She rose and leaned toward him, hands flat on the table. "I never told you anything about her. You think nothing of lying and lying. Don't you know the difference between lies and the truth?"

Unable to back his chair away from her, he tipped his head to the side as if he were attempting to solve a puzzle.

"She was an opportunist, you said. She got her claws into your father because he was lonely after your mother died."

"Shut up about my family." Despite the pain she suffered from her family situation, the comment angered her, from *him*, of all people. She half-rose, about to signal the guard, but sank back in the chair. "Nancy isn't evil. She's just . . . hard."

"Daisie was like that," he said. "A woman with no feelings for other people. She cared only for herself, not her mother, her husbands, and especially not me."

"How convenient," Hannah said. "You can blame her for the horrible, evil thing you did."

"You and I are the same, you see? After my dad died, she moved us—my sister Gretchen and me—to Denver. The way Daisie tells it, we were destitute, but that was a lie. Daisie's dad was a big shot. He had money. He was dead, but he must have left her money. He'd owned a nice place, a ranch in the Animas Valley."

His fingers kneaded the brow over his right eye. She'd seen him use this gesture before, and had a sudden image of him doing it as a little boy when life overwhelmed him.

"But then, she dumped me in an orphanage called Stanhope College. Isn't that stupid, calling an orphanage a college?"

Hannah had seen Stanhope College Orphanage years ago when her mother was alive. It was an impressive collection of sandstone brick buildings with arched, multipaned windows surrounded by grassy lawns and shade trees. She remembered being impressed by the complex's main structure, which featured a towering white cupola roof.

"Stanhope was supposed to take us poor little white boys—no Negroes accepted—and mold us into useful citizens. That's how they said it, *mold*, like squeezing us into a certain shape."

Jack's hand trembled as he pressed a thumb against his forehead. "Even though they had a gym and auditorium and offices and school rooms and dormitories, there were only a few kids there."

He was about five then, he told her, describing the way forty boys, maybe a few more, rattled around in dark, high-ceilinged spaces designed for three hundred, the gloomy buildings poorly lit and barely heated in winter to save money. The orphanage, in order to fulfill its purpose of training boys in the building trades, farming, or manual labor, sent them to school half a day and put them to work the other half.

"I was one of the littlest, and in the bathroom, the older boys would piss on my shoes. They slapped me and punched me in the ribs. At night, they snatched the blankets off my bed."

While he talked, Hannah's jaws ached from clenching her teeth. Finally, she said, "So, I should feel sorry for you, because you had an unhappy childhood? Because some nasty boy hit you when you were five—that gave you license to blow up all those people? To try—twice—to kill me?"

Her voice had risen again, and the guard's acne-scarred face appeared again in the window of the steel door.

Jack raised his hands as if calling a truce. "We're okay, officer."

The guard raised a warning finger. "Settle down, Miss, or you're out of here."

"I'm done." Hannah rose from her chair, but Jack continued the story, his voice breaking.

"My life was like something out of one of those old novels," Jack said, "where a boy is sent to a bad place and suffers. But that's not my point. It was the injustice of it. At the same time, I lived in this place that was little more than a concentration camp, Gretchen was enrolled in a fine girls' school."

She sank back into the chair, thinking of Nancy and Beau, lavishing their attention on the twins, hugging and kissing them, celebrating every little success: the first time they turned over, sat up unaided, pulled themselves to their feet. Meanwhile, they'd ignored her. Except when they needed her to do something for the twins, like Beau dangling the VW in front of her if she gave up going to college in California.

While these thoughts tumbled through her mind, Jack continued to talk. "I could count on one hand the times she visited me over the next few years." Finally, when he was nine, he said, Daisie married again, this time to Earl King, the wealthy rancher living in Toponas, the mountain town near Kremmling. "She came to the orphanage one Friday and drove Gretchen and me up to the ranch. I remember it was late afternoon in summer, one of those days when the world seems perfect."

Jack had been agog with excitement. Daisie'd never taken him anywhere for more than a few hours since dumping him at Stanhope. This was the end of his banishment for whatever unspoken sin he'd committed that separated them.

"It seemed like heaven, she and I together again after all those miserable years. And for once, she seemed happy. The next day, Gretchen and I rode horses that Earl had stabled in his barn. I'd never ridden before, but I decided to be a cowboy when I grew up, like the Roy Rogers or Johnny Mac Brown. We explored the barns and jumped from the loft down into piles of hay. Daisie organized a picnic dinner by the river, with a big, blazing fire where we roasted wieners and marshmallows."

Curses and cries erupted in the hall outside where they sat. Cautiously, Hannah peered out to see two prisoners punching and kicking each other, and guards racing up to pull them apart. A gash bloodied one prisoner's face.

"Don't pay any attention. It happens all the time." Sweat stained Jack's armpits and the back of his shirt. He wiped his forehead with a handkerchief. "After lunch on Sunday, Gretchen and I were playing checkers on a porch overlooking the pond. I'd just gotten a king. Daisie interrupted our game. 'Go pack your bag,' she said. 'We're leaving in an hour.' I didn't grasp what she meant at first.

"'Check-in time at Stanhope is 3 o'clock.' That's how she told me I wasn't staying at the ranch, living with her again. Gretchen would, but not me."

Hannah scarcely breathed, as though the slightest movement would shatter her. She imagined his lost hope. Had he huddled on his cot at night, ignoring the jeers of mean older boys, knowing his dream of a family was shattered?

His ankle chains clanked as he searched for a more comfortable position. His eyes were dry, betrayal having long ago burned away tears.

Sympathy stirred her heart, but she quickly smothered it. Think of the baby, the tiny boy lying in the haystack near Loveland.

Her mother had left her with no one who loved her enough, not Boomer, Clyde, and certainly not her father. Hannah's thoughts went to their brick house in Woodlake, where living after the loss of her mother was so painful that sometimes she wanted to die.

"That's what I saw about you from the very first," he said. "We'd both lost them. Our mothers."

"Except I didn't kill mine." Hannah rose, rattled the bars, and called for the guard. She was done.

37

Hannah barely noticed the road on the drive back to Denver. With her foot heavy on the accelerator, she navigated past Colorado Springs, then headed north. The barren prairie flashed by in the afternoon sun.

Jack's story of his soul-wrenching relationship with Daisie haunted her. Obviously, he was trying to justify what he'd done, struggling to elicit sympathy and forgiveness from her, without owning up to the lives he'd taken and the survivors he'd left with a lifetime of anguish. Weeks away from death, he still couldn't admit that, despite his mother's sins and omissions, nothing justified the carnage he'd inflicted on forty-three other people.

The car's open windows didn't relieve the scorching heat. Traffic had thickened, but she increased her speed, filled with unreasoning anxiety to leave behind the smell and hopelessness of the prison.

For as Jack had talked about Daisie—the way she'd abandoned him as a child—a wound seemed to rise in Hannah, a vile infection. She, too, was angry. At her real mother, Chantal, the woman Hannah'd always told herself she revered, her mother, who knew Hannah so well, she'd almost been able to read her daughter's mind.

It had been uncanny, when Hannah was young, how Chantal seemed to sense when Hannah was sad or frustrated. If she dragged home from school downhearted over a slight or a jeer about her birthmark, Chantal had only to touch her cheek, and the hurt drained away.

Hannah had hugged to herself a secret knowledge that, although Chantal loved Boomer and Clyde, it was Hannah she loved best.

By the time she'd been six or seven, Hannah went to the mountains with her mother in the summer, where Chantal set up her easel to paint one of her sought-after landscapes. Hannah helped Chantal lay out oil paints, brushes, canvas, and linseed oil, then played in the rocks or picked flowers or hunted lizards while her mother worked. At lunchtime they ate sandwiches and fed nuts to the ground squirrels from their palms. On the drive home, they sang songs or looked for out-of-state license plates on passing cars.

It was that closeness that had given Hannah the creeping uneasiness about her mother beginning when she was nine. It seemed as though her mother had put up a glass window between them. If Hannah hugged Chantal, her mother didn't embrace her back. Instead, her arms were lax and unresponsive. The photos Hannah snapped with her Brownie camera, which used to delight her mother, no longer elicited praise or even interest.

Afterward, Beau had told Hannah that Chantal refused to consult a doctor until late in the course of her disease. She'd known she was ill, yet she never acknowledged it, nor let on that anything was wrong.

A blue-black shadow sailed over the mountains, and rain swept across the highway, cutting visibility. The VW's windshield wipers beat rhythmically as the car crept in the midst of clogged traffic. Hannah's nose ran, and she wiped it on the lapel of her shirt.

How could Chantal? In the latter days of her disease, a tumor in her abdomen had grown to nearly ten pounds. How could her mother have cared so little for Hannah, for the toll it might take on the family, to deliberately ignore it?

The answer burned in Hannah's chest: Chantal had made a choice—through stubbornness or fear. She wasn't willfully cruel, like Daisie, who'd abandoned her son. Yet in a very real way, Chantal *had* abandoned her children, too. Left them, especially Hannah, hungering for love.

Traffic loosened up, and as the miles flew by, Hannah accelerated, pushing the car over the speed limit, weaving in and out of traffic on the slippery road. Passing on a curve, the VW came just inches from a Packard with a white-haired woman at the wheel. A split-second glimpse of the driver as Hannah sped by showed a pale, frightened face.

Hannah slowed, but now she blocked the faster-moving traffic. As she approached the looming bulk of Castle Rock, a white Colorado State Patrol car appeared in the rearview mirror, its flashing light signaling her to pull over. At the next turnout, she steered off the road.

The officer was young, in his twenties, dressed in a gray uniform with his tie tucked between the buttons in the front of his shirt. A bead of sweat dripped down his cheek from under the band of his cap.

"Driver's license and registration, young lady."

She pawed through the glove box and her purse, then gave him the documents.

"You in a hurry to get somewhere, Miss—" he looked down at her license—"Brightman?"

"No, Sir. I was returning home to Denver after visiting a friend in Pueblo." No point in telling him where she'd actually been.

With a probing eye, he scanned both documents. "These look all right, but I've been following you for several miles. I'm going to cite you, first for speeding and then for unsafe passing."

She pressed her lips together, but it wasn't enough to stop tears.

The officer inserted carbon paper between the pages of his ticket pad and filled out the citation. When he saw her crying, he frowned. "Miss, putting up a fuss will do you no good. Sign here."

She scribbled her name, tears staining the paper, mucous running from her nose. Leaving a copy of the citation in her hand, he departed, but her emotion didn't subside. It wasn't sorrow, she decided, but anger, giving her a glimpse of what Jack had felt.

Traffic roared by on the highway. Her hands shook so badly she didn't try to start the car. She felt boxed in. The car's interior was about the size of a prison cell, maybe smaller.

Her mother hadn't been cruel like Daisie King—she was nothing like Jack's mother—but Chantal had thought only of herself when she encountered life's cruelties. Her fear of the cancer creeping through her body had crowded out the love she'd always shown for her family, leaving them after her death with unresolved anger and despair.

Luckily, Hannah thought, she wasn't completely devoid of compassion in the face of her mother's failings, like Jack had been after his childhood with Daisie. She felt a lump of sadness for her father, who'd suffered through the last days of Chantal's terminal illness, then taken over responsibility for three children, sacrificing his dream of his own law firm for a safe but unrewarding position with the trucking association.

The wreckage didn't stop there: Boomer, a funny, upbeat sports nut, had joined the Army to escape the atmosphere of loss; Clyde, the quiet, thoughtful one, invented excuses to avoid returning home. Hannah had clung to her mother's memory to ease her pain.

Hannah saw herself clearly. She'd spent years blaming Nancy for her mother's faults.

38

Rather than taking Wadsworth Avenue to Paulette's, Hannah continued straight west on Colfax. She passed Berry's. The Woodlake Theater's marquee featured "The Fastest Gun Alive." Directly in front of her, the sun hovered on the lip of the mountains, its rays piercing her eyes like a knife.

She blinked in relief when she turned into her old neighborhood, where branches of the elms and maples shaded the winding streets. As she neared the house, the neighbors' obnoxious German shepherd was up to its old tricks, running alongside the car, barking and nipping at the tires.

Beau and Nancy's station wagon sat in the driveway, indicating that Nancy was home. Hannah let her engine idle while she watched the house. If she rang the doorbell, would her stepmother slam the door in her face? The drapes were tightly closed. When her mother was alive, drapes had nearly always stayed open. At night, lamplight had streamed out the windows as if no secrets could possibly be hidden inside.

Her fists tightened on the wheel. How naïve she'd been. Secrets lurked everywhere.

Finally, she turned off the engine. The brick walk to the front door was still slightly uneven under her feet. Should she walk right in or ring the bell? This had been her home since she was a preschooler, but she hadn't lived here for nearly nine months.

Standing on the step, she felt the earth-shaking realignment that had taken place since the skating party. The girl she'd been last year was as lost to the past as the one who played with dolls and ridden the playground teeter-totter a decade ago. Saving her sorrow for later, she pressed the doorbell, which played its familiar three-note tune.

The drapes on the front window twitched. No one came to the door.

She thumbed the bell twice more; finally, Nancy's shadowy face appeared, narrowly cropped by the sidelight.

"What do you want, Hannah?" Coming through the window, her voice sounded weak.

"Can I come in?" she shouted. "Just wanted to say hi to you. And the twins."

"Beau's in Colorado Springs at a conference. This isn't a good time." No excuses about meals or baths, only a naked refusal. "In fact, don't come around anymore. It makes things difficult."

Hard, cruel words. Hannah turned to leave, but then peered over her shoulder. Nancy looked lonely—eyes sunken in dark sockets, her face a ghostly white in the shadowed hallway.

"Please. I won't stay long, I promise."

Nancy hesitated, but in those few seconds, angry voices emerged from an open window in the house next door: Alvin and Margaret, who for decades had engaged in a running marital battle.

"Still at it, the old farts," Hannah said.

The corner of Nancy's mouth twitched. "Maybe their fights are an aphrodisiac." She sighed and opened the door. "Come on in. The kids are about to have their dinner."

The living room, which had once been the center of her parents' social life, looked like a storeroom, cluttered with broken toys, baby bounce chairs, cardboard boxes of outgrown infant clothing, and two bassinets, now surplus since the twins had graduated to cribs.

"Ignore the mess." Nancy called. She hurried to the kitchen, the only room with lights on, and turned off the stovetop burner, where hot dogs were cooking in a pan of boiling water. The sink was piled with dirty dishes.

Soiled clothes, wrinkled sheets, and a stinking diaper pail were poised at the top of the stairs, ready to be hauled down to the basement laundry room.

In the midst of the chaos, the twins stood in their playpen, eyes peering over the top railing. Since Hannah'd last seen them, they'd graduated out of babyhood—they were toddlers now. Jasper, always the quieter one, looked at her with an almost adult intensity. Marcus had gained a solid chest and sturdy legs, signaling he might someday follow Boomer into a spot on the high school football team.

They stared at her, their heads tilted at identical angles, puzzled by her arrival. They seemed to know she was someone important, but couldn't remember just why. She took a couple of steps, eager to hug them and kiss their cheeks, then hesitated. This wasn't her mother's house anymore, nor was it hers. It was Nancy's.

"Go ahead." Nancy drained the water from the hot dogs. "They'll remember pretty quick."

Squatting on the floor beside the playpen, Hannah poked her fingers through the slats, wiggling them at Jasper. He stared, then tried to grab them, but quick as a flash, she tickled his ribs.

He erupted in delighted laughter.

"Me, me!" Marcus tried to push him aside, but Jasper crouched, hanging onto the slats with both fists. Hannah diverted Marcus by blowing into his face. At first, he raised his hands to shield himself, but then lowered them, an invitation for another gust of air.

Joy bubbled up in Hannah like ginger ale. Despite their smells, vomit, fussiness, and killer curiosity, she loved these impish half-brothers. In the months since Nancy kicked her out, Hannah'd built an alternate life for herself. But she'd also felt a sense of loss, as if she were missing a thumb or a big toe.

"Sit them in their chairs, Hannah, and put on the bibs." Nancy sliced the hot dogs and tossed the bite-sized pieces, along with diced apples, into plastic bowls with their names printed on them. "Don't forget their little spoons."

Hannah lifted the boys one at a time from the playpen and installed them in their high chairs, their soft skin emitting smells of urine and baby shampoo. After her nine-month absence, the twins were heavier and bulkier than she remembered. Once food was in front of them, they ignored spoons and dug in with their hands as they had before Hannah left.

At the counter, Nancy popped the caps on two bottles of Coors with a church key.

"No kidding?" Hannah accepted the bottle Nancy offered, which felt cold and sweaty in her palm.

Nancy sank into a chair. "Take a load off." She tilted her head back, throat working as she guzzled a long drink.

Coors was *the* Colorado beer. The *Post's* society section regularly featured parties and charity events the Adolph Coors family attended, but Hannah'd never drunk one of its brews. Nancy's invitation was unexpected, possibly a temporary truce, but better than open warfare.

Nancy licked a bit of foam from the corner of her mouth. "How are things at the Merricks'?"

"Good." The crisp, malty beer slid smoothly down her throat. "Delilah's teaching tennis at the country club, and I'm working in the sport shop for the summer. It's fun, I meet a lot of people, and the money's nice."

"Delilah still hitting the sauce?" Nancy made a face and took another swallow.

"She's pretty much quit. I don't know how long it'll last, but Paulette's really happy." The beer wasn't half bad. It was strange, she and Nancy chatting like two girlfriends might, out for an evening.

How long had she known Nancy? Ten years, maybe. When Chantal was alive, she got a weekly wash and set at Nancy's beauty shop, Cut Country. Occasionally, Chantal took Hannah to Nancy for a trim. Back then, Nancy's peroxide jobs were renowned among

Chantal's friends for being natural-looking and not too brassy. Hannah hadn't known the ins and outs of bleaches, only that Nancy's blonde bouffant seemed glamorous. Not now. Nancy'd neglected to attend to her natural mousy brown hair; only the very tips still radiated with blonde.

"Don't get me wrong, I'm sympathetic with Delilah," Nancy said. "She's probably spent years at home, mostly not working. I know what it's like—damned lonely. Sometimes, with Beau on the road, the only people I see, other than the babies, are the dry-cleaning man and the yard boy."

That's only a taste of it, Hannah wanted to shout. Try the whole meal, having one or two pals in the whole world because hardly anyone wants a freak for a friend. When those two are sick or on vacation, or their parents ground them, you're the saddest lump of humanity on earth. That's alone-in-the-arctic loneliness.

Hannah bit her cheek. She should say something uplifting to Nancy, even if it weren't necessarily true. "Maybe Dad could get a job here in Denver. If he did that, he'd be home every night, not just weekends."

"He might give up the trucking association, but I doubt it."

Beer was making Hannah feel sentimental. "I'm sure he loves you. Why else would he marry you?"

Nancy raised an eyebrow. "Don't you remember? We *had* to."

Well, yeah. This was just too embarrassing, imagining her father and Nancy naked in bed. The kitchen felt uncomfortably hot. Hannah rose and opened the back door to let in cooler air. No more sounds from the quarreling neighbors' house.

Nancy finished her beer, threw the bottle in the trash and wiped up spilled food from the high-chair trays. She tucked the bowls in the dishwasher. "Speaking of which, are you using something, with this boy you're seeing?"

"What are you talking about?" Hannah could feel the guilty look smeared all over her face.

"Come on, I knew you were having sex with someone. Who do you think washed your sheets while you lived here—the love fairy?"

Hannah couldn't meet Nancy's gaze. The humiliation was enormous. This woman Hannah hated and dismissed as an interloper knew one of her deepest secrets.

"All I'm saying is, if you need good advice from someone who messed up, I'm your girl," Nancy said.

"I'm okay." Hannah dumped the empty beer bottles into the wastebasket. "Delilah and I talked."

"Well, so much for trying to be the stepmother-confidant." Nancy seemed amused, not at all put out.

In the silence, Marcus made a bid for attention, tossing a plastic baby bottle filled with apple juice on the floor, then whining for someone to retrieve it. Hannah scooped it up and returned it to the tray. To continue the game, he threw it again. Jasper clapped.

Nancy laughed and plucked two Oreos from the cookie jar. "Once in awhile, I'm not sorry we had them," she said, dropping one on each tray. The dishwasher hummed and sloshed. She removed the metal strip from a can of vacuum-packed coffee with its small attached key, readying the percolator for tomorrow morning.

The ground-coffee aroma gave the kitchen a relaxed feel, the way it had been when Hannah's mother was alive. No, even looser, more down-to-earth. "What was your first husband like?" Hannah asked.

"He was a nice boy. We were in high school together." Nancy filled the percolator with water. "After we graduated, he went to work as a bricklayer in his father's business. I went to beauty school."

Kenny and I will be different, Hannah thought. *We've got plans, not getting stuck in Denver, but seeing the world. He'll be a pro hockey player. I'll become a photographer for* Life *magazine.*

"Then the Japs bombed Pearl Harbor." Nancy plucked a cigarette from a pack sitting on the windowsill and lit it. "He enlisted in the Marines, we got married, and a week later he shipped out. The

South Pacific did bad things to our boys during the war. When he came back, his mind was really messed up."

"What happened to him?" She knew Nancy was a widow, but Hannah'd never heard the full story.

Smoke from Nancy's cigarette twisted in the air. "He shot himself."

The day's horrors seemed to fill Hannah's throat. She sank down at the foot of Jasper's chair, hands pressed against her mouth, as if the gesture could hold back the gut-twisting realities of love, hate, and insanity.

Nancy tossed her cigarette in the sink. She squatted down beside Hannah. "Don't worry, I'm at peace with it."

The pressure in Hannah's throat receded, but she felt dizzy.

"That thing with Jack Graham, it'll get better." Hesitantly, Nancy put her arm around Hannah's shoulder. "Come on. Help me put the kids to bed." They leaned against each other until they were on their feet. Nancy's scent of cigarettes and beer and face cream seemed comforting, in a strange way.

"I want to ask you something," Hannah said.

Nancy snatched her hand away. "You want to move back here?"

"No, no. I'm fine at Paulette and Delilah's."

Relief flooded her stepmother's face.

"The break's done me good," Hannah said. "At their house, I'm not reminded of Mother all the time. I'm not thinking, 'Here's where Mom and I played Crazy Eights,' or, 'There's the little table she refinished.'"

"Beau's been bad-mouthing me about—he says I kicked you into the cold."

"You did." The two words were true, but Hannah was over it and didn't feel angry. "What I want to know is this." She took a deep breath. "How about if I take a family photo? All of us. You could put in a frame on your desk. Or on your Christmas card."

Nancy raised her eyebrows. "Well, wouldn't that be something."

39

Clyde called after 11 p.m. from the Omaha train station. "The Zephyr left Chicago an hour and a half late," he told Hannah. "We won't be getting into Denver until at least 10 a.m. tomorrow."

"Oh, no!" She twisted a lock of hair between her fingers. "Delayed in Omaha is bad enough, but promise me you're not hiding out in Maine to escape the photo session."

"Omaha. Honest Abe," Clyde said.

Summer was rushing to a close, and this was it. Clyde had penned his last summer school exam at the University of Chicago, Boomer was swooping in from California on leave, and Beau and Nancy had called earlier in the evening to say the twins' mound of diapers and snack foods were ready to go. Early tomorrow, Hannah and Kenny would drive to Genesee Mountain, the location she'd selected for the picture session.

But if Clyde were missing, her plan for the family photo would be a failure.

"Hold on a minute." She perched the receiver on her shoulder and looked over at Paulette, playing solitaire at the kitchen table. "I've got a crisis."

Paulette snapped a queen onto a king. "Someone have a heart attack?"

"If only it were that simple. It's Clyde, his train's arriving late."

"Is that all? At least it's not a family feud, attempted murder, or plane crash."

Hannah stuck out her tongue at her friend. "You're such a turd." Those disasters already had happened, and she'd survived.

"I'll pick him up," Paulette said.

Back on the phone, Clyde gave her a hard time. "I don't get a limo? Paulette's truck is way beneath my standards."

"Not only that, your suitcase will get tossed in back with the lumber and old paint cans," Hannah said. He laughed, such a rare thing for Clyde, that her heart lifted with hope that this day would be a turning point, at least for some of the family.

After the call ended, she scooted around behind Paulette's kitchen hair and slipped her arms around her in a hug. "I owe you."

The corner of Paulette's mouth twitched. "You'll be getting my bill in the mail."

***

Paulette wasn't the only one who'd stepped in to help. Kenny rolled into the driveway just after 8 the next morning. Rather than the Model A, he drove his father's car, which had a trunk roomy enough to hold Hannah's equipment for the photo shoot. They loaded camp chairs, camera bag with flash and attachments, extension cord, a light, foldable reflector and stand, tripod, and her Rolleiflex.

"We got everything? Seems like an awful lot for a few snapshots." Kenny was nervous. During the months they'd been dating, Hannah had been living at the Merricks', so he had yet to meet her father or Nancy. He jangled the car keys in his shorts pocket and kicked the tires on his father's car.

"We're good." She stroked the soft blond hairs on his arm and gave him a long kiss, liking the taste of his toothpaste.

On their way out of town, they detoured to pick up Rosemarie, who'd ditched Shabbat services to ride along and assist Beau and Nancy wrangle the twins.

The highway climbed west out of Denver into the foothills. Rock outcroppings and forested hills concealed the Continental Divide, less than an hour's drive away. The usual Saturday stream of cars on weekend excursions to the mountain range's trails and lakes hadn't yet hit the road.

Hannah's nerves were jumping. Kenny seemed to be taking the curves too fast; other cars crowded too close; Rosemarie talked too much. When Hannah'd first proposed the photo, Nancy agreed, not enthusiastically, but agreed. Beau, however, offered a list of shop-worn excuses: work to catch up on, care repairs, urgent yard work. It was Nancy who'd finally said, "Beau, we're going to do this."

Since the night Hannah and Nancy had drunk beer together, they'd reached a truce, but her father seemed more remote than ever. It hurt like a bad bruise, throbbing with low-level persistence as she rose from bed each morning, worked at the tennis club, snapped photos for the small weekly newspaper, went to the movies or splurged on tickets to a concert at Red Rocks with Rosemarie and Paulette.

Kenny turned off the highway toward Genessee Mountain. The resident buffalo herd grazed in the nearby meadow: huge bulls with their shaggy manes and curving horns, smaller but still impressive females, and light brown calves. The road wound upward through pine and fir woods to the spot she'd planned, a stone lodge with a wide porch.

"I remember coming here with the Brownie Scouts when I was in elementary school," Rosemarie said. "It's the perfect spot."

Kenny parked the car and began unloading the trunk. "Where do you want this stuff?"

Hannah studied the lodge. The idea of using it as a location had popped into her mind a month ago. "On the porch. I want the rock walls as background." The granite's texture would provide excellent contrast with her family's smooth faces and colorful clothing.

They worked for awhile, Hannah directing Kenny and Rose-marie where to put the reflective screen and set up lights to counter the shade from the lodge's overhang. She placed her camera on the tripod and took readings with the light meter. During spring semester at school, she'd gained confidence in her skills, snapping dozens of photos for the yearbook.

A family with three young girls strolled by from the nearby tent campground and stopped to watch. The smell of pine resin hung in the air. Blue jays squawking in the tree limbs were as raucous as a family quarrel.

And speaking of family, here came the station wagon, her father at the wheel. Boomer hopped out even before Beau killed the engine. His body, which had been honed by high school sports, had bulked up with additional muscle since he joined the Army.

"Hannah Banana! I can't believe it!" He strode over and squeezed her in an enveloping hug that nearly smothered her against his chest, but it didn't matter. Tears stung her eyes. It felt like old times to have him around.

"How's my golden girl?" He drew back and pecked a kiss on her forehead. "Taller, no, but prettier? Absolutely!"

"Thanks, Booms." She cleared her throat. "You're looking pretty darn good yourself." He'd changed in the five years he'd been in the Army; his arms swelled with more muscle, his posture was straighter, and his hair, trimmed by a military barber, stood up like a private on parade. There was an air of independence about him; he'd dropped his habit of looking over his shoulder to see if Beau approved of him or Nancy liked him.

Boomer turned to Rosemarie and Kenny. "I remember this rosy young lady, but you, my man, are a stranger."

"Kenny Nilsson, a high school friend of Hannah's." He shook Boomer's hand and waved at Beau and Nancy, who stopped unloading the car to give him an assessing look.

"Any word from Clyde?" her father called.

"Nothing," Hannah said. "Paulette's at Union Station. As soon as the Zephyr pulls in, she'll drive him up here."

"I wouldn't depend on the railway system," Beau said. "Freight trains are a thing of the past, and passenger travel isn't far behind."

"Spoken like a true friend of the trucking industry." Boomer said, grinning. He and Kenny carried the cooler and other gear to a nearby picnic table.

Once the twins were unbuckled from their car seats and allowed to roam, they scrambled on hands and knees up the porch steps. Rosemarie clasped their hands and coaxed them down, then scoured the ground for pine cones and sticks for them to throw. Nancy clapped to encourage them, but Beau leaned against the picnic table with arms folded across his chest, making no effort to mingle.

A towering cumulus cloud approached over the mountains. Was it about to rain? How long should they wait? There was no way to know whether Paulette and Clyde were on their way. Maybe the train had encountered additional delays. Her scheme to bring the family together, hatched over a bottle of beer, seemed naïve now.

Kenny and Boomer moved off into the pines and began a rock-throwing contest to determine which one could hit a large stump.

Beau sank down on the lodge steps. Over the last few months, his hair had thinned and was mixed with more gray. "How are you?"

Hannah shrugged. It had been months since they'd really talked. She leaned against the rock column at the bottom of the stairs, her arms folded across her chest. What was she supposed to say: *I'm terrific,* when she really longed to ask him, *Why have you stopped loving me?*

He massaged the creases between his eyes with a forefinger. "Are you still having dreams about the night of the crash?"

"Sometimes." She hadn't talked about that night for awhile, and words stuck in her throat.

"Me too," Beau said. "It's robbing me of sleep. I don't want to nod off and see those terrible sights again."

"For me, it's been better the last couple of months," she said. Some nights now, she slept through until dawn without dreams of being a passenger in the plane or seeing a flaming piece of wreckage hurtling toward her.

"I don't know if you've heard, but they've set a date for Graham's execution—sometime during the week of January 12," he said.

"Yeah, I heard." She swatted a large black fly away from her face.

"I sometimes think, if I'd done something different, I might've prevented it," Beau said.

"Like what?" Hannah'd spent months thinking the same thing but she was impatient now, tired of dwelling on the past. "Nobody believed me, and nobody would've believed you either, even though you're an adult and a lawyer. It was just too bizarre, too terrible."

"Maybe if I'd been a better father, if we'd been closer, you might've confided in me earlier." His hands clenched and unclenched as they rested on his thighs.

Hardly likely, Hannah thought. No way would she have told her father about the married man or the night on Lookout Mountain.

"Dad, why are you obsessing about it now? We didn't know until it was too late." She felt impatient. If she could make a small break-through, why couldn't he? He was the mature person. Supposedly, he *knew* things, but the tragedy, like quicksand, seemed to have caught him, and he couldn't break free.

Beau tilted his head, tracking a dark cluster of clouds as it scudded eastward toward the plains. "Do you still think about her?"

Hannah shot him a puzzled look. "Who, Daisie King?"

"No, your mother. We didn't know about her, that she was sick, until it was too late."

"I think about her every day," she said.

"God help me, even with a new wife and new babies, I want her back." Guilt thickened Beau's voice.

Hannah sank down on the step beside him and ran her hand across his sagging shoulder. In front of them, a new version of their family—forged in the fires of disease, desire, and tragedy—moved on with life. The twins stretched their fat little legs climbing onto the picnic table benches. Nancy sat on a carpet of pine needles with her back against a tree, taking a moment's rest. Farther away, Boomer tutored Rosemarie on the proper arm motion for throwing rocks.

Kenny doused his head with water from the spigot. An odd feeling stole over her.

Life without Chantal had often felt to Hannah like a dark, powerful current threatening to sweep her away, separating her from joy. In the aftermath of the crash, she'd thought the struggle was lost. But she had friends—people who loved her—and passion for the images she created with her camera.

For first time, she felt wiser than her father. "That life's over, Dad. The new one's right here in front of us."

He didn't respond; instead, he squeezed her hand in a hard grip.

***

Nancy had packed extra clothes for the twins. Food for a picnic—bread, mustard, salami, cheese and fruit—filled a wicker basket. They gathered around the table. Marcus, who'd fallen in love with Rosemarie, cuddled on her lap. Jasper refused to sit down, but circled the table yelling and waving a piece of bread in his fist.

The group loosened up. Boomer told a humorous story about falling out of a fishing boat in Monterey Bay. Nancy offered to trim Kenny's hair before he left for college. Hannah described the difficulty following the path of a hockey puck while it was in play.

Meanwhile, Beau ignored them and chewed his sandwich.

When the picnic's remains were stowed in the station wagon, Nancy took stock of the twins. "Oh, my God." Jasper's cheek was covered with dirt. Marcus had slobbered mustard on his shirt. She handed out duties like an Army commander.

"Beau, wash their hands and faces. Boomer, get clean clothes from the bag. And Rosemarie, Honey, could you comb their hair?"

Within minutes both boys had been sponged with water from the campground spigot, combed, and dressed in fresh clothes.

Hannah asked Kenny to plug in the extension cord to the outdoor electrical outlet and rearrange the angle of the lights because a tower of thick cumulus clouds had moved over, blocking the sunlight. Her original plan had been to pose Beau and Nancy in the camp chairs, each with a twin on their lap, while the older generation of siblings—she, Boomer, and Clyde—stood behind them.

Her frustration mounted. Without Clyde, the arrangement didn't balance. Hannah set the timer and the camera clicked several shots with alternate configurations, none of which worked well.

Her father held himself aloof, leaning away from Nancy, his gaze focused on the granite peaks to the west.

"Beau, you're not smiling." Nancy said.

His head jerked back toward them. "What, I'm supposed to show my teeth like a grinning fool?"

Nancy's lips trembled with hurt.

After the camera's timer snapped each pose, Hannah glanced at the parking lot, hoping to catch sight of Paulette's pickup. Nancy watched, too, head tilted awkwardly for a sight line around Jasper's squirming body in her lap.

Finally, Beau called a halt. "We gave it a try, but it didn't happen. Maybe another time."

Hannah's face felt stiff, as though it were smeared with dirt. Her plan had failed. One event wasn't going to make people love each other, or even like each other. Kenny slid an arm around her shoulder and gave her a squeeze, but his sympathy made her feel worse. She rubbed her nose with the back of her hand.

They all pitched in to dismantle the equipment, a quiet and dispirited crew. The twins were fussy; Marcus rubbed his eyes with his fists.

Rosemarie plucked the Rolleiflex from the porch table. "Don't forget this. I'll bring it." The camera swung on a strap over her shoulder as she and Hannah walked to the parking lot together.

Beau had stuffed the picnic basket into the back of the station wagon and was fishing car keys from his pocket when the blare of a horn reverberated from the park roadway.

"Oh, my moon and stars, it's Paulette!" Rosemarie cried.

The pickup wheeled into the lot, tires screaming. Almost before it stopped, Clyde's skinny legs emerged from the pickup's door as it swung open. His dark hair flopped over the rims of his glasses as he raced toward them. "Is it too late?"

The family clustered around, Beau grinning like a madman, Nancy holding Jasper up in the air to see, Boomer with Marcus on his shoulders, Hannah giving Clyde a wet, sisterly kiss.

Kenny leaned over to Rosemarie. "Shoot the picture," he murmured urgently, "take it now."

Rosemarie raised the camera, clicked the shutter.

As it turned out, that was the shot that went on the Christmas card four months later. It was a fine photo, Hannah conceded, the first picture of the entire Brightman family.

40

In January 1957, fifteen months after the bombing, prison officials had strapped Jack to a chair closed the sealed gas chamber at Colorado State Penitentiary. Remotely released cyanide pellets dropped into a vat of sulfuric acid beneath his chair, and the deadly gas rose in a cloud around him. He groaned loudly, according to witnesses. Ten minutes later, doctors declared John Gilbert Graham, convicted bomber of United Flight 629, deceased.

Jack had been ambivalent to the last, confessing his guilt to Reverend Kellems the preceding day, but reversing himself and denying culpability hours before he died.

"He was one of the most puzzling, unknowable people I've ever met," said one of his attorneys in a statement to the *Rocky*.

Hannah had cried all night after the execution was announced on the radio. Her tears didn't flow for Jack, but for the baby boy in the haystack, for Daisie King and the others on board, for Lucy Graham and her children. Afterward, the guilt and anger that had been clotted inside her seemed to dissolve. A future opened up where the possibility of love was stronger than the impact of hate and violence.

Life had begun to shift several months before the execution.

Their farewell dinner the night before Paulette's September departure for California had left both Hannah and Paulette with aching hearts as they confronted their separation. Within a week, Hannah received a letter from Paulette announcing she'd rented a room in

San Francisco's North Beach neighborhood and landed a part-time job at the City Lights bookstore.

Meanwhile, Johnson Crombie, the owner of the *Jefferson Sentinel*, a weekly newspaper that covered Woodlake and other west Denver suburbs, offered Hannah a job. She snapped it up.

A skinny, intense man in his fifties, Crombie was uninterested in hard news. Instead, he sent her out to snap pictures of women's clubs, church suppers, and Little League signups. Then, midway through her first month, Alonzo stopped by his old home for breakfast with Delilah.

"You want a tip?" he asked Hannah, who was sipping coffee, nibbling on bacon, and reading the *Rocky*. "We're going to bust Chauncey Smalldone for gambling tonight." He gave Hannah the address in North Denver not far from Gaetano's. Just after 1 a.m., she crouched in a pile of dry leaves waiting for arresting officers, who'd stormed the house, to bring Smalldone outside to an unmarked police car.

The air snapped with fall chill and a three-quarter moon gleamed overhead. Her heart pumping with excitement, she inhaled several deep breaths to steady her hands on the camera. When Alonzo and the other officers appeared on the porch with the handcuffed Smalldone between them, she had clicked a picture, inserted a new flash bulb, and captured another frame.

The *Sentinel* wasn't interested in the picture, but the *Rocky* bought it, and it appeared on Page One.

True, she'd failed to snap the family photo, but Rosemarie's split-second save had opened a door for the Brightman family.

Since then, Boomer, now assigned to a new posting in Fort Bragg, North Carolina, had sent his first-ever gift to the twins: matching balance scooters, which the two unruly boys wheeled up and down the driveway. Nancy and Beau hosted Thanksgiving dinner. The leafs for the oak dining room table, which had been stored in the basement since before Chantal's death, were dusted off and inserted to extend the eating surface to its full length. Nancy bought a new linen tablecloth, cooked her first-ever turkey for the holiday meal.

Hannah had begun dropping by a couple of times a week to romp with the boys and give Nancy a few hours of free time. Occasionally Hannah and Beau met for breakfast.

The Christmas card turned out to be of those rare pictures people taped to their refrigerator door or slipped into the frame of a bedroom mirror. Everyone assumed that Hannah'd snapped it with a timer, but when asked, she gave proper credit to Rosemarie.

Not that the Brightmans had become an Ozzie and Harriet Nelson television family where all life crises were resolved by the end of the episode. Clyde forgot Nancy's birthday. Boomer never wrote letters.

Beau dragged his feet about taking a job that didn't involve travel.

Her photographic forays eased Hannah's longing for Kenny. They wrote letters once a week, but at night, in what was now exclusively her own room at the Merricks', she thought about him, the way his breath warmed the curve of her neck, tongue circled her nipple, hardness probed the slick flesh between her legs. As much as the heat of their secret moments together, she longed for his integrity. The things she confided—hurts, unacceptable thoughts, and unattainable dreams—were safe with him.

It was late March now. Kenny's university hockey season closed with his team as the league runner-up. He'd arrived home for spring break the night before, after driving across the frozen plains from Minnesota. The four of them—Paulette, home for a week from San Francisco, Rosemarie, Kenny, and Hannah—gathered in the Merricks' living room sipping 3.2 beer.

Hannah sat on the couch with him, her front to his back, and massaged his shoulder, still aching from a collision on the ice during a late-season game. Paulette and Rosemarie worked a jigsaw puzzle on the coffee table.

"I'm bored." Paulette took several long swallows. "It's Friday night, the moon is full, and the lake's frozen. Let's go skating."

Hannah's fingers clenched. "No frigging way."

"Ouch! Don't take it out on my delicate flesh." Kenny shrugged her hand away.

"I'll be happy if I never see the lake again," Hannah said.

"Come on, it's the last time this year the lake'll be frozen," Paulette said. "Who knows if we'll ever skate together again?"

Kenny tugged the hem of Hannah's sweater. "Come on, Babe. Why not? Dad was at the lake after work. He and a couple of other guys shoveled the rink. It's ready."

"Maybe if we go one last time, the lake will be fun again, like all of it never happened." Rosemarie twisted a lock of hair around her finger. "I remember when I was seven, I broke my ankle roller skating. I was too scared to get on skates again, but my father insisted. I cried and screamed, but it worked; afterward, I wasn't afraid."

That scenario wasn't going to happen, but Hannah let it go. "Okay, I'm in."

When they arrived at the lake, they piled out of the Model A with their skates, gloves, hats and scarves. Hannah wore a pair of jeans over long underwear. Her saucy red skating skirt had been left behind during her hasty move to the Merricks' and still lay in a cardboard box among leftover clothes in the Brightmans' basement.

A full moon hung over the frozen lake. Hannah waved at Kenny's father, Olof, who shouted a greeting. He stood near the snack shack with two other men, leaning on their snow shovels, talking. Their cigarette smoke drifted into the air. He and his companions had mounded snow scraped from the ice into a berm to border the rink. Olof, who'd grown up in Sweden's much colder winters, hadn't bothered to wear a hat.

Kenny crossed the parking lot to talk to them, skates swinging from his shoulder. Paulette and Rosemarie brushed snow off a bench and sat down to put on their skates.

Hannah paused, listening to waltz music drifting from the speakers mounted on the roof of the snack shack. The spot where she stood was a few yards from where Jack's Buick had been parked that night.

Looking back, she admitted she'd been a tiny bit fascinated. He'd been brash and not bad-looking. Nothing she'd experienced in her life had tasted so strongly of danger as accepting his invitation. She was lonely, never had a real boyfriend, nor drunk liquor. Her first sexual experience at church camp had been a quick, embarrassing fumble fest, nothing like the torrid lovemaking she'd read about in Frank Yerby's romance novels. Some girls her age shoplifted for excitement, but those stunts had never interested her.

That initial lure had lasted only a couple of weeks, until she was caught in the snare of her own recklessness and Jack's depraved plans. His haphazard and poorly conceived plots seemed now like schemes of an evil, disturbed child. First, the failed explosion at the Comet, settled with a minimal insurance check, then the lunatic truck-versus-train collision, which came close to putting him in jail. If the Mainliner had been delayed another half hour at the gate by mechanical problems or other circumstances, it could have blown up the entire terminal, causing an even more staggering death toll.

Maybe she, too, had harbored a drop or two of evil child, coveting a secret everyone would disapprove of.

The week before his execution, Jack had written her another letter: would Hannah come to the prison and photograph him being led into the chamber? His request was completely in character, another bizarre impulse in a lifetime of inexplicable actions. Such a photo would have launched her, at nineteen, as one of the nation's hot new photographers, but she'd shredded the letter in disgust. Her strange encounter with him was over.

Rosemarie and Paulette were already on the ice. Hannah slipped into her skates, walked on her toes through the snow and frozen grass. She skimmed onto the rink, blades cutting the ice with crisp, clean sounds. She waved at her friends as she took one fast circuit, body bent forward, arms swinging. On the second round, she skated backward. Her calves stung pleasantly, and her body hummed with rhythm.

She stopped to catch her breath. Nearby, Kenny was talking to a young man who'd been on his club hockey team last year. Kenny's cheeks were red from the cold, but like his father, he didn't need a hat. He spotted her and waved. Joy spread through her, like a photo image leaping to life. She blew him a kiss from her fingertips.

With her head tipped back, she gazed at the dark sky. The moon's rays and city lights rippled in concert overhead as if they were the music of the heavens, the song of the future.

Author's Note

The crash of Mainliner 629 on a flight out of Denver's Stapleton Field in 1955 has faded in the public's memory, although the plane bombing was the first such event in American history and perhaps the most horrendous criminal act in twentieth century America. Forty-four passengers and crew died when the United DC-6B exploded in a sugar beet field north of the city eleven minutes after takeoff.

I was an eighth grader in a Denver suburb at the time, but do not recall newspaper or TV coverage of the event. Yet, like the shards of the plane scattered for miles over the frozen sugar beet fields, pieces of the Mainliner crash story have landed in my life.

For example, the man arrested, convicted, and executed for the crime, John Gilbert Graham, attended our church. I wasn't acquainted with him, but we were connected through our minister, the Reverend Lloyd Kellems. The reverend visited Graham in prison during the final days before his execution and became spiritual counselor to Graham's wife. The jovial, red-faced Kellems baptized me as a ten-year-old, and I have fond memories of him.

Graham's wife attended my high school, although she graduated several years ahead of me. After he was executed, she changed her name and worked until her retirement at the Federal Center, Denver's sprawling complex of government offices where my father also worked. They never encountered each other, as far as I know.

It wasn't until I became immersed in research for **Night Flight** I discovered that our next-door neighbor—a friendly, dark-haired woman with a husband and adopted son—had been a key witness at Graham's trial. While working at a Denver electronics store, she sold Graham the timer that detonated the bomb, unaware of his evil intent. She does not appear in the book.

These random bits, the like debris flung miles from the crash site, may have been what impelled me in the summer of 2022 to set aside another nearly-complete thriller to write this fictional story.

I use real names—well documented in court records or written accounts—of John Gilbert Graham, his mother, Daisie King, and her second and third husbands. Names of other members of the Graham family have been changed out of respect for innocent persons drawn into unimaginable tragedy. The Reverend Kellems was mentioned numerous times in the news as spiritual counselor to the family.

While these connections are fascinating, the real story in *Night Flight* isn't the real-life Graham, but the fictional Hannah Brightman, a girl entangled in a deadly game with a violent man. Can she escape the trauma of this terrible tragedy?

Acknowledgements

Several non-fiction books were of immense help in providing facts about the crash of Mainliner 629 and its aftermath. One was Andrew J. Field's exhaustively researched book, *Mainliner Denver*. Also helpful was Edward C. Davenport's *Eleven Minutes*.

For an account of the Smalldone family's criminal enterprise in Denver during those years, Dick Kreck's book, *Smalldone: The Untold Story of an American Crime Family*, was invaluable.

An excerpt from UPI White House correspondent Merriman Smith's book, *Meet Mr. Eisenhower*, provided details about the president's fishing trips to Colorado.

The staff of Denver Public Library's Special Collections and Western History sections answered my questions with thoroughness and dispatch.

Keith Dameron, retired captain of the Colorado State Patrol, emailed photos of officers' uniforms and patrol vehicles in use during the period.

A posse of family and friends also pitched in. Lakewood High School classmate Mary Collier Ross called upon her sources for background on John Gilbert Graham's wife. Classmates Sandy Prose Kling and her husband, Paul Kling, provided details on Model A's, which were a popular 1950's-era restoration project for high school boys.

My brother, Neal Seitz, refreshed my memory about Denver area streets and chauffeured me around the city to visit actual sites appearing in the book, including the Grahams' house and the orphanage where the bomber spent his youth.

Georgia Taylor and her brother, Dale Alley, gave me much-needed assistance on the chapter about deer hunting. A fellow writer, attorney Charles Bonneau, advised me about legal strategies involving confidential informants.

The Monday Night Writers group and the Blue Moon critique group were uplifting cheerleaders and helpful critics. Special thanks go to writers Barbara Link and Joella Aragon; editors Jan Haag and Krista Minard; and cover artist Karen Phillips.

As always, my husband, Tony, is my backup, my sounding board, and my joy.